Shanghai'd

When I flew into China from Canada, I landed two days after I took
off. The flight was only eleven hours. When I returned, I landed
before I'd left. I always thought it was some dumb phenomenon
due to crossing the dateline. I couldn't have been more wrong.
China had taken a dizzying grip on my life and wouldn't let go
until it was done with me, or I was dead.
It was safe to say, I'd been Shanghai'd.

Nov 2021

Wendy
thanks again for
another great cut !!!

A Novel by
Kevin Weisbeck

Shanghai'd
An Owlstone Book

Published as a Print-on-Demand book
through the Amazon Company,
for the author Kevin Weisbeck.

Printed in the United States of America
This is a work of fiction. Names, characters, and incidents
either are the product of the author's imagination or are used
fictitiously. Any resemblance to actual persons, living or
dead, or events is entirely coincidental.

Cover design and Artwork
by Dan Huckle

Copyright © 2021   Kevin Weisbeck
ISBN 978-0-7777958-0-1

First printing, February 2021

Kevin Weisbeck

Dedication

A special thanks to the real Wuang Fang (aka Candy Wang). She was the tour guide on our trip and dragged us to Beijing, Xi'an, Shanghai, Suzhou, Guilin and the Longsheng area. That was where a small group of wooden barn-like buildings were huddled together to form the settlement of Ping'an. Too small for most maps, I honestly think the gang on our bus outnumbered the handful of residents.

Chapter 1

I spent the day trying to pull my mind out of China. It didn't work. Instead, my blank stare rested on the clock as the hands slowly swept across the face. My workday was sauntering down the path to a merciful end. Not that drilling holes in kitchen cabinets was boring, but it wasn't the thrill that Shanghai, or the streets of Beijing had been. That trip had been amazing to the point where I was having dreams about those places every night.

Ted gave me a slap on the back as we started toward the time clock. "What was it last night, Tang Dynasty girls, Geishas, or that hot little number behind the cash register at the 7-11? What was her name again?"

"Geisha?" I looked back at Ted as I slipped my punch card out of my pocket. "You know that's a Japanese thing, right?"

Ted cocked his head like a lost puppy. "What's the diff?"

The gang in the line up behind us all laughed. Barry, who was right behind me, muttered something under his breath. He hadn't caught why they were all laughing but knew that, once again, Ted was the idiot in the spotlight.

"It's okay," I consoled. "The two countries are right beside each other. It's an honest mistake. No Geishas. Last night I was back on the Great Wall and it was cold. The snow had started and climbing down was becoming treacherous. Did I tell you a couple of people died on the Wall when I was there?"

"In your dream or for real?" Ted asked.

"For real. There was a freak snowstorm after we left Beijing and it caught a bunch of tourists off guard."

Julie caught the tail of the conversation as she joined us. "They slipped?"

I didn't mean to smile, but her beauty had that kind of power over me. "Uh, ya. It's ridiculous how steep it gets in parts."

Barry cut the line and punched out. "It snows in China?"

"Yes, and the snow was starting to come down hard in my dream. I had just reached a steep set of stairs. They had this railing down the centre of them, so I propped myself up on it and ass-slid to the bottom."

I had thought of doing that in real life, even got a fellow tourist to take a picture of me sitting on that rail. A nearby guard had quickly yelled something in Mandarin and motioned that it wasn't allowed. It wasn't like I'd really slide down the damn thing. I'd have killed myself.

"That's way too cool," Ted chuckled. "Did you manage to slide that rail when you were there?"

"Hell ya. The darn guard chased me for about ten minutes. Thankfully, they've got shorter legs than us."

Julie giggled as she pressed me with her eyes. Was I shitting them? It was so hard to tell when I was in my story-telling zone. "Where are you going tonight, Andy?"

"I never know with these dreams. I could sure handle a trip to Shanghai again. I loved that place. You should see the buildings at night."

Without realising it, I had narrowed my conversation to only Julie. My eyes had locked on hers, and hers on mine. It was as if we were in some small diner, sitting across from each other, sharing a moment like best friends, or perhaps lovers.

"They, uh, light the buildings like Christmas trees. One building looked like two big glitter balls stuffed on an Eiffel Tower, except the balls are constantly changing colour. You'd love it."

2

Kevin Weisbeck

"I'm sure I would," Ted chuffed.

I quickly pulled my eyes away from hers. This wasn't any diner, and we weren't alone. What was I thinking, letting my guard down like that? Had anyone notice? I'd get ribbed for a week if they had. You see, Julie was in a class all by herself. Sure, she was single, but only by choice. That girl could have landed herself a lawyer or doctor at the drop of a hat, if she wanted to. For some crazy reason, she didn't feel the need.

"Uh, yes." I managed a sideways glance at Julie as I finally punched my card. The girl was still staring at me, and was that a smile? I dang near snapped my neck when I looked away. Damn she was cute.

That night, supper at home consisted of a frozen pizza and a Monday Night Football game. Miami, my team, was playing New England and, even though New England was the better team, the score at the two-minute warning was close. But that wasn't why I was smiling. Julie, and that stupid moment, was lodged in my brain like a fat kid in an economy airline seat.

Was it a moment? We'd never dated, never would, but we'd sure shared something. Was there some kind of crazy friendship that I hadn't clued in to? I don't always catch the signs. Maybe she knew I liked her, and this was some form of charity? I knew girls like that. They loved making losers feel good, like some kind of paying it forward.

Tannehill passed the ball to Landry, bringing the ball to the New England forty-two-yard line. Sadly, I was too wrapped up in my thoughts and missed seeing it happen live. Thank God for replays. I was also on my laptop, focusing on vacation pictures. One in particular had caught my eye. It was the one I took on a cruise of Shanghai's Huangpu River. The Bund, Shanghai's skyline, was lit to perfection. Julie would have loved seeing it.

Tannehill hands the ball off to Jay Ajayi. Jay's the new guy on the team and he runs the ball down to the eight-yard line. I set the laptop aside. Things on the field had just got serious. If the Miami Dolphins won, they'd be in the playoffs against Pittsburgh

A Dream Escape

and then maybe Oakland. It was a much better fate than the alternative, which was yet another early end to the football season.

I lifted another slice of pizza out of the box as a time out was called. They always needed to get those shaving cream and beer ads in. There were even two car rental commercials before getting back to the game.

The ball is snapped. Jay Ajayi for five more yards. No one's calling a time out. New England wants to kill the clock before Miami can score, and Miami wants to score, leaving no time left for New England. Only one team will get what they want.

Suddenly, the phone rang.

"Seriously?" I screamed. I edged to the end of the cushion. The laptop teetered beside me like a forgotten friend in a corner pub.

The phone rang again. Meanwhile the teams were lining up over the ball. Tannehill saw something in the defence and starts calling a different play. He snaps the ball, keeps it, and lunges forward.

The phone rang for a third time. I started to get up, my eyes glued to the TV set. Then out of nowhere a thought came to me. What if it was Julie? That got me moving.

I was standing now and edging blindly for the phone. The dog pile on the goal line grew and the referees moved in. There was no call yet. The phone rang again, and I stretched my arm in the direction of it. I fumbled for the receiver and pulled it out of the cradle, cutting the fifth ring short. Then the referee's arms went straight up. It was a touchdown!

"That's what I'm talking about."

The person on the other end of the phone sounded confused. "Hello?"

"Sorry." I quickly added, "just watching the game. Can I help you?"

"I'm Amanda with Scotiabank. I'm calling about your account. Is this Mr Jones?"

"It is. What's wrong with my account?"

"Nothing, maybe. We've been seeing some odd activity. Can I have your mother's maiden name."

4

"Smilphton, that's with an ph, not an f."

"Thank you, Mr. Jones." There was a brief pause. "Were you out last night trying to use the card?"

"No, I was home all night, sleeping. Why?"

"Someone was at an ATM trying to access money with your card. There were three failed attempts, so the card was flagged."

"That's impossible." I reached for my wallet and fumbled the card out.

"You have your card, Mr. Jones?"

"I do."

"They may have cloned your card. We'd like to cancel the card and issue you another one. You could pick it up at your branch and change the password there. Would that be okay?"

It seemed like a lot of work. The bank was a few blocks out of the way. "And if I don't want that?"

"We have the right to terminate our responsibility." She waited a second. "That's the fraud insurance. If some one tries again, and is successful, we wouldn't cover the loss."

"Hey, we don't want that." I had saved a few hundred dollars and didn't need some a-hole with a knack for computers taking it from me. "Cancel the card and I'll be in after work tomorrow."

"Thank you, Mr. Jones. I'll be here in the afternoon at the courtesy desk. I'll have your new card ready, and I can help you set it up."

"It's Amanda, right?"

"It is. I'll look forward to seeing you."

"Same."

I hung the phone up wondering if she was cute. She sure sounded cute, and friendly. Ah, who was I kidding. They all sounded cute over the phone. I scooped the leftover pizza, walked it into the kitchen, and slid it into a microwave-warped plastic container. It had just become tomorrow's lunch. On my way back to the living room, I downed the last swallow of Pepsi and turned the TV off. The laptop was folded up and placed on a stack of magazines beside the empty Pepsi bottle. "Good enough."

A Dream Escape

Entertaining wasn't a priority, or even on the radar in my place. The guys at work were great guys, but I saw enough of them at work. I didn't need to see them after work as well. And let's not even talk about Julie. My home would be the last place I'd ever want to take her. She didn't need to know I lived in a dump. At thirty-three, I should have had more, but between the lack of good choices, the all too often bad choices, and the choices not made, I had ended up here.

None of that mattered now as I headed for the bedroom, because soon I'd fall asleep, and I'd be in China. Whether I was walking amongst the terra cotta soldiers in Xi'an, or helping the families in Ping'an pick rice, it would be a lot more exciting than eating pizza or drilling holes in kitchen cabinets. I slipped on a pair of pj bottoms and smiled in the mirror as I brushed my teeth.

Here, I was shy and more of a goof than a catch. In my dreams I was whatever I wanted to be. Nobody knew me there. I could be that American football player or Canadian Mountaineer. Nobody would know any different in China.

I rested my head on the pillow and let my eyes close. It was nine o'clock pm, but not where I was going. It would be morning wherever I woke up… and where would wherever be? I was hoping for the hotel in Shanghai. It was a five-star suite with a California King-sized bed that cradled me better than my own mother.

When I opened my eyes, I looked around and tried to shake the cobwebs. They were always as thick as crocheted afghans during these transitions. I was on a bus. It was familiar, the hard seats and the free bottled water. Candy Wang, our guide, was collecting passports in order to check us into our next hotel. My back twinged as I dug through my pocket for mine. These bus rides were crippling.

Outside, the back-up alarm on the bus was beeping as Mr Ma, guided the bus into a parking stall. As he did, Candy started telling us about the Temple of Heaven. Outside the people were bundled up like little piggies in blankets, which meant I'd woken up in a rather chilly Beijing. Why was I dreaming of this place?

And was that a snowflake?

Chapter 2

U p until now, the dreams had been fairly generic and mimicked the events of my vacation. An attractive young Asian woman, named Candy, had been and still was our tour guide. As expected, she wanted us to stay close behind her like sticky rice. There was no need to lose anybody. Finding them amongst this mass of people would be chaotic to say the least.

I remembered that kind of chaos as those first few nights after returning from the actual vacation. I had been severely sleep-deprived from the flight and my dreams had come at me in waves of confusion.

On the day I flew back, the twelve-hour flight had landed me in Kelowna five hours before I'd left Beijing. Oddly enough, it had made for one hell of a long day. Add to that the two weeks of sleeping in beds made of cement and it was no surprise that I wasn't my usual self. Those first few nights back had grabbed a hold of me like dog shit on the underside of a shoe. Each night the dreams wrapped me up in challenges that made no sense. How many grains of rice do you need to start a car, or how far is the swim to Hawaii from Shanghai verses Hong Kong? Don't forget to factor in shark attacks. Nope, nothing from those first dreams made any sense.

A Dream Escape

Like the scrambled pieces of a puzzle, the dreams soon fell into place and instead of feeling like nightmares, they became welcome adventures. It was a lot like looking through virtual photo albums and reliving the experiences. That being said, I knew they were dreams and enjoyed pushing the boundaries. Sometimes I got back to the bus late or strayed a little further than we were allowed. It didn't matter because things always worked out. At the end of the day, I always went for an after-supper nap and woke up to an alarm clock telling me I had to get up and build a few more cabinets.

But I'm getting ahead of myself. Right now, Candy had finished checking us into our hotel. "Passport, Mr Andy."

I looked up to see Candy holding a little blue book. It was mine. They needed all the passports every time they checked into a hotel. "Thank you, Wuang Fang."

"You remembered, Mr Andy." She seemed surprised that I could pronounce her Chinese name as good as I did. "You speak good."

"*Xie xie.*" Which meant thank you if I was pronouncing it right. If wrong, it probably meant I wanted to eat her neighbour's camel. I'd had a couple weeks before my vacation to practice. "*Ni chi la ma?*"

"Oh, yes. I have eaten. Thank you for asking." Candy gave me a second look before handing off the next set of passports. "I hope you bring jacket, Mr Andy."

I watched her as she worked her way down the isle. She never gave me a second look when I was actually in China, but this was my dream, my way.

On the temple grounds, I quickly found the exercise equipment and used it to work the kinks out of my back. Again, getting ahead of the group was no big deal. They'd catch up to me in time, they always did. I was blindly looking through the crowd when I first saw someone staring at me.

I squinted for a better look, but the woman had disappeared as fast as she'd appeared. She was a tall white woman with long loose curls of dark chestnut hair. Close to five foot nine, she couldn't have weighed more than a hundred and thirty pounds...

8

maybe thirty-five. I used the girls in the stack of magazines back on my coffee table as a comparison.

I jumped off the equipment and quickly gave chase, but she was gone. Unlike the local Chinese, this woman was quite exotic, with pronounced cheekbones and a strong jawline. So, why had she been watching me?

Why would a girl like that be interested in a guy like me? Did it matter? Hell, this was my dream. I could attract whomever I wanted. I smiled at the thought, a girl like that gawking at me. I might never want to wake up.

"Sticky rice, Mr Andy, sticky rice. Candy no want to lose you." She smiled and put a hand on my shoulder while she did a quick head count.

Was this flirting? I looked at the hand and noticed she wasn't that eager to remove it. Yes, these dreams were a huge improvement from the real world. Like a mother duck, she started off again and we all followed.

I only followed because our next stop was a restaurant. Yes, in dreams you get hungry. In China you get extra hungry because the potential for a great meal is always at the next restaurant. We all made our way down a tight street, through a couple blocks of back alley, across a busy lane, and into what looked like a crack in the wall. I had to look twice to see if there was an actual door or a crack.

Within minutes of sitting down, the food was served and as expected, the fish had bones, the rice was gummy, and the vegetables were non-existent. This wasn't my dream meal. On more than one occasion the group at the table had grumbled about the food. Even in these dreams, the good meals were few and far between. It was the one thing I couldn't control.

As always, there was time to check the area out if you ate quickly. I had eaten next to nothing and was roaming the lobby when en elderly man approached me. He was the typically shorter, dark haired local with leathery skin. What wasn't typical was the fact he was wearing a cream-coloured suit, a fedora hat, and there was no contempt in his aged expression. Chinese men always looked angry, but not this guy. The crow's feet emerged when he smiled, and there was a playfulness to his grin.

These were details that I wasn't used to seeing in these dreams. Candy's features were clear, as was Mr Ma's, but I'd seen them every day. I never saw that same detail in my fellow tourists, or that old lady who had cooked us rice in Ping'an. I barely noticed them in real life. As for the rest of China, it had been a blur of neon, endless attractions, and round faces that were wrapped up in their own lives. No, this guy's face wouldn't have been this clear unless I'd seen it before, and I knew I hadn't.

"*Ni hăo*," the man started.

I returned his gesture. "*Ni hăo*." The face didn't even look remotely familiar. "Do I know you?"

"Of course not. Do you have a minute?"

I looked back at the room where the others were still eating. "Well, I really shouldn't." I had to remind myself that this was a dream. As real as it seemed, it wasn't. "What the hell. Where are we going?"

He led me to the back of the restaurant where an old silken screen hid a shabby wallpapered wall. The man pushed on a panel and a part of the wall sprung open. He stood back and motioned for me to enter. "After you."

"Uh, I don't know." I could hear the voices of my group in the distance. They were still having fun. "I mean, I have no idea who you are or what's going on back there."

"Not a problem. My name is Mr Chin and I know what you're thinking… Mr Chin? The man has no chin. If anybody should be Mr Chin, it should be you. You have a very nice chin. Chinese people, we are ripped off. We get no chin, no nose and our hair is always this colour. We have baby, hair is black. We have girlfriend, hair is black. We get old, hair still black. It just not fair. Me want grey hair, like you, or chin like Jay Leno."

"Isn't that a little too much chin?" I asked.

"No such thing." He held out his hand for me to enter the room. "Now you know me. Tell me who you are."

"I'm Andy."

"Andy, do you play poker?"

Was he kidding? "Love the game."

Again, he motioned for me to enter. This time I did. Inside, the small room had three tables. Each table had five or six men gambling and a beautiful female dealing the cards. I eyed each dealer, trying to figure out which one was the cutest and eventually gave up. They all had adoring Chinese features, as did two of the three girls serving drinks.

"Pick a table, Mr Andy. Are you good for two-fifty?"

I reached for my wallet and Mr Chin stopped me. "No! We settle later. Maybe you win and put money *in* wallet."

"That would be nice, Mr Chin." I picked the second table solely because that dealer shot me a coy hint of a smile, that and her waitress had eyes that looked a lot like the eyes of the woman I'd seen at the park. The game stopped momentarily while I grabbed a spot between two men that looked like life-long customs agents. I shot them a smile hoping for any expression, but they were too cool for that. A few stacks of chips were placed in front of me, and I tossed two green ones into the centre.

Mr Chin slapped me on the back, before starting for the door. "Good luck, Mr Andy."

He looked back at me from the doorway. This time the man's smile wasn't as obvious. He had hardened and those cheery crow's feet had faded.

"Uh, thanks."

The game was Texas Hold'em and my first-hand netted me an easy win as I flopped a full house. And why not, this was my dream. A tray of treats was set down beside me, along with a beer. The cashews were delicious as I slowly worked my way to the bottom of the bowl.

I won three of the next five hands before the losing began.

Chapter 3

Ten minutes soon turned into three hours, which quietly stretched into four as I tried to recoup my losses. At times the cards gave me hope, but those moments were few and far between. My once, two hundred and fifty, had soon dwindled to sixty. My luck wasn't coming back, so I decided to call it a day. Poker was a fun game when you were seeing aces, not so fun when it was threes and sevens.

"I should probably settle up. I need to get going."

Mr Chin had already returned and stepped forward with a smile. The dealer took a second to count the chips. It was actually sixty-two. She announced the number in Chinese, "*liushi-er wan.*"

Now I'd learned a little Chinese and thought that sixty-two was *luishi-er*. So, what was the '*wan*' part all about? I was about to ask him when my waitress came forward. I'd only caught fleeting glimpses, but she sure looked like the Caucasian woman from the Temple of Heaven.

She leaned into my ear and whispered, "Andy. Can we chat for a second?"

I nodded, solely because I was speechless. The accent I heard from her, the one I'd never expected, was British. I'd be lying if I didn't admit a strong fondness for those women. I stared intently and followed her to the far end of the room. She took my wallet and flipped through the cards while I watched. There was a

Kevin Weisbeck

Visa card, a library card, two nearly expired Amex gift cards, and a discount card for a grocery store called *The Pig Barn.*

I thought I was a card short and wanted to say something, but she cut me off. "I don't see a platinum card in here. You know you owe him one hundred and eighty-eight thousand dollars, right?"

"Shit." My knees wobbled. "Is that what the '*wan*' part was?"

She nodded.

"He didn't say thousand. He just said two fifty."

"And you didn't ask?"

"In hindsight, maybe I should have."

"What am I going to do with you, Andy. This was reckless. You should be with the tour looking for over-priced jade trinkets."

"I know. I'm really sorry."

"Oh, don't be sorry to me. I'm not the one who owes Mr Chin all that money."

I looked over to Mr Chin. The man's smile had returned, and why not. I owed him a hundred and eighty-eight thousand dollars.

I leaned forward and took a deep breath. Her perfume was a familiar one. I'd smelled it before. I couldn't place where, but I knew dreams were based on familiarities, and this was definitely a freak'n dream. "I don't have that much. Hell, I'll never have that much. Seriously, what's he gonna do, slap me awake and send me back to my bedroom?"

"What? Uh, look Andy. This isn't a dream. This is real shit and you're knee-deep in the stuff. You fucked up and fucked up bad."

"No. This is a dream, and it went south, no big... uh... can I call you Olivia?" And why not? It was my dream.

"Olivia? Fuck, whatever. What are you going to do?"

"In a little while I'm going to wake up and everything will be fine. Do you know why?"

"Enlighten me." Olivia looked over to Mr Chin.

A Dream Escape

I shifted and stepped past her. "Because I have an alarm clock. It's gonna wake me any minute now because I've got cabinets to make."

"No." Olivia stopped me. "This isn't what you think. Let me talk to him."

I chuckled as I stopped and let her step past me. "Knock yourself out."

She walked over to Mr Chin and they talked. While she did that, I calmly grabbed another drink and a handful of cheese puffs. They were tasty and since I'd be waking soon, I'd call them breakfast. She returned and took the beer out of my hand.

"He said he'd forgive the money, but you're going to do him a favour. He won't call it right now, but he will call it someday. You won't be able to say no."

"Got it. Don't say no, do a favour, kiss his ring." I shot her a wink. "Do I have to kiss his ring?"

"What the hell are you babbling about?"

"Marlon Brando, Al Pacino, James Caan." I held my hand out. "Come on. That guy comes to the Don during his daughter's wedding day, and he asks a favour. In return the guy owes him a favour." I gave her a poor, but honest impersonation of Marlon Brando. "Someday, and that day may never come, I will call upon you to do a service for me. Until this day, consider this justice a gift on my daughter's wedding day."

I smiled at her silence.

She didn't smile back.

"Then I kiss his ring and leave. What? You don't watch movies? It was a classic."

"Except he will want a favour, and he isn't wearing a ring." She sighed. "One more thing." She took a couple steps away from me.

"What's going on?" I asked.

She watched as two men got up from the table and grabbed me by the arms. They held me while Mr Chin brought a phone book over. "Mr Chin needs to save face."

"Whoa! What the... I'll do what you want. I give you my word."

14

The first shot caught me in the ribs, taking my breath away. The second swing of the book caught me across the jaw. If this was a dream, it hurt like hell. A third hit me in the thigh and a fourth and final shot was an open-handed slap across my face.

"I never trust a man's word," Mr Chin laughed. Then he grabbed me by my extra-large chin. "You're a good man, Mr Andy. I like you." He turned to Olivia. "Does he understand my terms?"

Olivia nodded and headed for the door. What would they do with me if I didn't? She looked back only briefly and in that second, she saw something in my eyes that comforted her. It was fear.

I dropped to my knees when the two men let go. Mr Chin also took a step back and grabbed my pretty young dealer by the hand. He led her around the table, and she knelt down beside me.

Mr Chin put his hand on my head. "This is Lucy and she'll make you feel better... if you know what I mean. And don't ever make me do this again. I do not like being the bad guy. Now get up. You're making yourself look bad."

I let Lucy, if that was her real name, help me to my feet. She took me by the arm and helped me out the door. From there she walked me to her room on the twentieth floor.

"Where are you taking me?"

"I have room. I take care of you. I do good job, you no be diss... point... You no be upset with my care." She leaned me against the wall as she slipped the card in the door lock. The door opened and I made my way to a king-sized bed where I flopped on my back. Lucy followed and as I tried to catch my breath, she began to massage my sore leg.

"That feel good?" she asked.

"It does." I was still trying to figure everything out. It sure was a weird dream. My body wasn't supposed to hurt like this. Then Lucy unbuckled my belt and started to slip my pants off. I almost said something but was more curious to see how far this was going to go. I hadn't had a dream like this since I was a teenager.

Her hand found the bare skin of my sore leg and she continued the massage. This wasn't to soothe my pain as much as it was to eliminate bruising. The blood needed to be worked through the flesh. A bruise would be proof of an assault. I let her work her magic as the pain eased.

After a few minutes she stopped, disrobed, and climbed into bed with me. I closed my eyes, and let her kisses ease the pain. Now this was my kind of dream. I tried to enjoy her kiss, but the fog of sleep was coming way too fast.

Before we could get into it the alarm clock went off, reminding me of the cupboards that had to be made.

"Damn it!"

I casually rolled over to see a naked woman on the bed beside me and Lucy, if that was her real name, wasn't breathing.

Chapter 4

I fell out of bed and couldn't pull my eyes away from her blue skin. I couldn't call out her name, couldn't shout for help. The words were caught in my throat like a mouthful of chewed up soda crackers. Instead, I got to my feet and put my hand on the smooth silky skin of her hip. I was about to give her a gentle shake, tell her to wake up, but she was cold.

My hand recoiled as if being carpet shocked. I scrambled to the ensuite and dropped to my knees in front of the toilet. My head hung in the bowl as I brought up as much of last night's pizza as my body would allow. Guts wretched and ribs hurt, but I didn't stop. Each time I thought of her, I heaved again. Soon, there was nothing coming out. Tears streamed down my cheeks as the stomach acid burned in the back of my throat. My God, was she really dead?

No way. She couldn't be dead. Shit, how the hell did she find her way to my bed? She was a dream, a freak'n dream and nothing more. I flushed the toilet, and the disgusting mess swirled into a fresh pallet. I heaved again, but there was nothing. The clean bowl calmed my stomach, relaxing the tense muscles in my shoulders. I slumped back on the cold floor and tucked my knees up into my chest. Closing my eyes spun the room, as if I'd been drinking, so I kept them open. What the hell was going on?

A Dream Escape

The aching in my ribs slowly eased with long steady breaths. Had Mr Chin really beaten me with that book, or did they hurt from the violent convulsions? I put my hand up to my face. I'd been hit in the jaw. My teeth hurt, but this was a dream, just a fucking dream.

Her skin had been so cold, and it was blue. And was that a needle sitting on the nightstand? There was a two-foot length of rubber tubing beside the needle. She had done drugs. That was it. She had done drugs after I had fallen asleep. This wasn't my fault. Maybe not, but how would I explain this to the police? Mr Chin gave me a beating and Lucy, a consolation prize, was dead. And where was this Mr Chin, they'd ask. And what do I mean, she was my dealer in the dream.

"Shit."

Then I heard a noise, like a door closing. It wasn't a slam, nor was it a gentle close, like something a husband might do when he's off to work and the house is asleep.

And was it the front door? As I ran through the bedroom, I had to take a look. It wasn't anything more than a morbid curiosity. I'd never seen a dead body before. What I saw, stopped me in my tracks. The body was gone, and the nightstand was bare.

I rubbed my eyes. "What the hell?" Was the dead woman a dream?

There was a chair beside the bed, opposite the nightstand. I always folded my clothes and put them there. It was something I'd done since I was a child. They weren't there. My pants were on the floor by the foot of the bed. There was a shirt hanging off the corner. That just didn't happen, unless…

I looked down at my shrunken manhood. "What did you do last night?"

Suddenly the ten-minute snooze went off. It was after seven and time to get up. I jumped across the bed and sprawled to shut the clock's snooze off. Careless Whisper, by George Michaels, ended abruptly with a slap.

"Shit, shit, shit."

Was this a situation? Where the hell had Lucy gone? I sat up on the edge of the bed and cupped my face in my hands. I had

18

touched her cold skin. It wasn't the kind of thing you'd forget. Sure, she wasn't here now, but she sure as hell had been.

That meant I had crawled all over her last night, hadn't I? Wait. There was a better chance that I'd passed out first. I couldn't remember doing anything. She was massaging my leg and that led to kisses, but the rest was muddled. Had she climbed on top of me and placed her hands on my chest? Damn it. It didn't feel like a dream.

And who was at the door? Could the dream have lingered? She had been there in my bed, but that was only because I wasn't fully awake. I was still half out of it when I was puking. It had to be. That made a lot more sense than a dead and disappearing woman. I sat on the bed until the music came on again. This time I properly shut the alarm off and got dressed.

"Hey Andy, you look like shit," Ted announced. "Are you limping?"

"I'm sure I do, and yes, I am. Rough night." Breakfast was McDonalds, and the drive to work cleared my head. Everything was making more sense now. My ribs and leg hurt a bit, but that was from falling out of bed and barfing my lungs out. The pizza had made me sick, like hallucinating sick.

"What the hell happened?"

"You wouldn't believe me if I told you."

"Does it have anything to do with your dreams?"

I started in on my poker story and Barry came over to listen in. By the end of it, three others had joined us. I hadn't noticed them at first. What a shame that my dreams were the needed distraction from their daily ho hum.

Barry gave me a pat on the back. "I don't know what's wrong in that noodle of yours, but I like it. You've got hookers, hitmen, and a hot British gal. I wish I could get in on this. That British gal, have you... You know?" He made an okay sign with his pointing finger and thumb. Then he repeatedly slipped a finger through it.

A Dream Escape

I shook my head. Only Barry would ask that kind of question. Still, I smiled at the thought. She was a beautiful woman. "She wants me. I was too busy with the other one."

"You mean the dead girl?"

I registered the sarcasm, and it buckled me. That was Julie's voice. I looked up to see her walking away.

"Awkward..." Greg said as he downed his coffee and also walked away.

The others took the cue and left for their workstations. There was a lot of paperwork to sort. Barry remained. "You like her?"

"Julie? She's hot."

"She's also miles beyond anything you and I might end up with."

"Thanks for the reminder."

Barry laughed. "No. I mean you're having these crazy dreams and we all listen. It kinda makes you something special. It's like we hear these stories, and they resonate like a good book. Did ya hear what he dreamt about last night, kinda thing."

"Doesn't that make me a freak though?"

"No more than us for wanting to hear them. I know I'll never get to China or find a dead hooker in my bed. You're kinda cool, in a freakish kind of way. I say just go with it."

Just go with it. I gave that logic some thought. It was simple, honest, and what I wanted to hear. I'd enjoyed these dreams because that was what they were. Last night had been cool, in a twisted dead hooker kind of way. I could have lived without parts of it, being beaten up and all. On the other hand, I'm pretty sure I'd had sex, albeit with a woman who turned a horrifying shade of turquoise. That being said, it was the only action I'd had in months. I'd take it.

And tonight, I'd be sleeping with one eye open.

Chapter 5

S taring at the bedroom door, my eyes burned from the lack of sleep. I tried to watch a late-night rerun of Jeopardy, but it wasn't easy. Some of the answers I knew, others were poor guesses. I normally didn't stay up this late when I had to work the next day, but after last night, I had second thoughts on falling asleep. If I could be guaranteed rice fields or tea leaves, I'd have no problem resting my head on the pillow. What if I went back to Beijing? What if Mr Chin was waiting for me?

"What is Jean Webster." The question was 'Who penned Dear Enemy and Daddy Longlegs?'

TV's Alex announced I was right. It brought my mock score to sixty-nine hundred points and that made me chuckle. I put my legs up on the coffee table and bumped the Ketchup-blotched plate with my foot. It had held an oven baked box of fish and chips, which was delicious. Triangle shaped beer-battered Cod and fries.

Again, I looked back at the bedroom door while Alex set up Final Jeopardy. The category was China. "What?"

A shiver ran the length of my spine. Why China? They usually had some dumb question that only the nerdiest of nerds might know. What's the fourth largest city in Rhode Island, or which President was afraid of spiders and teddy bears.

The show broke to commercial which meant I had lots of time to think about China. I seriously didn't need the grief. The image of the blue body came back to me causing my hands to tremble. I remembered hurling several slices of pizza into the toilet and watching it swirl away. The second commercial pulled me from the thought. It was an add for a new Chinese restaurant. The guy in the add looked and sounded a lot like Mr Chin. It wasn't a perfect likeness, but dreams were seldom exact. They tended to exaggerate features.

Final Jeopardy finally came back. Was I over-thinking this whole China dream? I had to have seen that commercial before and these residual people were carried over. They were no more real than the roles they played. Mr Chin was a variation of Mr Shing from the advertisement.

Alex read the question, "Other than a straight flush, what beats a full house, Andy?"

The answer was four of a kind. It was what had dropped me down to sixty-two thousand, which was what had caused me to drop out of the game. It had cracked me in the jaw with a phone book and caused me to wake up next to a dead hooker. I grabbed the remote to change the channel, but Jeopardy was on every channel.

"What the hell is this?"

"Come on, Andy. We need your answer." Alex was looking straight at the camera. He was looking at me through that camera. "We'll go to commercial while you think about it."

The commercial came on and it was Mr Shing. "Andy, my friend, come to bed. We need to talk. Lucy was a no-show today. I think you know something about that. I'm not angry." He smiled. "But we need to talk."

"No!" I said as I accidentally kicked the plate onto the floor, waking myself from the nap. My heart was racing as I watched Alex ask, 'What is the fourth largest city in Rhode Island?'

"Shit. I had dozed off." I shook the cobwebs. "Pawtucket, I mean, what is Pawtucket?"

Alex looked to the camera, "That's right, Andy. Now off to bed."

Chapter 6

Morning eventually came, and I had succeeded in doing everything in my power to stay awake. I'd cooked two other meals in the oven, watched some of the worst movies imaginable and, jogged two laps around the block. That being said, I'd bummed a cigarette on the second lap from a stranger who was returning from the bar. I smoked it down to the filter. It was disgusting.

One of the meals I cooked last night was a frozen lasagne. It was small, so I'd eaten half and packaged the rest of it into two lunches. I tossed one of them into my lunch kit after dressing for work.

In the break room, Barry tagged me right away. "Whoa man, what happened to you? I thought you looked bummed yesterday. You dun taken it to a new low."

"I know. I got a little messed up last night. Too busy thinking about those damn dreams."

"How so? They're just dreams. They have no merit on real life."

"Dreams can fuck you up. I couldn't stop thinking about that dead girl last night. I was kind of…"

"You stayed up all night?"

"I did. Every time I closed my eyes I thought of that girl, thought of that beating I took. It was crazy."

A Dream Escape

"But there was no beating. There was no girl. You don't owe anybody any money, and there isn't anybody out to get you. And sadly, there isn't any British girl with the dark locks. It's all made up in your head." He tapped his temple with a bent index finger.

"Well, you put it that way and it makes me sound stupid."

"If you're losing sleep over this dream, then you are."

"You're losing sleep?" It was Julie.

"I, uh, well…"

Barry saw the struggle and decided to let me take that fall under the bus on my own. "I'll catch up with you later."

I nodded. Then I turned to Julie and stood there with my mouth partially open. Bloodshot eyes told the story. I had to shrug. "What?"

"Was it because of that girl that died?"

"Yes, but she didn't die. She never existed. Sleep and dreams, that's all it is, yet it's messing me up."

"Fear doesn't stem from logic, Andy. It comes from emotions."

"What are you saying, I'm all emotional?"

Julie placed a hand on my shoulder and laughed. It wasn't flirtatious or harbouring any deep meaning. It was one friend consoling another. "Andy, you've always been emotional and that's not a bad thing. Most guys lack in that department and it's nice, no refreshing, to see a guy acting human instead of all testosterone and macho. Not all girls like macho, ya know."

"Most do."

"Then most girls are idiots."

"Is this when I'm supposed to argue your point?"

"Ha, good one. I'm glad you had a rough night. Even in dreams, when people die, you should be rattled. But it was a dream, like you said, so get some sleep tonight. Have an adventurous dream and come see me when you get in tomorrow. I love hearing your stories."

With that she smiled and took her hand off my shoulder. I watched her leave and, although I knew girls like that never dated

24

guys like me, I smiled and let my mind wander into that world of make belief.

After work, I had to run a few errands, so I grabbed take-out for supper. There was nothing like a burger and fries before bed. Half the Cola was dumped down the sink and the last two bites of the burger were tossed over the fence to Rusty, the neighbourhood dog. His name came from a homeless person who had died a while back. The dog was a scrawny Shepherd that always did tricks for food, or a pat on the head, much like Rusty had. There wasn't an official owner of this dog, because this block was all rental townhouses and none of us could have pets, officially. When it got cold, each of the tenants, me included, took turns taking the dog in for the night.

It was only six-thirty when I started my wind-down ritual of stacking my clothes on the chair beside the bed, but tired was tired. I was beyond caring about what came from the other side. I didn't want another day like today. The hours had dragged and every time I stood still, I started to drift off. At last coffee, I fell out of my chair. Everyone had watched me teeter like a falling tree and laughed when I finally went over. Barry had called out 'timber' before catching me.

Oddly enough, my sleepless night had knocked me to a higher level of cool. Julie was befriending me, and all the others had seen or heard about it. There were a few that kept to themselves, but even they had popped by to see if I was okay. They seldom said hi to each other, let alone anyone like me.

My head hit the pillow and I forced my mind full of positive thinking, reinforced suggestion, and the Bund. Could I force that place into my dreams? Beijing was okay, but I still had a few reservations about going back. Mr Chin might find me walking the Great Wall and shoot me. Could he shoot me? Nah, the Bund in Shanghai was a lot better place. Thirty-some million people and hundreds of thousands of places to hide. It doesn't get any safer than that.

I needed several minutes to let the jelly in my skull settle. When it did, I awoke in a bed. It was a California King, as soft as duck down and warmer than a mother's hug. When my eyes focused, I saw that I was in a suite. It was a modern contemporary with windows the size of walls. They all looked out over high-rises, rooftops, and canals that stretched as far as the eye could see.

I looked past the clock that read eight-thirty and saw my suitcase. It had been opened and half the stuff taken out. I'd unpacked. That meant today was a trip to the silk factory followed by the Bund.

Bingo on the whole positive thinking thing, because this was Shanghai.

Chapter 7

After a breakfast of bacon, eggs, and beef noodles, I grabbed a coffee and headed down to the Lobby. The tour group was starting to assemble, and the faces all looked eager to get the next adventure underway. The usual ones had already started to complain. The weather was cold, the breakfast didn't have dumplings, or the beds were too hard, too soft. Mine was just right.

I walked past them to Candy. "*Ni Chi la ma?*"

"*Shide. Qing bang wo yixia?*" She looked distressed.

"Okay. Not sure what you just said, but I'm in."

"How do you explain weather is not the fault of China. Everyone wants good weather. We in China want good weather. We cannot make it so. How do I say to them that?"

"Two words." I'm sure my smile was sinister as I leaned toward her. "You tell them to, pump sand."

Candy giggle as she recoiled. "Candy would love to say, pump sand. I must be diplomatic."

"I understand. I could tell them for you."

"Thank you, Mr Andy, but I must say no. They are just frustrated."

"I know, but they're also on vacation. They don't have to worry about flights, bus trips, meals, or getting everyone booked into these hotels. You get all that crap. They should shut up and say thank you."

"Not how it works, Mr Andy." She warmed me up with a smile. "Thank you for noticing what I do."

"No problem. And if you want me to tune them in, just say the word. I'm your guy."

"We don't need trouble today." Candy gave me a playful swat on the arm as she passed. "I need to get bodies loaded on the bus."

I watched her leave. She looked good in pleather, which was a good thing, because it was all she wore. It seemed to be the go-to fabric for the women here, and why not. Most of them kept their figures in pretty good shape. Both men and women were fit, and it had to be the result of their fast-paced lifestyles. They generally ate like crap, with a solid diet of grease, but wore it off by walking everywhere.

As the last one on the bus, I missed getting a morning beer from the cooler. All that was left was water. No doubt, the bus driver underestimated Canadian's love of beer at any time of the day. The far end of the bus was vacant, so I worked my way back there and grabbed a window seat. As the bus started to roll, I rested my elbow on my knee and chin on my palm. I quietly watched the hotel as it grew smaller. Today I'd lay low, go with the flow. I didn't need any trouble. I could always make something up when I got to work. Maybe I'll tell them there's an Area 51 in the heart of Shanghai. Yes, that would work, and it's run by Irish dwarfs.

It was an hour and a half to the Bund and a good hour to the silk factory. The first time I'd been there I almost bought a comforter. They did the hard sell and it worked. Who wouldn't want the best comforter, which was silk? They kept you warm in the winter and cool in the summer. It was like they were made of magic. Sadly, they also had a magical price tag. Maybe I'd get one today. I could go to bed early tonight and just curl up in it. It wasn't like I'd have to worry about returning it.

"Deep in thought, that's a little scary. Even for you." The voice was female, smooth as melted chocolate, and British. "How are you doing? I missed you yesterday."

Kevin Weisbeck

I looked up to see Olivia spin around and take the seat beside me. God, she smelled good. "Ah, hi. What's up?" I cringed at my not so smooth delivery.

"I was looking for you yesterday. You must have found a good hiding place."

"Oh, I wasn't hiding. Why would I be hiding?"

"Do you remember Mr Chin?"

There, the elephant was in the room and she'd just pointed it out. "About that. You said you'd help me. That guy kicked the shit outta me."

"It could have been worse... a lot worse."

She pulled out a package of gum and tossed a piece in her mouth before offering me one. I declined. She started chewing, in a sexy tomboy kind of way, and I couldn't pull my eyes off her.

"How could it have been worse?"

"He could have killed you."

"I know you have a hard time believing this, but I'm not that worried. Ya see, this is all just a dream. I've been having these dreams about China ever since I visited this place. I got back home weeks ago."

"News Flash my good boy, this is no dream. Did it feel like a dream when you had your ass handed to you?"

"Dream pain, nothing more. I felt great when I woke up."

Olivia quickly recoiled her arm and gave me a shot in the ribs. It hurt like hell. She gave me a second shot in the leg. "Hurts, don't it?"

I doubled over and winced. "Cause this is a fucking dream, damn it. It won't hurt when I wake up."

She thought about it for a second. It made sense under my logic, which didn't prove a thing. "You're going to have to trust me on this one. And here's some more bad news. Mr Chin wants to see you."

"No problem. I'll look him up next time I'm in Beijing."

She faked a smile and raised her eyebrows. "Sorry sport. He's here in Shanghai. He's asked me to take you to him."

"And you said yes? What, do you work for him?"

29

A Dream Escape

"Hell no." She scratched her head. "If anything, I work for you."

"Great. Bring a message to Mr Chin. Tell him I'm sorry about the money and as soon as I can dream my bank account a little bigger, I'll pay him."

"He's already dealt with the money. You owe him a favour now, remember?"

"Whatever."

"He wants to talk about Piáoliang Shui."

"I'm sorry, what?"

"More like who. Scarlett was the dealer that you took back to your place. She was also the one that I had to retrieve the next morning. You do remember her, don't you?"

My jaw dropped. "Lucy?"

"Scarlett, Lucy, do you remember what the hell happened to her?"

"I have no idea. I woke up and there she was. I honestly expected to wake up alone. I always wake up alone."

"You don't know how she died?"

"I'm guessing it had something to do with the drugs. I saw some shit on the nightstand." I brought my eyes up to hers and held the stare. "You were there? I mean, I heard the door close. That was you, wasn't it?"

"I couldn't necessarily leave her there. You were all…" she put a finger in her mouth as if gagging.

"How? I mean, why was she there? How were you there? That was my bedroom."

"Shhhh."

I cleared my throat and lowered my voice. "Are you saying what happened wasn't a dream?"

"That's what I've been telling you all along, Andy."

"This is messed up."

She broke eye contact, sat back, and patted my leg. "When we get to the silk factory, there'll be a car waiting. You'll need to get in it, but don't worry, I'll be with you."

I sat back and turned my gaze to the passing countryside. This world was suddenly looking a little more real.

30

Chapter 8

A charcoal black limousine picked us up and all eyes were on me as Olivia ushered me into it like a rock star. Unlike in North America, where limo's were used like taxi cabs, this was a big deal. Candy cautiously inched toward it as if she might hop inside herself, even if only to get kicked out. At least she'd get to see what it looked like inside.

Candy, had she made it in, would have seen red leather, black marble, and gold accents. She'd have seen a sink, a wet bar, and a TV playing a Jackie Chan movie. There was black shag carpet, red throw pillows with gold stars and enough champagne glasses to accommodate a Liz Taylor wedding. What she might not have noticed was the inch-thick glass between them and the driver, the bullet-proof windows, or the set of tires that could be shot full of holes and not lose air.

"Talk to me, Olivia. Who is this Mr Chin?"

"He's a businessman, and a very successful one. He has hotels in Shanghai, Beijing, Hong Kong, and New York. He owns Oil Companies in Alberta and Texas, and he owns three casinos in Vegas."

"And those are his legit endeavours, I'm guessing."

"Exactly."

"And what does he want this time?"

"He told me he wanted to talk to you, so we talk."

A Dream Escape

I shifted in the seat. It was comfortable. "You know more than you're telling me."

Olivia nodded and I followed her eyes as she looked up. I took a second to look at the ceiling, then back to her. When I mouthed the word camera, she nodded.

And with that, the conversation was over. Her eyes lingered on mine and whether it was nerves or a sudden surge of confidence, I winked. It wasn't an obvious wink, and she'd have missed it had she blinked. She didn't. She returned an equally discreet smile.

Suddenly, I was ten feet tall, and why not, this was my dream. "What's a cute dame like you doing in a place like this?"

She rolled her eyes, but the corner of her mouth curled slightly. "Where'd that come from?"

"Hey, if I'm gonna die, I might as well die with a smile on my face."

"And I put a smile on your face, do I?"

I eyed her long lean torso, slowing down for the curves. "I'd bet that everything about you could put a smile on my face."

She shook her head as the car came to a stop. "Isn't betting what got you into this mess?"

"Touché, but you my dear, would be a sure thing."

I got out when the door opened. Olivia followed and took my arm as we were ushered up the cement steps. At the top of the stairs, Mr Chin greeted us. He had two thugs with him. "Shall we walk, Mr Andy?"

"Not with them."

"Then not with her."

She went to slip her hand out of my grip, and I reined her back in. "She's with me."

Mr Chin turned and started to walk away. He motioned for his men to stay. Olivia gave my arm a congratulatory squeeze as we hurried to catch up.

"What happened, Mr Andy?"

"You mean with Piáoliang?"

He stared, daring me to act stupid, lie, or deny her death.

"Everything was fine, I thought. When I woke up, she was dead. There was a needle and a surgical tube on the nightstand." I waited for a second before adding, "I'm sorry this happened. She seemed like a nice girl, but I never chose her vices."

"I found her on the street," said Mr Chin. "She was starving and had just been beaten up by her John. I fed her and hid her for a couple days until she was strong enough to tell me who he was."

"Then you bought her off the man?"

Mr Chin gave a hearty and uncontrollable laugh. "Something like that. You a funny man, Mr Andy. I like you."

"Good thing, huh?"

He held out a fist to pump. "Good thing indeed."

I gave it a tap and we walked to the edge of the water. Across the Huangpu River, the skyline rose from the ground like flowers made of glass and steel. One in particular, stood out to tourists. It always had. The Oriental Pearl Radio and TV Tower was impressive during the day, but more breathtaking at night. It was what they all came to see, and what they all brought their cameras for.

"She's beautiful, isn't she?" Mr Chin asked.

"She's a Pearl alright."

"She should be. You see that tower off to the right, the Shanghai Tower? It's one hundred and twenty-seven floors, stands over two thousand feet tall and has one hundred and six elevators, some of them the fastest in the world. It cost two and a half billion dollars to construct. The Pearl is a mere fifteen hundred feet tall, counting the spire, and has six elevators. It was a bargain in comparison. Still, the cameras all point to the Pearl. Do you know why?"

"It's a cool building?"

"Have you seen these buildings at night?"

"I have."

"Then you know how the night sky fills with colour. The Shanghai Government wanted a stage and so they asked the fine people who owned these buildings, a favour. Would they give them that stage? The people didn't hesitate because they knew better than to say no." He turned to me. "Do you know better?"

I got the point. "What do you want from me?"

"That's why I like you, Mr Andy." Mr Chin dropped a firm hand on my shoulder. "You're eager to pay your debts."

"I'm not sure about eager, but we can work with that."

"Good." Mr Chin pulled his hand back and turned to leave. "I'll put you up in a room. We'll talk more tomorrow."

I tightened my grip on Olivia's arm. "I think we should do this today. I might not be here tomorrow, and I'd really like to get this whole favour thing off my back. It's a heavy burden to carry."

"Even for a dream?" Mr Chin asked.

"What do you know about that?"

"I've heard you say that this is all some silly dream." He chuckled.

"I don't know what to think."

"Does this feel like a dream? I know it seems amusing. I have to ask, if this is a dream, why not tell me to go to hell? Why not get a gun and shoot me?"

"I don't know."

"I think you do. You know that in a dream you have nothing to worry about. You could easily ignore me, except…"

"Except?"

"I think there's a part of you that wants this adventure, that wants this to be real. Why is that, Mr Andy?"

I felt Olivia's arm slide around my back and I struggled to keep a smile off my face. "I have no idea, Mr Chin."

The room we were given was on the forty-second floor. We had to take an elevator to our elevator. In this room the floors were marble, and the walls and cabinets were cherrywood. I couldn't stop myself from checking out the craftsmanship. The hinges were installed without screws and there were no drill holes for the shelves. It was incredible, a work of art. Was this some strange dream hoax, or did this technology really exist?

"What are you looking at, Andy."

My temple bounced off the door as I tried to pull my head out. "Ouch!"

"Shit. Be careful." Olivia headed straight for the wet bar and pulled a cold beer out of the fridge. "Ah, that's better."

"Hey, am I paying for that?"

"She shot me a wink and tipped the bottle my way. "Want one."

"Sure." I took the bottle she handed me and popped the top. "Are you staying here tonight?"

"I am." She pointed to the left side of the bed. "Dibbs."

"Seriously?"

"It's a big bed," she smiled. "Ya got silk sheets and a comforter that weighs as much as I do."

I returned the smile.

"Relax, big boy. There's nothing gonna happen in that bed. You're the reason I'm stuck in Shanghai and hey, I'm curious to see what happens when you fall asleep. Do you disappear, or turn into a mouse and scurry away?"

"Oh, very funny."

"What?" Olivia had clued in. "You thought I wanted to sleep with you?"

What could I say? Yes, and I look like a fool. No, and I look like a fool. Say nothing, and I am the fool. "I'll take the right."

Olivia smiled as she strolled in front of me on her way to the bathroom. Her slacks were unzipped, slid down her legs and were left behind on the floor. The blouse was methodically unbuttoned, removed, and draped across the back of a chair. Now, down to a bra and panties, she bent over to roll her nylons down her leg. This she did at a leisurely and deliberately slow pace. I'm sure her backside felt the heat from my stare as it burned through what little she'd kept on. The wiggle in her cheeks as she walked through the bathroom doorway was meant to torture me, and torture me it did.

When the door closed, I finally took a breath. I also reached down and rearranged myself. What the hell was she thinking? What the hell should I be thinking? I turned my thoughts to Julie and the gang. I'd be at work in an hour or two. Would I have a story for them. The image of Olivia walking to the bathroom returned and I looped it through my brain over and over. Maybe I should call in sick tomorrow. That way I could sleep in.

Lord knows I won't be drifting off now.

Chapter 9

Sleep came quickly for Olivia. She was gone the moment her head hit the pillow. It gave me the chance to study the curves of the sheets, as they clung to her contours. The guilt of having to get up for work finally forced me to close my eyes. I awoke two minutes before the alarm went off.

My face was washed, teeth were brushed, and a lasagne was retrieved from the fridge. Outside, the air was mid-summer fresh. Until I'd brushed my teeth, I could taste the Chinese smog. When I had been there, the air had been thick with the stuff. It left a metallic taste on the sides of my tongue and at the back of my mouth. You couldn't wash it down with water or pop either, although some of their beers did a good number on masking it.

I pulled into the parking lot the same time as Julie, and she waited for me to get out of my car.

"Dare I ask about your dreams?" she joked.

"Ask away. I had a good one last night."

"Beijing?"

"No, Shanghai."

"Did you run into that Olivia girl?"

"I did. I actually shared a bed with her last night."

That comment made her squirm. "Did you wake up all…" She took a discrete glance at my crotch. "You know."

"Oh my God. Of course not. I was a gentleman." I shot her a stern but forgiving look. "I did run into that guy that beat me up. I made a deal with him, a favour for my life. It was the least I could do after owing him all that money and killing one of his hookers."

"You have some pretty messed up shit going on in your life, don't you?"

"I do."

"And now this guy wants a favour?"

"It okay. Like you said, it's just a dream. I kinda hope it's something crazy. Maybe I'll get to rob a bank or blow something up."

"What if he asks you to kill somebody."

The childish smile that had stretched across my face immediately vanished. "Why'd you have to say that?"

"Anything is possible." She swiped her card at the door to let us both in. She held it for me as I stood dazed. "Stop thinking about it. He probably just wants something blown up. Maybe a gas station."

"I sure hope so. I don't think I could kill anyone, even in a dream." I reached behind her and grabbed the door. "After you."

She ducked slightly to get under my arm and gave me a shove as she passed. "You're such a dork."

"Huh?"

"Are you going to tell everyone you just slept, and that nothing happened?"

"That's what happened."

"You should have fun with this. Make something up. Maybe this girl had some crazy move she used on you? Right?"

"Crazy move, Like what?"

"Maybe she's really bendable."

I'm sure I was blushing. "I guess I could stray a little from the truth."

"I say go big."

"Who are you. I always thought you were this proper girl next door type."

"I am, but I also have a warped sense of humour, thanks to you guys. Like this weekend I'm going to a friend's wedding. I'm gonna mess with the bride. I'm making trifle."

"Isn't that the dessert with busted up cake, pudding, and whipped cream? How would that mess with her?"

"Imagine the look on her face when I tell her it's all that's left of her wedding cake."

"Oh man, she'll freak."

Julie smiled. "What can I say. She never should have kissed my boyfriend back in grade seven."

"Hold a grudge much? Where is this wedding, in town?"

"An hour away, in Summerland. And don't worry, I won't let her suffer long. What do you think I am?"

I pulled out my timecard as we approached the clock. "I have no idea anymore."

"Exactly, so watch yourself." She dropped her card in the slot. "I'm just saying, you have quite the audience, so have fun with it. Who's gonna know otherwise."

"True enough."

At first coffee I told my story. Julie stayed in the background for support. After each lie, I looked up to see her eyes locked on me. She was smiling. As it turned out, Mr Chin wanted a huge favour, and Olivia couldn't wait until we got in the apartment. She was half-naked and pawing at me on the elevator. We made it into the room, but never made it as far as the bed. And she did this thing with toes that…

I had to stop. I made a point of looking straight at Julie, like I couldn't continue with her standing there. Each guy gave her the same stare, begging her to leave. She didn't. Instead, she stalled long enough to end the break. She knew I'd painted myself into a corner. What the hell could you do with toes?

As the buzzer sounded, I gave her a thank-you smile. She winked as if to say you're welcome. Partners in crime to the end.

At the end of the day, Julie was out first and sitting on the hood of my car. She slid off as I walked up. "That toe thing, where were you going with that?"

"I'm not very good at making shit up as I go. Thanks for the bail-out."

"Naked on the elevator?" she laughed.

"I know, and I wouldn't have done it on the floor either, not when there's a king-sized bed only a few feet away. But that makes me boring."

"Not wrong there. Doing it on the floor sounds good, but a bed is always better if you've got one." She slipped her hands in her pockets and became quiet.

I unlocked my car and watched her as she stood there. It was awkward, like she wanted something. "What?"

"What do you mean, what?"

"I get the feeling you want to ask me something."

"Why do you say that?" she asked.

"No reason, so you don't want to ask me anything?"

"Stop! I need a favour and it's a big one. Can I ask it later, and get a yes now?"

I hesitated for a second but realised that I was already nodding. We both knew I couldn't say no... not to her.

Chapter 10

After an amusing day with Julie and the guys at the factory, I woke up to see Olivia staring at me, much like I'd been staring at her before I fell asleep, only non sexually. It felt like my head had just hit the pillow back home, and other than a lingering fog, I felt fully rested. And why not? Being here meant I was sleeping in my bed back home.

I broke the morning silence. "Why are you staring?"

She scrunched her nose and asked, "have you ever thought of parting your hair down the middle?"

"No, why?"

"You've got the facial features for it. I don't think a side part suits you. It tilts everything to the left."

I cocked my head to the right. "Better?"

"Look, I just want to help." She reached her arm out from underneath the covers and let her fingers glide through my hair. When she pulled her hand away, the part was down the centre. It was crooked but gave her an idea. "Go to the mirror and check it out."

I would have, had I not gone to bed in my underwear, and had her touch not awoken me. Instead, I gave her a goofy smile and clutched at the covers.

"Suit yourself, but I think you rock it."

Kevin Weisbeck

She left the covers behind as she got up, grabbed her clothes, and made her way to the bathroom. I watched those perfectly rounded cheeks wiggle their way out of sight before getting up. I looked over to the clock. It was nine-thirty.

Like a married couple, I yelled through the door. "I'm guessing we're not doing the Lingering Garden tour today?"

Her voice came back at me. "Just got a text from Mr Chin. He wants to see us as soon as we can get there. He's at the restaurant across the street."

"Does that mean he's buying breakfast?"

Olivia kicked the door open. Her pants were on, but the blouse was yet to be buttoned. The hair was already dazzling, and she still had the brush and blow dryer in her hands. "I would change that attitude, unless you want to get on his bad side."

"What are you talking about? The guy said he loved me."

"He didn't say love. He said like, and that can change with one snotty comment."

I barged past her to get to the mirror, I tried to straighten the part down the centre. I couldn't. "I don't know about this."

"That's because your hair was cut for a side part. It wouldn't take much to fix." She started to play with it until she noticed I was staring at her chest. That bought a playful cuff across my head. "What are you, a virgin?"

"Come on, you walk around with…"

"Let's go. We shouldn't keep him waiting." Her fingers started on the buttons as she made her way to the door. "Grab whatever you brought. I don't know if we'll be back."

"What? Did I say something wrong?"

The door to the suite opened and closed as I finger-combed my part back to the side and grabbed my socks, shoes, and jacket. Olivia was waiting for me at the elevator when I caught up to her. "What do you think he wants me to do?"

"He's a businessman. Don't expect anything too crazy."

That was almost disappointing. That being said, I didn't have to tell Barry and the gang the truth. I would, however, tell Julie nothing but the truth. She probably had a sixth sense for knowing whether or not I was lying. And what was Julie doing

41

right now. Back home it was just after midnight so a good guess would be sleeping. Damn, these dreams were so real.

Ding. The elevator doors opened. We entered and as the doors closed, Olivia turned to me and locked her lips on mine. She pinned me against the wall and used her hands to grab my hair while she drove her mouth against mine. I could feel her teeth bite hard on my lip. I tried to pull away, but couldn't, and I wasn't sure I wanted to. Instead, I put in a feeble fight as she pinned me with her chest. I wasn't going anywhere. Damn she was strong. Then her knee came up into my groin and the kiss was over.

She let me drop to the elevator floor in a heap. "That's for lying to your friends about having sex with me. I'm not one of Mr Chin's sluts."

"How the…" It hurt too much to finish the sentence. "Fuck…"

"You'll live. And don't ever let me catch you staring at my breasts again, got it?"

I groaned and got to my knees. "Look, I didn't mean anything by that. I was just giving the guys a thrill. I wasn't implying that you were a…"

"Don't finish that sentence. I think you're a great guy, so how do you think I felt when I found out you were talking about me like that? And what, on God's green Earth, would ever make you think I'd want to do anything with my toes?"

"I was scrambling. I didn't know what…"

"Well, now you can tell them I drove your nuts up your ass."

The doors opened and I managed to get to my feet. "I'll be sure to pass that along."

I followed a step behind as I tried to walk off the pain. We made our way out of the hotel and to the crosswalk. Crosswalks in China were death zones. There were six car lanes that obeyed traffic lights but didn't obey crosswalks. There were scooter lanes on either side and the scooters didn't obey lights or crosswalks. They did, however, watch the cars and pedestrians very closely.

Without looking, Olivia stepped out into the scooter lane and proceeded to cross. I stood there with my mouth open. No less than thirty scooters dodged and wove their way around her.

She waited at the other side of the lane. "Coming?"

"Hell no!"

"It's easy. I just did it."

I wanted to tell her she was hot, and that nobody wants to run over the beautiful people.

"Step out and keep the same pace. Don't look at them, and don't speed up or slow down. They'll adjust to you."

I watched as the light changed. The cars stopped, but the scooters kept coming. "I can't."

"I've got a tattoo, a kitten paw print, and against my better judgement, I'll show it to you if you make it across. Just don't look at them. Look at me and walk."

I took a deep breath, imagined where that paw print might be, and stepped out. I kept my pace and didn't stop until I was beside her. Three times a scooter had come close enough to do a breeze-tug on my shirt. "Shit."

"Now let's hurry. We've still got a green light."

We half-ran the rest of the way and I stayed close to her as we manoeuvred the other scooter lane. On the other sidewalk, Olivia lifted the front of her shirt and slightly pulled down the top of her jeans. There was indeed a small kitten paw print, but it wasn't worth dying over.

"That's it?" I didn't mean to sound so disappointed.

"There's a couple more," she tugged the jeans down a little further to reveal part of a second paw, "but you'll have to earn them."

Mr Chin was watching us from inside the restaurant. I saw him as we entered. I waved and regretted it immediately.

I was such a dork.

Chapter 11

Mr Chin rose to his feet and held out an open palm.
"Please, join me."
I took a seat, my eyes panning the spread of food.
It was good. I really should tell Candy about this place. Olivia
remained standing and never took her eyes off the man.

"Help yourself, my friend. You must be hungry."

"Thank you." I started with a spoon full of scrambled eggs,
several dumplings, and a slice of shredded sweet wheat bread.

Olivia remained polite with her decline by putting a hand up
when Mr Chin offered. Her eyes left him to check out the envelope
sitting on the table between us. It was a manila, with the red
buttons and tie string. There were no visible markings. From the
thickness, Olivia calculated the document inside to be several
pages. Maybe there were pictures. Regardless, that envelope
contained Mr Chin's favour.

"Look at him eat." Mr Chin pointed like a proud father.
"You have a healthy appetite. I love this guy."

"See." I turned my head. "He said love."

Olivia's eyes rolled. I'm sure she thought I'd get us both
killed.

"Now down to business. First you owed me money, and
then there was that whole tragic set of events that led up to one of
my employee's untimely demise." He shrugged, like this was the

shit that happens. He continued, "I am willing to forget about the money. I am also willing to forget about your unfortunate night with my dealer, as long as you do me this one tiny, almost insignificant, favour. Can you do that for me, Mr Andy."

I stopped chewing. "Whatever you need."

"I have an envelope that needs to be delivered."

"You don't have Fedex here?"

"I need to make sure this envelope makes it to its destination. Fedex employees are good, but I prefer to use somebody with more at stake. That way I know there won't be any careless mistakes, like an envelope lost behind a seat. Do you understand?"

I stuffed half a dumpling in my mouth. It was delivering a fucking letter. How hard could that be? I had hoped for a bank to rob, a plane to hijack, or hell, a building to demolish. This was a dream. I was prepared to do any of those things. Instead, I get to play mailman. "No problem. Piece of cake."

"I'll need you to do it right away."

Olivia stepped beside me as I got to my feet. She continued to study Mr Chin as he handed the envelope over, along with a piece of paper with an address. She noticed that Mr Chin had a gun in a holster under his right arm, which meant he was left-handed. Also, as burly as he was, he wasn't out of shape. There was no potbelly on this man. Finally, she noticed an odd tattoo on the inside of his left wrist. It was a Chinese symbol, but one she'd never seen before. She'd share all this with me after we left.

"Shall we?" I moved my chair out of Olivia's way. "And thank you for breakfast, Mr Chin. It was delicious."

My words were delivered with confidence, with moxie, like a young James Bond. It wasn't like I was that cool in real life. If I were, I wouldn't have been nutted in the elevator earlier. Bottom line, none of this was real, so I was playing the game.

Olivia grabbed at the envelope and I pulled it away from her. "Uh, this is my job."

"You make it sound like a paper route. This is serious shit."

"You want to know how serious?" I started to unwind the thread.

A Dream Escape

Olivia gave an uncharacteristic shriek. "No!"

It almost made me drop the envelope. "Whoa. What the fuck was that?"

"Open it and we're dead. These things are always booby-trapped."

I held it out to arm's length. "You mean it could blow up?"

"No. It means that they'd know it was opened and believe me, you think you've got troubles now. Open it and see what real trouble looks like."

"That's the thing. This is a fuck'n dream and I don't give a shit. I was looking for excitement and all I got was post office delivery boy."

"Then do it for me. Maybe you are dreaming. Maybe this is all make-belief. For me this is very real. You piss this guy off and he'll kill us. That means that tomorrow you'll wake up in your bed, but I won't."

I thought about that. It was true. I'd wake up, get a bite of breakfast and go to work. What happened to Olivia and Mr Chin? "That kinda makes sense."

"Like hell it does. Wake up, Andy! This isn't a dream. Get it through your head, if anything happens to you, you're done. You don't wake up from gun shots or car accidents. And this guy isn't the type to go after just you."

I rubbed my ribs. "What do you mean?"

"Sure, he'll kick the crap out of you, but that's just the tip of the iceberg. What he'll do to your family, to your friends, that's what I'd worry about."

"You lost me."

"He needs you. If we don't get this right, he'll go after the person you care about the most. It could be your Mom, a child, or a girlfriend."

I started walking. "That sounds so diabolical. I'd hate to be me if I fuck up."

"Okay. Don't take me seriously. I don't care." She lifted her shirt and showed me the bruising on her ribs. "Do this for me and I'll show you all the paw prints and then some."

"Did Mr Chin do that?"

"No. I fell against a phone book a few times. What's it gonna take for you to get serious about this?"

"The rest of those paw prints would be a pretty good motivator."

Olivia put her hands up. "You win. Let's get this delivered and I'll show you whatever you want. At least I'll be alive."

"Great. So where is this place." I handed her the slip of paper.

"That's odd. It's right around the corner."

"I don't care. There's no reversies. You're showing me kitten tracks as soon as we dump this off."

Olivia studied the address while we walked. It truly made no sense. Whoever the recipient, they could have picked it up. Mr Chin could have dropped it off. It was a four-minute walk at best. "That's it up at the top of the stairs."

"What is this place?" I asked.

Olivia studied the building. "It's an embassy."

"Who's embassy?"

She read the plaque at the gate. "Pakistan." She pointed out three different cameras. "No wonder he didn't want to do it."

"What the hell is in this envelope?"

"I don't know, but suddenly I want to." She grabbed the envelope and started on the string.

I had to stop her. "What about the whole, he'll kill us, thing."

"That was before the Pakistan Consulate got involved." She started in on the string again and opened it up. Inside there were photos and a blueprint. It was of the Three Gorges Dam.

"Why would the Pakistani Government want blueprints on this place?"

"The Chinese government would kill if they found out this information was handed over." A flash from a camera came in from the side. "Shit. We've got to get out of here."

The man with the camera pulled a gun as Olivia and I bolted. One slug embedded itself in the gate pillar. A second slug hit a parked car, setting off the alarm. Olivia grabbed my arm and shoved me into a crowd of people. The mayhem of the two shots being fired had the crowds running in every direction.

Olivia dragged me into traffic. Car brakes squealed and horns honked. We wove our way around the vehicles to the other side. I was following as close as I could without hopping in her back pocket. A group of tour busses were unloading, and the crowd of white tourists made it easy for us to disappear.

"I have a safe house not far from here. We can hide out there."

"A safe house. What are you, CIA?"

"Wait until you see this place. Then ask me again."

Chapter 12

The safe house would have been a ten-minute jog as the crow flew. When you're being chased by a maniac with a gun, it's hard to see where that damn crow is. Olivia ducked down an alleyway and I was a step behind her. It wasn't like I had a choice. She had a firm grip on my shirt.

"How much further?" I asked.

"Hate to say it sport, but we're heading the wrong way."

"What! Why?"

"Because," she scoffed, "I don't want them knowing where we're going. We'll lose them and double back."

"Good point." I broke free from her grip but kept close. When she dodged left, so did I. When she ran into traffic, so did I, although I kept her between the oncoming traffic and myself. They never hit the pretty ones."

After sprinting two blocks, I started to slow. "Hey, I think we can…"

A distant pop came from behind us. There was a whiz and then a store window exploded. Olivia cut between the buildings. "I say keep running."

We resurfaced at a Metro station, jumped the turnstiles, and headed for the first tunnel. Down one flight of stairs we took a right and pushed our way through the people on the platform. A train was just arriving.

"Where are we going?"

Olivia dragged me through the doors as they opened. "Wherever this thing takes us. We'll start on an alternate plan once we get there."

As the train started rolling, Olivia saw the gunman. He wasn't the one with the camera. We'd likely lost that guy. This meant the guy with the camera had called in backup. And by now Mr Chin had been informed that the drop hadn't happened. The Pakistan Consulate hadn't received the envelope, and shit had officially hit the fan.

"Any thoughts on our other plan yet?"

Olivia looked up at the train route. "We get off at the next train station and move fast. There might be people waiting for us. Follow me close and get ready to do what I say. You might not want to do what I ask, so don't think, just do."

At the next stop, the doors opened, and Olivia was on the run. I was winded and trailing her by a good ten feet. I was also looking around to see what she saw. I saw nothing. "Hey, wait up."

She made it out to the street level and stopped. I was panting as I caught up. A white BMW was slowing for the light when she pointed to it. "That one."

"What?"

She ran around to the driver's door. "Get in."

The driver's door opened and the woman behind the wheel was pulled out of her seat. Olivia took her place and reached across to open the passenger door. "Get the fuck in, or you're on your own."

I got in and scrambled for my seatbelt as she sped off. Looking back, I could see the woman, in a cream-coloured skirt and jacket, sitting in the middle of the lane. A bullet shattered the image as the car's back window blew inward. Olivia turned an abrupt left through a red light.

"You just stole a car," I shouted.

"We just stole a car, and you don't have any bullet holes in you so, you're welcome."

"Why are you doing this?"

"You mean keeping us alive? As long as I'm getting it right, why worry about it?"

"I'd just like to know who my personal James Bond is. Is that asking too much?"

"No, it's not. Let's just say I'm not affiliated with any organisation. I'm not CIA or KGB, and I don't have a double-o number like the MI-6 folk."

"What now?"

"Now that they shot out the back window, we stand out. We need to ditch the car, so keep your eyes peeled for something you like."

"There's a couple of black BMWs sitting there. Maybe we should steal one of those."

Olivia looked over and saw them sitting side by side in a parking lot entrance. "Oh shit." She cranked the wheel, and the two black BMWs gave immediate chase.

Mopeds, scooters, and cars were actually pushed aside as she bullied her way past them. One scooter lost it getting up onto the sidewalk, and two others were nudged into the ditch.

As fast as Olivia was driving, the two BMWs remained on our heels. "This is getting ridiculous," She shouted. "Kick the windshield out!"

I just stared at her.

"You want to live? Kick the fucking windshield out."

I leaned back in my seat and cocked my legs. "If I kick this, will it come out?"

"Likely not with the first kick, but hit it square and hit it hard."

I recoiled and kicked. The windshield spider-webbed and came free on my side. I moved over for a second kick but couldn't line up properly.

"Hurry it up!"

"I can't spin around enough."

Olivia shoved at the windshield. It didn't move. "Why can't you spin around?"

"My seatbelt."

"When did you put your damn seatbelt on, and why!"

A Dream Escape

"You drive like a …" I fumbled for the latch. "I'll undo it."

"Hurry." She turned a quick left and slammed the car against a wall. It helped her turn. It spun me in my seat. I was lined up and after I caught my bearings, I kicked. The windshield folded up onto the roof as if on a hinge. It hung there for a couple of corners before sliding off the back of the car.

"Okay Andy, we're getting close. Put your feet up against the dashboard and hold on."

I was done asking questions. She yanked the e-brake and launched us down a back alley. It narrowed like she knew it would and the car was quickly wedged between the two walls. Bricks tumbled across the hood as the car crumpled. I was folded into the dashboard but followed Olivia as she scrambled over the hood. We rolled onto the ground in front of the car.

"Come on!" She headed around the corner and no less than four shots hit the trunk of our car as I got to my feet.

"In here!" Olivia ducked into a restaurant and put a finger to her lips as she made her way past the Manager. The man nodded and pointed to a back room. I could see that they were friends.

We sat quietly for two hours before the man knocked on the door. It was four slow knocks. Olivia opened. "*Xie xie*, Mr Liu."

"You have a lot of people looking for you. The police are cleaning up the car right now. It looks like a couple more hours. I bring you food?"

"I would like that." She pulled out two thousand Yuan and handed it over. "I hope that'll cover a serving of Chow Mein and Almond Chicken."

"I'll also bring you some vegetables. Who's your friend?"

"I think it's better if we call him, nobody."

Mr Liu held out his hand. "Good to meet you, Mr Nobody."

I took his hand and gave it a shake. "Same."

It took several hours before we could get going. Olivia wanted to make sure no one saw us leave, and a couple times we had to stay put while black BMWs trolled the streets. It was safe to say we were being hunted.

By seven o'clock, we'd backtracked, and the safe house was in sight. The four-story building was abandoned. Years of dust sat in the lobby as we passed a handful of men in overcoats. They sat huddled in a corner around a small fire.

Olivia headed straight for them. "*Ni hǎo.*"

"Miss Olivia, so good to see you. Do you need a room?"

She pulled out fifty Yuan and handed it over. "I'll give you another hundred tomorrow if you don't tell anybody I'm here."

"We can do that. You want the usual, Room 114, or do you want a nice view on four for your friend."

"Room 114 will do, thanks." Olivia gave him a fist pump and headed for the stairs. I sheepishly looked around and trailed closely behind her. This place would need a major upgrade to be considered a dump. Halls were littered with broken furniture, and the smell that lingered was definitely urine. There was no door on our room and the view was a back alley full of garbage. A stained mattress sat in the corner with three scary looking pillows, or was one a dead animal?

"I am not putting my head anywhere near that... that... whatever that is."

"Why not? This is all just a dream, right?"

"Fuck that."

Olivia laughed as she reached up and pulled the vent cover off the wall. Inside there was a plastic bag. In the bag were pillowcases and a gun. "Here, take one."

I took one of the pillowcases and slipped it over the pillow. "Thanks."

It was getting dark, but it wasn't crazy late. I'd have to get up for work soon, so I took the right side of the mattress and stretched out. Olivia took her spot beside me. She gave me a funny look, unbuckled her jeans and started to slide the zipper down.

"Anybody want to see some cat paws?"

"What, here? Really?" I placed my hand on hers, stopping her. "I'll take a rain-check."

Chapter 13

I awoke with a cramp in my calf that had a stranglehold on my leg. I bent around, rolled onto the floor, and tried to stand. I made it as far as my knees and froze until the pain subsided. I'd only ever had a cramp like that when I'd played football, a weekend warrior thing with friends and beers. An odd thought briefly crossed my mind. My leg had twinged when I'd kicked out the windshield. I looked back at the bed, hoping Olivia wasn't in it. She wasn't.

I got up, got dressed, and headed for the bathroom. My hair and teeth got brushed, and then I poured myself a much-needed coffee. There was no lasagne for today's lunch, so I had to rummage. Three double-decker peanut butter and jam sandwiches won out. There was an old spotted banana and a handful of stale chocolates that I'd found in the crisper. It would set the mood for the day, and it would be a long one.

The car started, which surprised me. It was almost out of gas when I left work yesterday and I'd forgot to fill it. That worked in my favour. I stopped for gas, grabbed a bag of chips for my break and poured myself a tall Columbian Dark Roast. That tasted like every morning should.

I backed into a parking stall, and not seeing Julie's car in the parking lot, sat there and sipped at my brew. I promised I wouldn't push her to reveal what that favour was, but I was getting worried. Sure, I'd probably say yes to whatever she wanted, but a heads up would have been nice. Was she moving? Maybe she wanted to borrow money. That would be alright.

I waited as long as I could, but she never showed so I went inside.

"Hey Barry, you seen Julie?"

"Why ya looking, Buddy?"

"No reason. She wanted a favour and I kinda said yes without knowing what she wanted. Now I'm curious."

Barry didn't miss a beat. "A date. She's going to this wedding on the weekend. She needed a date. I said no."

"She asked you first?" I tried to spit the words out without sounding completely crushed. "I mean it's no big deal. I'm sure she just doesn't want to go alone."

"Oh, the date's not for her. That girl could get anybody she wanted. No, this was a favour for a friend of hers. I saw the picture. The girl looked like she stopped a heard of charging buffalo with her face. Hoof prints everywhere. You didn't really say yes, did you?"

"Shit."

I grabbed a template and my drill and started drilling hinge holes. My safety glasses were dirty, so I stopped to clean them. As I was doing this, the boss walked up.

"Andy, you're on drawer facings today."

That was Julie's station. "She called in sick today?"

"She took a couple vacation days."

Barry, always the nosey one, came over as soon as he left. "She sick?"

"Vacation."

"Well, that's boring." He shook his head as he walked away.

"Hey Barry." I waited until he turned around. "You wouldn't have her number, would ya?"

Barry didn't say a word. He just started laughing as he made his way back to his station. Imagine any of them having her number. I set my tools back in the drawer and moved over to her station. I'd never done her job, but I'd gawked at her enough to know it wasn't that hard. Most of it was pre-drilling holes for corner brackets and attaching the slider mounts.

After lunch, the boss checked in on me. It was a casual talk and I almost asked for Julie's phone number. That way I could get back to her and make up some excuse. I had a prior engagement, or a lawn to cut. Maybe I needed to wash my hair. Didn't girls use that excuse all the time?

And why was I thinking that doing this favour would have her falling into my arms? Was it a guy thing? Like I could win her over by moving a couch or changing the oil on her car. That shit didn't work in the real world. It only worked in the dorky dreams of losers that chased girls way out of their league, like Olivia.

At the end of my shift, I got in my car and left for home. I was glad I didn't see Julie in the parking lot. In person I wouldn't be able to say no. She had that… that thing, and it overpowered logic.

Tonight's supper consisted of the vegetables in the crisper. My mother had dropped them off last weekend. There were radishes, lettuce, baby carrots and beans, all from her garden. A salad would have made sense, but instead, I cleaned them up and put them on a tray with a bowl of ranch dip.

I watched a taped football game while I nibbled. It was a game from two years ago, an older game when the Dolphins had embarrassed the Denver Broncos. It didn't happen often, and I never got tired of watching it.

The phone rang twice and twice I let it ring itself to the answering machine. There were no messages left. I had flinched, and even got up, but as I got closer to picking it up, I got further from feeling I could say no to her. Hell, maybe it was just my mother wanting to see if I wanted to come over for supper on the weekend. I didn't have call display and couldn't take that chance.

Bottom line, losers didn't date prom queens for a reason, and no favour was ever going to change that. The phone started to ring a third time and I walked past it to the bedroom. Olivia was probably waking up and that girl was ridiculously hot.

Sadly, my chances were far better with her.

Chapter 14

I t wasn't the lovely curves of Olivia that I woke up to. Nor was it silk sheets or a mattress that screamed luxury. It was a stench that was choking my throat shut. I'm talking a metallic funk that settled on the back of the tongue like pine sap. For the first time in a long time, I woke up not feeling hungry.

"What are you thinking?" her voice asked.

I rolled over to see my partner in crime lying beside me. Even with a matte of tossed hair, this girl owned the room. "How can you look so good in such a cesspool?"

"Awe come on. It's not that bad."

"I'll spring for a hotel tonight," I offered.

Olivia opened my wallet. She'd taken it while I slept. "You need to keep an eye on this. Oh, and you don't have enough cash to do a hotel and dinner."

I reached for my back pocket out of habit. "I have credit cards."

She tossed me the wallet. "Use them and you might as well send up a flare. You know the idea is to stay off the grid and out of sight, right?"

"I suppose. So, what's the plan?"

She smoothed her hair with her fingers, got up, and grabbed the envelope. "Blueprints to the largest damn in the world. It could only mean one thing, that someone wants to do a little damage."

"Terrorism?"

"That's the thing. That guy with the camera, and the one with the gun, were Chinese government. They don't do terrorism. That being said, the building was the Pakistani Consulate. I know a guy that might be able to make sense of this but getting to him won't be easy."

"We have the government after us now?"

"Looks like it."

I had to ask. "Can't we steal a car?"

"Look at you, Jason Bourne."

"What do you mean?"

"When I first saw you, you were a dork. You lived in a tour bus and looked at these dirty buildings with the awe of a child at Christmas. I felt bad for you but look at you now. You've pissed off a Chinese Billionaire, kicked out a windshield, and slept on a mattress that's seen at least twenty people OD or die on it."

"What!" I jumped up and immediately stripped the pillowcases off the pillows.

"And just like that, the old Andy's back."

"No, he's not. Being a bad ass doesn't mean I have to wallow in the filth of dead people. I can still be cool."

"You've come a long way, so I'll take your word on it."

"Thanks. It's a lot easier when you know you'll wake up."

"Enough with the dreams." Olivia took two steps toward me and drilled me in the arm with her fist. It was a blow that made me step sideways to catch my balance.

"What the hell?" I grabbed for my arm.

"Oh. I'm sorry. Did that hurt?" She swung again and caught me on the chin. She'd pulled that one a bit but wanted to make sure I felt it. "How about that one."

I stepped back and brought up my fists. "Hey, I don't wanna hurt you."

She dropped her arms. "I wouldn't go there if I was you."

"Why'd you hit me?" I put an open palm to my jaw.

"What do you care? It's just a dream." She made a fist and edged toward me.

I put my hands up in self-defence. "Doesn't mean it doesn't hurt, now."

"Take it easy." She opened her fist and raised her hands. "I'm done. How does your jaw feel?"

"It hurts."

"But it shouldn't hurt when you wake up, right?"

"Right" Although I had to wonder about that. Mr Chin had beaten me bad, and I had been hurting the next day, but not because of the dream. I was hurting because I'd fallen out of bed and barfed out my guts. And don't forget I'd staggered into the doorway on my way to the bathroom. The pain was easy to explain. "You mean…"

"Look around, Andy. Breathe in that air, taste that smog. Feel those muscles that ache and those eyes that sting from shitty sleep. I hit you for a reason, and when you wake up tomorrow, you'll feel your jaw. When you do, you'll know that this isn't the dream. This is the reality. Dreams don't hurt you like that." She clapped her hands together as if knocking the dust off them. She had presented a flawless case.

"You hit like a girl." I had to throw that in. "I'm not sure this'll still hurt when…"

My head snapped back as her fist reconnected. I saw stars briefly before dropping to one knee. Not that it was all that manly to cower from a woman, but damn she hit hard. I'd be feeling that one for a while.

Olivia dropped to one knee beside me and tried to soothe my jaw. "I'm so sorry for that, but you were right."

"Fuck me, I hate being right."

"You should feel that tonight when you start dreaming. If you don't, then don't worry. You'll know that this is a dream and that I'm not real."

"You're pretty confident about this."

"Seriously? I know this isn't a dream. Even when I dream, I know it's a dream."

That caught me off guard. "What do you dream about?"

A Dream Escape

"I don't know, sandy beaches, shooting ranges. I dream a lot about guns." She thought some more. "Days ago, I'd had a dream about this homeless person. He had holes in his clothes and no laces in his shoes. He also had teeth made of gold, every last one of them. I noticed it when he smiled. He closed his mouth and swallowed. When he opened his mouth again, the teeth were gone. That shrivelled up mouth was all I could see. Suddenly, he was wearing a tuxedo. Weird, huh?"

"I once had a dream about a duck that could play the trumpet, so not really."

"You want me to hit you again?"

"No. You can dream, and you throw a mean punch. How is that gonna get us out of this jam… if this really is a jam?"

"Why? Are you getting worried?"

"I don't even know anymore. I'll admit it's getting a little hard to tell the reality from the dreams lately. On the one hand, I'll be curious to see how I feel when I wake up tomorrow. On the other hand, I know I work at a cabinet factory and that I have friends like Julie and Barry."

"Which one feels right?"

"The cabinet factory."

"How can you say that? Do you hang with these people all the time?"

"Uh, no. Actually, I never see them unless I'm at work. I live in a very small house and it's not the best for company."

"Well, given that world or this one, I can see why you'd gravitate to that one. You gotta girlfriend in that one?"

"No, I don't."

"Whatever."

"Look. It's not like we get to choose our lives, or our dreams."

"Not with that attitude you don't. Why are you single? Can you not find the right girl, or is it something else?"

"I'm sorta working on one."

"Julie? Doesn't she want you to go on a date with her ugly friend?"

"You shouldn't say ugly. People have feelings."

"Sugar coating it won't change the fact that this girl needs her friend to hustle a date for her, and it was a hustle, wasn't it?"

I dropped my head. "I think so."

"There's nothing like that going on here. It's all adventure, intrigue, and filth. That's real."

"Like our problem?"

"I've been thinking about that."

"What do you mean?" I asked.

"We need to get to my friend, right?"

"I suppose, that's if you think he can help."

"I do. Are you ready to try something real adventurous?"

Confidence was percolating through my veins like beer through a straw at a stag party. I got up and pounded a fist into my chest. "Hey, I live for adventure."

"Easy sport. We need to lay low today."

"Why?"

"Because your tour is going on the Bund cruise tomorrow after supper. I say we hook up with the gang. We'll stay at the hotel with them and ride their bus to Suzhou."

"That's a little risky, don't you think?"

"Not if it works. Then it's bad-ass."

My eyes widened. "I could do bad-ass."

Chapter 15

The phone only had to ring once to get my attention. I had beaten the alarm clock by a good two minutes but was still caught up in my morning drowse. I picked up. Who could be calling me this early? Was my Grandmother okay? She was the first to come to mind. At seventy-five, she'd out-lived my grandfather by a decade. That didn't make her invincible.

"Hello?"

"Oh good. You're awake."

I didn't register the voice. It was familiar, but not family familiar. I needed a few more words to figure it out.

"Hello? Are you there?" she repeated.

I had almost made the mistake of asking who it was when it clicked. I was talking to Julie, and here I had dodged her all of last night. She'd obviously grown desperate enough to call me at six in the morning. Was it too late to act like the answering machine?

"Hello, Andy?"

Shit. It was way too late. "Hi, Julie?"

"Did I wake you? I mean I thought you'd already be up getting ready for work."

I would have been, had I not taken Olivia up on her offer to show me the next cat track. After seeing it, we'd spent the day sitting in the filth getting to know each other. I had wanted to make my move but chickened out several times. I kept telling myself, what if the dreams stopped? What if she never came back? This was my chance to sleep with a hot Brit. She saw through my clumsy advances and respectfully kept it to just the tattoo. Still, spending the day with her had made falling asleep difficult, and waking, a little cloudier than normal.

"Just had a late night."

"I tried calling you last night."

"Sorry. I was out."

There was a slight pause. "You remember I said I had a favour?"

"Uh, yes." I tried to sound chipper. "What do you need? I'm your man."

"I need a date for tomorrow."

A smile formed across my face as I gave her the bad news. "Oh, damn. You said tomorrow? My parents need me to move a bunch of stuff for them. They're doing a late spring cleaning."

"Oh."

There was a hurt silence.

"Damn it. Maybe I can call them and tell them to find someone else."

"No. Don't do that. It's not that big a deal. I just thought if you weren't busy."

"Hey, I'm really sorry I can't help you out." The silence became awkward, so I added, "I better get ready for work."

"Uh." Her confusion hung in the air like a bed sheet on a clothesline... during a rainstorm.

I let the awkwardness linger for a moment. "Again, Julie, I'm sorry I couldn't help."

"No, uh, I should get going too. If you're not coming, then I can leave right away. I still need to load the car."

More silence.

"Have a good weekend, Andy."

"You too. Enjoy the wedding. Have a slice of cake for me."

"Sure."

A Dream Escape

The connection ended and I dropped the phone in its cradle. "Yes! Oh, Olivia you'd be so proud of me. No one's taking advantage of this guy today."

Damn if Olivia hadn't toughened me. She'd given me a worth that I'd never felt before. It made me realise I had rights, not with her of course, but with everybody else. Hell, I'd even start standing up to her, as long as she was okay with it.

The alarm clock startled me when it went off. There was something terrifying about Alice Cooper raging through a cheap clock radio speaker. My hand came down hard on the top button. Then I tried to shake the rest of the cobwebs as I headed for the bathroom.

While most men stood to pee, I had learned to take a seat. I'd cleaned that toilet once and was amazed at all the splatter. I'd almost lost my lunch as the stench of old urine wafted from the base and the underside of the seat. Mothers do not get paid enough.

After finishing my business, I washed my hands and reached for my toothbrush. That's when I remembered Olivia striking me. As soon as I opened my mouth, that side of my jaw stiffened, and was that a bruise? I ran the brush over the teeth and thought a couple were actually loose. How was that possible?

Rubbing my jaw made it sore to the touch. That was most likely from the second pop she gave me, the one I hadn't seen coming.

The toothpaste was painfully spit into the sink and I watched as the thin threads of blood squirmed toward the drain. At least one tooth was loose as I stuck a finger in my mouth and gave it a wiggle. I dropped the toothbrush in the sink and stared at the mirror. What the hell did this mean?

I slapped at my face. It stung like I knew it would, but I had to sober up. The skin reddened and my eyes watered. Nope, I was awake. "What the fuck?"

I slapped myself again, harder this time. It hurt as much as Olivia's right hook. If the punch to the jaw had come in a dream, how could it have hurt me? I'd have to rethink all this, but it would have to be later. Right now, I had to get ready for work, that is, if my job was real. Shit. Of course it was.

Kevin Weisbeck

My friends are real and so is Kelowna. There's Barry, Julie, Ted and the gang. I didn't have any friends in China. That being said, I was on vacation. Did I have a job to go back to in that place? I'd been too busy dodging bullets and watching Olivia to care. Except she was a dream, but she had struck me, dropping me to one knee. That felt real. I rubbed my jaw. There was no doubt, it was real... I think.

As a last ditch move, I grabbed at my skin and gave it a pinch. It hurt like hell. The jaw hurt like hell. This was impossible. And then something Olivia said hit me. She knew what I was telling the gang. She'd even chastised me for telling them we had sex. How did she know that?

I dressed and grabbed my lunch before heading out. At work, Barry noticed the bruising on the jaw. I made up a story about slipping on the bathroom floor. Barry looked at me as if I was a woman telling him that story. It was a little far-reaching and certainly a cover up. It took a minute, but I eventually assured him there wasn't a brute of a husband knocking me around back home. A part of me wanted to invite Barry over, just to prove to Olivia that I did indeed have friends on this side, but I didn't. Why couldn't I?

That night I went to bed early. Normally, Friday night was a Play Station night. I'd play into the wee hours, but I wanted to see Olivia. I had questions. I had to prove this wasn't a dream, and I knew how I'd do it.

When I got home, the first thing I did was go to the bathroom and get the rubbing alcohol. The second thing, I grabbed a knife out of the block. It wouldn't be easy, but I had to cut myself. No, it wasn't like I needed to lop off a finger, but it had to be something I'd find on the other side.

I opened the palm of my left hand and made a cut just below the thumb. It wasn't much more than a deep scratch, but it bled, and it would leave a mark.

65

Chapter 16

Whether it was the dead people that had slept on the mattress, or just a combination of all the bizarre events, I woke up with my head spinning. I wasn't tired, and yet I wasn't that awake either. My senses were muddled, not that I couldn't smell the stench of this darn place. Maybe a better explanation would be an overload of sorts, one that I'd have a hard time escaping. I would escape it though, because I was a man with a plan.

Olivia was lying beside me, her gaze weighted on me like a thick blanket. "How's the jaw?"

"Hurts, but you already knew that." I looked at my palm and held it up for her to see. "Any idea how I cut myself?"

"Look at this place. It's no wonder we haven't done worse. You probably cut it on a piece of glass. The shit is scattered everywhere."

"Wrong!" I turned my hand around and my eyes dropped to the wound. "I did it on the other side."

"Please, Andy. Give it a rest already. There is no other side."

"I have friends on the other side, a job. Explain that."

Olivia's eyes softened. "You poor thing. You have friends and a job on this side. You work at a cabinet factory and you've got friends there. It's just that you aren't there now. You're on vacation

Kevin Weisbeck

in China." Then she reached down and picked up a broken car emblem. It was on my side of the bed and very sharp where it had been broken. She looked at my hand and shrugged.

I ignored it. "But the tour is going to Suzhou. I know because I've already been there. We'll be on the Bund Skyline cruise tonight and I've done that too. The boat will have wooden floors, a couple of inside decks and we'll be able to go outside and take pictures. How could I know all that?"

"You've been handed a hundred brochures since you got here. I'm sure the cruise is in one of them. Now let me look at that hand. You can't be roaming around in here without a bandage on that thing." She pulled out the tail of her shirt and stripped a length of fabric from it. It was wrapped around my hand and she tied the end tight. "Let me know if it gets painful. That would mean it's infected."

I looked at her shirt, missing the strip off the bottom. It exposed a bit of her midriff. It was sexy. How many more could she pull off before it became obscene? I smiled.

"You're an ass, Andy." A playful, but grateful, hand cuffed me softly across the head. "Now stay put and I'll get us some breakfast. We'll stay here until tonight."

"Why do you get to go out there? Besides, I'm not hungry, whatever it is."

"I have cash and they aren't looking for me. I can go out in the streets. And I'm used to the shadows and tight spaces." She got up and started for the door. "I'll be back."

"And if I don't want to stay?"

"That's where Shui and Hong come in. You met them when we got here."

"Those two lumps? Seriously?"

Olivia laughed as she turned to go. "Don't underestimate them."

I decided to walk her out and hang with my two bodyguards. We watched her leave and she muttered something in Chinese.

Curiosity got the better of me. "What did she just say."

A Dream Escape

The big one, who I assumed was Shui, answered. "She said I could shoot you if you try to leave. Personally, I don't think you're that stupid."

I nodded. "You speak good English."

"I is a farm boy from Nebraska," he offered. "Can't you tell?"

I couldn't. He was a six-foot tall Chinese man and although he looked like he might have been in good shape years ago, he wouldn't be chucking any hay bales today. "Sure."

Hong asked, "how do you know, what do you call her, Olivia?"

"Yes." I wanted to say we went way back, but we didn't. We didn't even go back a week. How did I know her? I shrugged. "We're just friends."

"Okay, because this is the kind of place friends hang out."

'Well, I've got myself in a bit of trouble and she's helping me."

"You know who she is?"

I wanted to say that I did, and that I'd seen her hike her jeans and panties down far enough to see a couple paw prints. I'd even kissed her, although she promptly kneed me in the nuts shortly afterward. "Not really. Who is she?"

"Oh no. I'm not going to piss her off by telling you. I don't need that."

"Seriously? Come on. You have to tell me now."

"You ask her." The man looked up and laughed as she re-entered the hotel lobby. "I dare you."

"I will." I joined her as she walked past them back to the room. "That was quick."

Olivia set down the teas, opened the bag, and pulled out a couple sandwiches. "Sorry they didn't have peanut butter." It was meant as a joke.

I just stared.

"Okay spit it out. What did those two say?"

"I don't know. It's more what they wouldn't say." I took a sip of my tea.

"What didn't they say?"

"They wouldn't tell me who you are."

"That's an easy one. I'm your Olivia."

"Nice. I walked into a bad situation and probably would have been beaten to death on the spot when out of nowhere, here comes, Olivia. Don't get me wrong, I'm grateful, but you're a girl with no last name, no fear, and a knack for scaring the shit out of people."

"I don't scare anybody."

"Just the two guys down there, Mr Chin, and me."

She put her arm around me and placed a peck on my cheek. "Do I scare you?"

"Not if this is a dream. If it's not a dream then, shit ya."

She loved the squirm as I worked myself free from her grasp. Fear was power and that wasn't a bad thing. Thing is, it wasn't a good thing in this case. "I guess we'll have to change my bad girl image. Would you like to go for a walk? I'll play nice and let you hold my hand."

"And the catch?"

"Awe come on. I don't deserve that. Finish your sandwich and let's go."

I put the last bite in my mouth, washed it down with a swallow of tea, and held out my hand. "I'm going to regret this, aren't I?"

She took my hand. "You know me better than anyone. You've been closer to me these last couple days, than anyone else I know."

We walked through the lobby and down into the basement. The once-white paint on the walls was peeling, and what wasn't peeling was stained a dingy mustard yellow. A long corridor took them into a room with a wet floor. The puddles had to be a half an inch deep. In the corner, a few buckets, a mop, and an old trunk were stacked as if no one was coming back. On the other side of the room there was a hole in the wall the size of a small dresser. Olivia dragged me toward it.

I pulled back. "Seriously? Is that a sewer?"

"Oh, don't be like that. Only small people judge."

A Dream Escape

She crouched down and made her way through the hole. I, again, was dragged along. Inside the sewer, it didn't smell any worse than our room. A large tunnel disappeared in both directions. In the dim light, the sidewalk ran along the water, or waste. The flowing whatever-it-was was low enough that the sidewalk was dry.

"Is there any crap in that?" I decided to take the wall side of the sidewalk.

"It's grey water."

"Meaning?"

"No shit, just water from the street drains."

"That doesn't mean no shit then." I thought about offering her the safer wall side but didn't. "How high does the water get?"

"Depends on whether it rains or not."

It was always about to rain in Shanghai. I decided the wall side was mine. I also kept a firm grip on her hand. It was a lot softer than she was. The woman held my hand like she didn't want to let me go. Was she worried I'd bolt, make a break for the light? Maybe she enjoyed holding my hand. Could it be, she liked me? That was the story I wanted to believe.

"Where are you taking me?" I asked.

She smiled. "It's a place I like to go, when I want to be alone. It's a great place to think. I don't know if you've noticed, but China's a busy place. It's hard to find a place in this city where you can be all alone."

"But you're showing me. What if I start hanging out there all the time? Wouldn't that bother you?"

She gave my hand a squeeze. "That might not be so bad."

I wanted to ask her if she was serious but bit my lip instead. I had to play this one cool. I simply kept my eyes forward and squeezed back.

We'd only walked fifty yards when the dimness of the tunnel started to give way to daylight. There was no talking, just the absorbing of the moment. The small, rounded light in the distance soon became the opening to the Huangpu River. Olivia pushed the iron gate open so that we could have an unobstructed view.

I looked out over the water, making sure to keep her hand in mine. I noticed the grooves cut into the cement wall of the river leading up to the street. Instinct was edging me to step out and climb them, show Olivia I was capable. Why do men always want to show off for pretty girls? She must have sensed this and gave me a gentle tug to hold me back.

In the distance, a tour boat was making its way to a dock. It would be dark in about eight hours and we'd be boarding one of them. Then off to Suzhou where we could escape to wherever the wind carried us.

"So now you know one of my biggest secrets," she said.

"I do. Thanks for that."

She took a seat and I sat beside her.

"How'd you know the gate wouldn't be locked?"

"I'm the one that cut the lock off," she admitted. "I doubt there's a lot of people trying to break into the sewers, Andy."

I took my cardboard cup of tea and tapped it against hers. "To tonight."

She took a sip, leaned against me, and rested her head on my shoulder. "And to believing and letting go."

My eyes widened a little. Was that what this was? Was I really starting to believe her?

Chapter 17

Down by the docks, the wind was picking up. It was a chilly breeze that cut through my clothes like little wind-blown shards of ice. The temperatures were turning as a Siberian front rolled down the coastline. And while the morning had hovered close to twenty Celsius, those numbers had spiralled throughout the day. It was down to four degrees as evening approached, and with the wind, it felt like winter was on its way.

"You cold?" I offered to wrap my arms around her.

She nodded and let me. "This is what you get for being stuck below Russia. We'll steal a couple of jackets when we get the chance."

"Andy?" a voice chimed.

I let go of Olivia as I turned around to see my tour guide. "*Ni hǎo,* Candy."

"I see why you've spent so much time on your own. Are you here to take the Bund cruise with us?"

"I am. Is it possible to…"

"An extra ticket for your friend?" She extended a hand to Olivia. "Yes, of course. I'm Candy Wang."

Olivia wanted to laugh but quickly shook the thought. "I'm Olivia. Thank you so much."

"We're off to Suzhou tomorrow," Candy added. "You're welcome to come if you're willing to share a room with Andy. He's paid for double occupancy."

Olivia nodded through a shiver. "That is most appreciated."

Candy started a head count on the others and ran off to get the tickets. The group hovered around, braving the cold, staring at Olivia, and wanting to ask. Instead, they talked about her amongst themselves.

Olivia slithered her way back into my arms and waited to board.

When Candy returned, everyone shuffled through the slow-moving line of people that led to the boat. It was warmer in the boat and Olivia quickly dragged me to a seat as deep in the crowd as she could find. Blending in was more important than enjoying the cruise. We'd seen the Shanghai skyline earlier, although it wasn't as lit up as it was now.

The boat left the dock, and everyone stared out the windows in amazement. The buildings looked like an urban forest of Christmas trees, bouncing off the water as we made our way down the river. I took her hand. "It's beautiful, don't you think?"

Her hand recoiled. "Shit."

Talk about mixed signals. "What?"

"Don't look around. We've got a problem."

It was instinct to look around, but I refrained after she put a death grip on my knee with her hand. "Ouch."

"Don't turn around, I said." She leaned into me. "I don't think he's seen us yet. Mr Chin is on the boat about eight seats back."

"How did he know we'd be here?"

"I don't think he does. He's with some young girl. I'm sure she's bought and paid for. They're just laughing and drinking champagne."

"Why didn't he take one of his yachts? He has yachts, doesn't he?"

"Not how it works here. In China, if you have money, you flaunt it. What better way than to drink champagne amongst a boat full of people that are stuck drinking sodas. And that girl is less than half his age, which screams power and wealth."

"Are you too old for me?" I asked. Olivia was maybe two years my elder. "Just saying."

"Right. Because nothing says power and wealth like a guy who hides in sewers and can't pay his poker debts."

"You got me there." I tried to sneak a peek behind us. "What are we gonna do?"

She was about to tell me when Mr Chin locked eyes on her. They were angry seething eyes. They wanted to see her dead. Pretty sure they wanted to see me dead too. The bromance was over.

"So much for not being noticed," Olivia quipped.

"He can't touch us here, can he?"

Olivia cautiously pulled her eyes away from the man. "No, not here, and likely not him. He's not one to get his hands dirty. He's on his phone though, so my guess is that we'll have company when we get off."

The boat was starting to make its way toward the Pearl Tower. "So, what can we do?"

"Follow me."

Olivia got up and started for the other side of the boat. I followed close. We both saw the gun as Mr Chin opened his jacket to reveal the chrome nine-millimetre. Olivia returned a smug sneer as if to tell him it didn't scare her, and it didn't. To her it was a girl's gun. The fact it was chrome didn't change the fact that it would take three or four shots to stop her.

She opened the door to the outside and the cold wind slapped us hard. Her hair was blown across her face as she made her way to the back of the boat. I felt as if I should have been holding a shirttail.

Surely, Mr Chin wouldn't follow us outside. There were enough people, witnesses, to prevent anything from happening here. She grabbed me and shoved me up front. "Go."

I took the lead and we both looked back as the door opened behind us. It was Mr Chin. He followed us to the back deck. Now the gun was drawn.

"You in big trouble now, Mr Andy. You should have done as you were told. All I asked was the delivery of one envelope. No big deal. Now you make me mad. I will have to make delivery myself. Hand over the envelope."

I leaned into Olivia. "Do we still have it?"

"Taped to my back," she whispered.

We were at the back of the boat with nowhere to go. "Let her go. I'm the one that screwed up."

"You noble man, but no. She in it like you, now." Although the gun remained trained on me.

Olivia stepped between us. "You don't want to do this."

"That's right, but you interfered. I have no choice."

"You don't need us as enemies."

"Sometimes you have to cut ties to make new ones. I'll mention that to your boss, next time I see him. I'll let him know you didn't suffer."

"You aren't going to do this," Olivia scoffed. "I don't think you have it in you."

He changed his aim to her. "Now I shoot you first, Miss Prescott."

Mr Chin was about to squeeze the trigger when his young girlfriend showed up. "*Zhè shi zěnme hui shi? Shi qiāng ma?*"

When he turned to chastise her interruption, Olivia shoved me over the side. We tumbled into the water as the first shot left the shiny barrel. Three more shots were fired into the darkness as the boat continued its way along the colourful skyline.

Once it was far enough along, Olivia broke the silence. "Andy. Where are you? Are you okay?"

"Water's damn cold." I swam over and met her halfway. "How about you?"

She sounded a little out of breath as she grimaced. "Been better."

I noticed she was holding her side. "Are you cramping up?"

"No."

That worried me. The only other thing it could be, other than a freshwater shark attack, was a gunshot wound.

Chapter 18

The south bank of the Huangpu River was closer and the obvious choice. There was no way of knowing how bad Olivia's wound was. She started for the shore, swimming slowly, and I trudged along at her side.

We'd made it halfway when I had to ask. "What's that smell?"

"No idea what you're talking about… and whatever you do, don't swallow."

I thought about it for a second and didn't ask again. She changed course when one of the sewer openings came into view. "Over here."

It took thirty minutes to reach it after leaving the boat. My shoulders were burning by the time I pulled myself out of the water. The gate was locked, but a bar was missing allowing me to pull Olivia through it. She took my hand and let me help her up. Then she flopped against the wall and I flopped beside her.

"Let me see." I tugged at her arm.

"Relax. I don't think it's that bad." She grabbed the bottom of her shirt and pulled it up. The bullet had entered from the side, hit the rib and exited out the front. The entrance hole was small, but the bullet left a gash of torn skin. "See. Superficial."

"You call that superficial. You need stitches, and you're looking at a serious infection if you don't clean it."

"Probably right. You go get the car and I'll change into something a little dryer." She smiled while I considered the options. "Or… I can relax and catch my breath while we make a plan."

"Make a plan?" I pulled at my shirt and tried to rip off a strip for her wound. It was a lot harder than she made it look.

She finally stopped me. "It's okay. I think the cold water has stopped the bleeding, for the most part. I'll just stuff a little piece of shirt in each hole." She tore a couple smaller pieces off her shirt and rolled them up. They fit. "See, works good."

I bent down, picked her up and carried her down the tunnel about fifty feet before setting her back down. "You sleep and I'll stand watch."

I got up and peered out the gate. I had no way of knowing if they'd come looking for us, but I also knew I couldn't take the chance. I spent an hour watching out over the water before my nerves calmed.

"Are we safe?" She was awake, but her words were weak.

"I have no idea where this sewer goes. I don't see any holes in the walls." That would have been too easy. "I'm gonna go check it out."

"Wait until morning. I'll go with you."

"Don't worry. I won't go popping my head out anywhere. And I won't be long."

"I'll take that as a promise." She wouldn't have been able to stop me. "I'll stay here." She dropped her head back down and closed her eyes. She was out in minutes.

I spent a few hours wandering the dimly lit tunnels counting my left and right turns so I could backtrack when needed. There were a couple of other gates that were locked, and they turned me back. I saw no signs and, true to my word, didn't poke my head out. Around three in the morning I made my way back to Olivia, did a final check of the river, and took a seat by her side. She was lightly snoring, and I smiled. The bleeding had stopped.

I took her hand in mine and rested my head on her shoulder. It was hard for me to close my eyes, and yet I did.

A Dream Escape

From the couch I awoke to see the TV had gone to an infomercial about a frying pan that not only cooked eggs to perfection, but it didn't scratch. It could be mine for three easy payments of twelve ninety-nine. I had to wonder what kind of idiot bought frying pans on a payment plan.

What time was it? I grabbed the remote and brought up the TV guide. It was later in the afternoon, so I started to look for a hockey game. All I could find was the Rangers verses the Maple leafs, barely worth watching.

When I looked around, I saw that the red light on the answering machine was flashing. It flashed twice and then stopped. Twice again and then stopped. It repeated this until I got up and hit the button. The first message was recorded just before four o'clock.

Hi Andy, it's Julie. My friend got married and I played that trick on her. You know, the one about the cake and that dessert I was making. She freaked out. Hey, maybe I shouldn't be calling. I've had a few drinks already. I guess you're still helping your parents. Shame. I could have used you here. I feel like dancing.

That was weird. Wouldn't she have had her own date for dancing with? Maybe the guy didn't dance. I continued to listen.

Oh wait. Somebody was too busy to come out and dance with me. That's okay. Maybe another time. See ya Monday at work.

Was that flirting? I almost wanted to replay the message. Instead, I tried to blink the sleep out of my eyes and started the second message. It came about fifteen minutes ago.

Andy, I'm drunk. I wish you were here. The food was great, and the champagne is amazing. I've had a glass for each time a good song came on and you weren't here. You're gonna get shit on Monday for saying no to me. Anyway, I'm gonna git going now cause I gotta pee, big glasses and small bladders, bad combo. Have a good night and I'll see ya soon.
Bye.

Kevin Weisbeck

*I guess I should hang up now. I don't want to. I wanna talk.
Bye.*

I shook my head, turned the TV to an old Big Bang Theory rerun, and got up to forage. It wasn't like I was get-up-and-cook-a-meal hungry, but I wanted something. Maybe a bag of chips would do.

I opened the pantry, grabbed a bag of salt and vinegar, and returned to the couch. What was her game? She wanted me there, but not with the commitment of being a date. Instead, some friend would be stuck with me, yet she'd steal me for dances. Made no sense.

Big Bang Theory quickly grew tiresome, so I started flipping through channels. There was tennis, golf, several news channels and a movie, The Shining. That's where the channel changing stopped. I leaned back and decided to watch Jack terrorise his family. Within seconds, I was drifting off.

Chapter 19

I awoke to snoring and scrambled to get my bearings. Was it me? Was the movie over? It was a light snoring and almost pretty, that's if nasal dysfunction could be considered pretty. I lifted my head off her shoulder and listened for the British accent in it. There wasn't any. That meant all people snored the same. I'd learned something. Then I remembered my parent's dog. That damn thing snored like my father and when the two of them got going, they cleared the room.

Outside the sun was starting to cast an orange glow through the tunnel. I got up and walked over to the gate. The river was quiet, as far as boats went. I took it all in for a minute, the calm and the peacefulness of not being chased or shot at. In that moment there was no Mr Chin, no bullet hole in Olivia, and no cold as the morning sun brought a very welcoming warmth.

The light was now turning the dank tunnels into actual passageways. I could see the sidewalk, the signs on the walls. Maybe some of them would give me a clue to where we were. I stepped over Olivia's legs and watched her lips as a smile tried to form. She was happy dreaming. I was just relieved to see her getting some rest.

Down the corridor, and around the corner, there were no signs. There were no arrows pointing to freedom. There were metal rungs leading up to manhole covers every hundred feet or so, and there were locked gates. I climbed up to one of the manholes and stared through a hole. It was quiet out there. I tried pushing up on the cover, but it didn't budge. The thing must have weighed as much as a small car.

I slowly shuffled my way back to Olivia, working the blood into my legs as I did. This was not a dream. My legs ached. Who gets this kind of detail in their dreams? I slid down the wall and took my place beside her. Olivia and this tunnel were as real as it got. Her shirt was spotted with blood and I wanted to check it out, but she was sleeping. Did I have the right to look at the wound? Hell, if she caught me looking up her shirt, she'd get the wrong idea and crack me a good one. What the hell... you only live once.

I lifted the shirt up and checked the wound. The blood had soaked through the balled-up bandage, but no further. We'd have to tape it and douse it with alcohol at some point.

Then I noticed her bra. Some of the lace was visible. I hesitated but pulled the shirt up a little higher. The fullness of her breast filled the bra in a way that had me holding my breath. She had showed me her tattoo. That was a far cry riskier than this. A part of me wanted to pull the shirt up even further, but what would I see. It wouldn't be worth the risk of her catching me. Branded a perv, it would ruin everything we'd built.

The shirt dropped to her side and I leaned back. She was a beautiful woman, and as out of my league as Julie was. Thank God we were stuck with each other, for now. It wasn't ideal, but I'd take it. I dropped my head back down on her shoulder and let the thought of her carry me to sleep.

It was shortly after midnight when I woke up on the couch. There had been a third call and that was what had brought me back to this world. I'd missed it but the light was flashing. I reached over and hit the play button. It was Julie and she was about ten drinks past her limit.

What the fuck, Andy. Where are you? I danced with a plant and lost my shoe. I drank too much. Hey, what time is it? Is it late? Why aren't you home? I don't believe you're helping your parents move this late. Old people get sleepy. All the old people here have gone to bed.

Where the hell is my shoe? I'm walking back to my room like a one-legged penguin. Did I tell you I drank too much?

Hello. Are you there? Oh wait, I got your machine. You know you're no fun to talk to when you're not home. Opps. I'm at my room and can't find my key thingy. I'm gonna let you go.

Bye, Andy.

I don't mean like bye, never see you again. I'll see you Monday. Bye until then.

Bye.

She dropped the phone and cursed through the dead air as she fumbled the phone out of her purse and hung up.

"Shit, Julie." I listened to the call again before deciding not to delete it. These calls were keepers. This girl had never acted so out of control. The third time through the message I dropped my head on the pillow and closed my eyes. I fought them open and tried to see what was on television. One of the Baldwin brothers was doing a take on Donald Trump. I watched and laughed at the satire. Donald wouldn't have been anybody's first choice for president, but he was far better than his running mate and the people had voted. Now they were stuck with him. It would be a very interesting four years, that's if the man survived the full term.

Three commercials almost put me to sleep until the Saturday Night Live's game show skit returned. It was funny, but not enough to keep my eyes open.

Back in the sewers, I was alone. I'd been covered with a blanket and there was a note.

Hey sleepyhead,

Our day has started so I'm off to get a few things dealt with. I have a good idea where we are, and I'll send Hong and Shui to come and get you. They'll keep you below the streets and take you back to the hotel. I'll get us a car and meet up with you there.

I'll also get us something to eat. Don't expect me before dinner. And whatever you do, do not take off. I have things under control. We'll have a bite and then leave for Suzhou. I have contacts there that can make sense out of this.

Oh, and hey, I had a weird dream last night. You were gawking at my bra. Crazy huh. Like you'd ever do anything foolish like that.

Anyway, I'll see you soon. Listen to Mr Hong and Mr Shui.

Olivia

I studied the note for a second. The handwriting was uniform, soft, and flowed with the ease of leaves fluttering to the ground during an autumn breeze. It was far too gentle for a girl as hard as Olivia. She was a no-nonsense gal, ready to shoot it up or take a bullet. Who was this woman?

With the note folded and safely in my pocket, I got to my feet. My pants were close to dry and I walked over to the gate by the river. Boats were everywhere and the day was very much alive for the rest of the world. I slipped my hands in my pockets and slowly backed into the shadows as my stomach growled. My mood was a familiar one. This was me feeling sorry for myself. Could I really be missing Olivia that much? That would be stupid because none of this was real.

I tried to shake the thought as I stared down the dark tunnel. I couldn't.

Chapter 20

M r Hong was the one to break my trance. I'd been deep in thought wondering about my friend's back home. I wasn't sure, but I'd dreamt I was talking to Julie and she was pissed. Not pissed angry, but pissed drunk as a skunk and swimming in a champagne bottle. She was going on about me missing some dance or, hell it was hard to remember. That was the way it was with these dreams. When I got back to Kelowna, I'd have to razz her about it. Dreams didn't have to make sense, so maybe we were in high school and it was a sock hop. Had I stood her up?

Mr Hong's words were abrupt. "Let's go." I had to figure it was a Chinese thing.

"Where are we going?"

"Olivia's waiting."

They started down the tunnel and I got up and followed. I'd been doing a lot of following lately. Why was that? Was I that kind of person, the one that liked to be led? Did I have responsibility issues? My mother had always bossed me around, in a motherly kind of way, and I had always let her. Hell, it was my mother. She knew best, as did my father. Come to think about it, I never did a whole lot of thinking for myself.

"Hey, did you bring anything to eat?" That was my stomach asking.

"We'll eat when we get there."

"No that's fine. I just haven't eaten yet today and it's like mid afternoon. Getting a little case of the growls. So how far is this place? I mean, six tunnels, five?"

"It's not far."

"Great. Hey, you guys don't like talking all that much do ya?"

"No."

"Good thing I'm not shy. I had this crazy dream about a girl I work with. She's a hot one, blonde, nice figure and a voice like an angel. I bet she sings, not that I've ever heard her. But in my dream, she's bitching me out. You know what that's like, eh." I waited for a response. It was stupid in hindsight. "Of course you do. We've all been there."

Mr Shui cut me off. "Quiet."

"Why? Are the rats gonna rat us out?" I looked at both of them. Mr Shui almost smiled, so I continued. "I know you want to hear the story. Anyway, she was mad because I didn't dance with her. Can you imagine? I'm no Brad Pitt, which means if she had wanted to dance with me, I'd have danced. Hell, I'd have danced until my feet fell off. Did I tell you how cute she was, that her nose scrunches in the cutest way when she smiles or how her eyes look like little crescent moons? Hard not to stare at them, if you know what I mean."

Mr Shui turned to Mr Hong. "Are we sure about this?"

Mr Hong nodded.

"You two holding out on me? You have a chocolate bar or something? I'll take anything. Heck, we find a chewed-up piece of gum on the ground and I'd be all over it. Just kidding. I wouldn't eat that, but you get my point. Kinda running on empty's all, so if you have anything…"

"Shut it!" This time it was Mr Hong. He'd obviously missed his morning java.

"Sure. I can do that." I dropped my head and obediently tagged along. It wasn't like I could remember the details to that damn dream.

A Dream Escape

Two more corners passed us by before we stopped. The metal rungs led up to the surface, daylight, and food. Hopefully Olivia had ordered lots of fruit. Normally I shied away from the stuff for deep-fried meats and gooey sauces, but not today. My body wanted the healthy stuff.

Mr Hong went up first and put his shoulder into the manhole cover. It didn't budge at first but lifted with the second attempt. He climbed out, followed by me, with Mr Shui bringing up the rear. Up top they'd found a back alley, and around the corner, a hotel with a restaurant.

"Now we're talking." I peered through the windows looking for Olivia and didn't see her. What I did see had my skin crawling. I couldn't let them know that though. "Are you guys eating with us?"

"No." Mr Hong barked. He was a master at conversation.

I moved between them as they made their way to the hotel entrance. Every hotel had the same door system. It was a rotating turnstile. I'd let the eager Mr Hong go first, which he did. I was expected to follow, which I did not. Instead, I caught Mr Shui off guard and shoved him in with his friend. He turned back to grab me, but the door was closing behind him. By the time the two of them had made their way around, I was fifty yards down the sidewalk and in full sprint.

The crowded streets were in my favour, but Mr Hong and Mr Shui gave a good chase. It was no surprise that I could run faster scared than they could angry. Three blocks into the chase, I ducked into a bakery. From inside I waited and watched as the two thugs bolted past. They blindly wove their way through the people and disappeared out of sight.

These were Olivia's friends? Why would they be bringing me to Mr Chin? I'd seen him in the restaurant window when I scanned it looking for Olivia. Was she in on it too, or had she been double-crossed? If so, she was in trouble and I had to find her.

I was about to leave the bakery when the aroma of the baked breads put a hold on me and wouldn't let me leave. I had no money, no change. Even my passport was with Candy. Who knew where that was?

Kevin Weisbeck

I looked back at the shopkeeper and took a deep breath. In front of him were these ham-filled buns with cheese. They smelled incredible. I looked back again and saw the lady was busy with a customer, but beside me was a little girl, five years old. My hand was already reaching for a bun when I pulled it back. The little darling was staring at me with a smile. I tried to shoosh her away, but she was having none of that.

"I haven't eaten in a long time."

Not able to speak English, the girl continued to smile and stare.

"I have no money."

Again, just a smile.

I quickly pointed off to the side. "Look a pony."

She kept her gaze on me.

"This sucks." I patted her on the head and left the bakery, without the bun.

I had to find Olivia.

Chapter 21

In a little park, littered with a handful of trees, I waited for the darkness to settle in. It was an uneventful wait, except for the little boy and the hotdog. Not experienced at being on the lamb, or trying to stop whatever it was I was trying to stop, I had never felt such hunger.

The boy was in the right place at the right time. Walking through the park, he didn't want the hotdog his mother had just bought for him. He hated hotdogs. The mother, on the other hand, had bought it to tide him over until they could get home. Had she listened to her son and bought the bag of shrimp-flavoured crisps instead, everyone would have been happy... everyone but me.

I listened to the argument as the two strolled down the path. Ten feet away from them, I hid behind a bush. I watched the little boy hold the uneaten dog over a trash bin. I willed the kid to drop it. Just let it go. The mother scolded him until the little boy stopped. The hotdog had been bought and he would eat it, if he knew what was best for him.

My heart sank. Would I have picked it out of the garbage? Hell ya, but that was a moot point. Even if the boy had taken a bite, he looked healthy enough. There was no runny nose, or spots and I was hungry. Such a shame to lose out on a free meal. Was I really that hungry?

Kevin Weisbeck

I got my answer when the little boy did the unspeakable. Mom would have her hands full in the future with this kid. The little boy dropped the hotdog on the ground and then started shedding crocodile tears like it had been a horrible accident. I bought it, at first. The mother did not and yanked the little boy by the arm down the path scolding him all the way.

I did a quick shoulder check and saw two elderly people coming. I'd have to wait. They were just passing through, but always with old people, it would take a while. The sight of them almost hypnotised me. It was like watching a swinging pocket watch. I was willing them to hurry when I noticed the magpie. The black and white bandit had also seen the hotdog and was bouncing down the path from the other direction. Sure, it was easy for him. He had no pride.

"Damn it." I almost choked on my spit.

As the elderly couple passed, the bird circled the sandwich. He needed to gauge how he was going to do this. Should he eat it there, drag it off, or could it be carried away. The first attempt was a lift, except his tiny bird feet couldn't get a good grip. The drag off was the next attempt, with a little better success. As the old couple moved along, so did the hotdog.

I watched the meal travel down the path and tried to convince myself that this wasn't strange. Willing an old couple to hurry, and cursing the damn bird to failure, wasn't abnormal. Wanting a hotdog, riddled with beak marks, was perfectly fine.

It was time to move. The couple was far enough away, and they wouldn't look back. They were old and deaf. But the bird saw me coming and knew exactly what I was up to. It jumped in front of the hotdog, spread its wings, and started to squawk. I wasn't buying it. I grabbed the dog and dusted off the bun. I was about to take a bite when I realised that I'd misjudged the old couple. They had both turned around.

Embarrassed, I broke the hotdog in half and tossed the smaller piece to the ground. Slinking back to the bushes, I ate my half and patiently waited for the darkness to clear the crowds from the Bund's walkway.

A Dream Escape

It had to be close to seven before I felt comfortable enough to step out into the open. The park was only a hundred feet or less to the railing. I walked up to it and looked across at the skyline. This wasn't the view I'd seen from Olivia's secret spot.

There was no guarantee she'd be there, but we'd been split up. There was nowhere else to look. She had to be somewhere. Surely, she'd be looking for me. Did she know that these two had betrayed her? Was she okay? What if she went to the hotel lobby and they jumped her? I had to shake the thought. It wasn't like I'd be able to do anything about it. I had to hope I'd find her secret spot and she'd be there.

Looking back at the skyline, I knew I wasn't at the right spot. I started walking to the west. The pace was fast, and it didn't waver until I saw the skyline that I'd seen from the sewer opening. Yes, this was close. I moved to the railing and leaned over. It was just a rock wall.

I ran my hand along the rounded metal, feeling every chip in the paint with my fingers. Every fifty feet I hung over the edge and looked for the opening. It had to be here. I looked across at the skyline and nodded. This was the view, and those were the buildings. So where was the damn hole?

Add to this, the fact that the hotdog was repeating on me. The boy was right to drop it. I'd been re-tasting that stupid thing since I ate it. It was the meat that kept giving and giving. It made me wonder if there was a dead magpie in that park.

The hole finally came into view. I did a quick pan to the left and right. I was alone. It only took a second to climb over the railing and get to the other side, because that was the easy part. The hard part was scaling these rocks like a professional rock climber. Were you a rock climber if you were going down? Climbing kind of cites climbing, which meant going upward?

I did well, finding footholds, until I ran out of railing to hold onto. Now I was officially at the mercy of gravity. Each move was painstakingly thought out. The idea of slipping and falling into that cesspool of a river scared the shit out of me. I was finally fully dry from the last swim.

Kevin Weisbeck

I was halfway down when I heard voices. They were two male voices above me, and I'd heard them before. It had to be Mr Shui and Mr Hong. I wanted to pop my head up. Instead, I scrambled down the wall. The gate slowly swung open with a creak that would have made Alfred Hitchcock proud. I made my way into the opening and quickly closed it.

I had hoped to find Olivia, with no luck. Where the hell was she?

Above me, the voices carried in the cooling night.

"Where the heck could he have gone?" the one asked.

"Big city. He could be anywhere," the other answered.

"Without him, we don't get paid."

"What about Prescott?"

"Good point. She'll be looking for him. Do you think he's dumb enough to go back to the hotel?"

"More important, does *she* think he's dumb enough?"

"Let's get back there."

The footsteps leaving were fast, like they were running. I was also running. I made my way to the lobby to see Mr Shui and Mr Hong appear. I froze as I watched from behind the stairway.

Olivia was waiting for them. "Where's Andy?"

Mr Hong quickly grabbed her. Olivia didn't have a chance.

Mr Shui started for the room that her and I had shared, the one with the stained mattress. "I'll check to see if he's here. Tie her up."

I slipped back into the basement and to the safety of the sewer.

"Damn it, Olivia. What do I do now?"

Chapter 22

I sat with my back firmly pressed against the wall of the tunnel. A heavy rain had started up and the water level was rising. I watched it without worry. Still a couple inches below the sidewalk, I was safe, for now. Olivia's safety was weighing heavy on me. She was in the lobby tied to a chair. She had considered these two friends, but money talks and we didn't have as much as the bad guys.

This was a basement full of junk, most of it buckets, mops, chairs, wall decorations, and boxes of mouldy curtains. One item, however, was exactly what I was looking for. It was a tile of mirror. I snapped off a corner and headed for the lobby. Stopping short of the doorway, I held the mirror out to see how Olivia was doing. There was no way I'd pop my head around the corner unless I knew it wouldn't get shot off.

Olivia was sitting there, tied to her chair as expected. Mr Hong and Mr Shui sat across from each other, ten feet away from her. The two men were talking. She was looking off at the door. I poked my head around the corner and tried to catch her attention. It didn't work.

I had also found a pen and a couple sheets of paper. It was something I thought I'd use for writing a note, but now I had another idea. I bit the cap off the end of the pen and slid the ink refill out. Now I had a clear tube. Without hesitation I tore off a small corner of the page, crumpled it, and put it in my mouth. I chewed it, grimacing at the taste of old paper, and put the tube up to my mouth.

The first spitball sailed through the air and hit Olivia in the side of the head. All those years of delinquency had paid off. It stuck to her hair and caught her attention. She gently shook her head as if a bug was on her. I repeated the process and this time I bounced one off the side of her nose. It was a thirty-foot shot, and a proud moment.

She turned her head, found me, and mouthed the words 'Fuck you'.

I smiled and gave her a wink.

She winked back and mouthed another word. I strained to catch it. Was she saying 'enough'? I mouthed the word back at her and she shook her head. That wasn't it. She mouthed it again and I watched until Mr Hong started to get up. I leaned back against the wall out of sight and thought hard. Enough, A nuff, A knife. That had to be it.

The mirror was quickly held up and seeing the two men sitting and talking to each other, I poked my head around the corner and mouthed the word knife. Olivia nodded. I nodded back and slipped back into the basement. She wanted a knife. It made sense because she was tied up.

Was there a kitchen in this place, and if so, were there knives? It was time to find out. The basement had a few trapdoors, and I could only assume that one of them led to a kitchen. I had seen how the Chinese-owned stores back home worked. There were trapdoors through floors that gave easy, yet somewhat tight, access to storage. The hotel likely had a kitchen that accessed large freezers down in the basement.

I climbed the first ladder and opened the trapdoor to see a room that looked like it used to house laundry machines. Now an empty room, the one wall had plumbing fixtures hanging out of it. The second trapdoor opened up to the kitchen. Bingo.

It wasn't a fully functional kitchen as the ovens had been removed and all that was left of the sinks were the drain elbows. There were, however, drawers and cupboards. I quickly went through them until I found a half-decent steak knife. The blade was rusty, but I could fix that as I retreated back to the sewer.

The water was still not quite up to the sidewalk, but it was close. I wet the blade and rubbed it against the cement in a sharpening motion for close to half an hour. The blade went from a rusty orange to a dull, brushed silver. The finish wasn't mirror shiny, but the edge was sharp enough to split a hair.

Yes, I'd made a plan, and hopefully it was a good one. I'd start with a nap, because it was too early, and the two thugs were wide awake. No, I'd go back in the wee hours of the morning. I'd get her attention and slide the knife to her while the captors were sleeping. For now, I slipped the knife in my sock under my pant leg.

The phone was ringing when I awoke. I was on the couch and the TV had cartoons playing on it. What time was it? The sun was up. Had I overslept? I looked at the clock to see that it was close to eight in the morning, and that I was in place in Kelowna. Who'd be calling? I grabbed the phone as I tried to pull myself from the sewers of Shanghai.

"Hello?"

"Where the hell have you been?"

"Uh, who is this?"

"Are you kidding me? I've been leaving messages on your phone, trying to get your attention and that's the thanks I get, who is this? Fuck you, Andy Jones."

The call ended with a click and I was even more lost. It took a couple minutes of a dazed stare at Sponge Bob Square Pants before I could figure it out.

"Oh shit. That was Julie."

Should I star-69 her number and call her back? Why the heck was she calling me? Then I remembered snippets of a drunken rant about dancing. Had I talked to her or was it the chatter from messages. And where was I last night? Why didn't I answer? Could it be because I was with Olivia, or sharpening a knife in order to save Olivia?

Kevin Weisbeck

What the hell was happening to me? I shook my head and looked over to the kitchen. Food. Damn if I wasn't starving. That was the problem. I sat up straight, shook more of the daze, and tried to stand. The legs almost held me, wobbled, and I went down. My head struck the corner of the coffee table.

Mr Hong grabbed me by the shoulder and struck me a second time across the face. Blood trickled from the cut above my left eye.

"We found your spitballs. Thought you could hide from us, make us look like idiots?"

"Hell no. You do a good enough job of that on your own."

Mr Hong lifted me to my feet and drove a fist into my gut. "Such a brave man. Let's see how brave you are later."

"Why. What's later."

He smiled as he dragged me off to the lobby. Olivia tugged at her ropes as the two men tied me to a chair that Mr Shui had put beside hers. I noticed her right eye had started to darken. They had hit her, likely because of me and my spitballs.

Mr Shui chuckled. "Looks like Mr Chin gets two gifts in the morning."

Chapter 23

At five in the morning, it was still dark, and Mr Hong was starting to drift off. Mr Shui had left and returned with a coffee and a paper. He was sitting with one leg up on the other, reading the third page. Olivia was staring at me. Actually, it was more like a scowl.

"Hi. You mad at me?" I asked.

She was about to answer when Mr Shui looked up, frowned, and then let his eyes fall back to his paper.

"No," she replied.

"You look upset."

"My face kinda hurts."

"Mine too."

"Next time, maybe spitballs aren't the best plan."

"I get that, now."

Mr Shui looked up again. "I'll get duct tape if you two don't shut up."

I pursed my lips and looked down.

Mr Shui went back to reading. That was when I straightened my leg. With my other foot, I quietly lifted my pant leg up, exposing my sock and the handle of the knife. That put a smile back on Olivia's face. She motioned for me to swing my leg behind her. I knew to move slowly. We didn't need the attention.

I shifted in my seat and waited until Mr Shui turned the page. As expected, the man found an article to sink into and I raised my leg. I held it steady as Olivia found the knife and worked it out of my sock. My leg started to cramp. Mr Hong started snoring and I gritted my teeth as the blade slid out of the sock. With the knife now in Olivia's possession, I dropped my leg back down with a thump. Mr Shui looked over.

"Sorry. Leg cramp."

"You want me to take care of it?"

I smiled. "Fuck you, asshole."

"Pardon me?"

"What are you gonna do, hit me again? You're such a chump."

With that he got up and hit me hard enough to knock me over. It was also hard enough to wake Mr Hong. He opened his eyes to see Mr Shui lift me, and the chair, and set it upright again. Then he wound up to strike me again. This time Mr Hong stopped him. "No. He's not ours."

"I don't care."

Mr Hong grabbed him. "Well, I do. I don't need Mr Chin being upset with me because you want to beat the crap out of his property."

Both men had their backs to Olivia, a horrible mistake even if she hadn't cut herself free. The ropes dropped to the floor, the chair was lifted, and it came down hard on Mr Hong's head. It didn't shatter like they did on TV. Instead, it held strong and gave his head a solid wallop. He crumpled in a heap and by the time Mr Shui turned around, the knife was slicing across his face. It opened his cheek and nose like a ripe tomato. She followed it up with a punch that surprised even me.

I watched the man fall. "Way to go, One-punch."

"Do not call me that."

"It was a compliment."

"Shut up and look for keys."

I found them in Mr Hong's pocket. "Got'em."

"Let's go and find a black BMW."

"Really? Why a black BMW."

A Dream Escape

"The BMW is the prize car in China. Mr Chin has a fleet of them. They're all black with the windows smoked in. His personal one is a golden stretch BMW."

"So, he's a narcissist?" I asked.

"Big time, and if you're working for him, you get one of his cars."

"Even these thugs?"

"Let's get going, unless you want to wait for them to wake up."

We left the lobby and saw the car parked across the street. Olivia took the keys from me as I used the fob to unlock the doors. "Hey."

"Sorry, Andy. You've taken a few good knocks to the head. Besides, I'm the one with the plan.

I didn't put up a fight. I'd seen what she did to Mr Shui. I took the passenger side, not even thinking to open, or hold, her door for her. The car sped off and I was sucked back into the plush leather seat. Olivia manoeuvred the street like there was no traffic on it, but there was. There was a lot of traffic.

"Uh, you can slow down."

"Not yet." She wheeled into the tunnel that led under the Huangpu River and shot out the other side.

"You're gonna attract cops."

"I'm not worried about the police." She slowed the car down and pulled into the BMW car dealership. There was an empty spot, and she took it. "Stay put."

She exited the car, crouched down and transferred the front and back licence plates to the white BMW beside us. It was the car to her left and she popped the passenger door open. I watched her ass wiggle back and forth as she stretched across the seat and fiddled with a handful of wires under the dash. Thirty seconds later, the car was started, and she was motioning for me to get in.

I crouched as I made my way to the passenger side. "Isn't this theft."

"They have a flunky that walks around counting cars. We left a BMW for a BMW. The numbers are good. I bet it takes them days before they realise it's gone. Meanwhile Mr Chin will be looking for us in a black one with smoked windows."

"And the police?"

"Mr Chin would be a fool to call them."

Olivia wheeled the car slowly out of the parking lot and onto the street. Nobody cared. It made leaving Shanghai a lot easier.

"What's the plan, and don't tell me you have friends that will take care of me."

"Sorry. I didn't see that one coming." She hung a right and did it without using the signal light. "I did a little digging and found nothing. I'd have to go with terrorism. It's the most likely."

"Why?"

"Why else would you need blueprints? Besides Mr Chin owns land at the mouth of the Yangtze River. Since the dam was built, the acidity of the Ocean has crept its way up the river. His land is becoming useless. I'm sure he's not the only one hurting either."

"Not to rain on that theory, but it seems a little extreme."

"It does. Another theory is that they want to control the ship locks of the dam. Everyday, ships travel up and down the river. They all pass through those locks. Now what if one of those ships had a special cargo?"

"Or a person," I offered.

She thought about it. "You mean like an assassination?"

"Say a ship or private boat gets stranded in one of the locks. They could board it and do whatever. With the blueprints, they could control the locks, make it look like an accident."

"I love the way you think?"

I'd never heard that before. "Most call what I say verbal diarrhea. I just spit out whatever comes to mind."

Olivia gave my leg a pat of approval. "Well, it comes in handy when we've got no leads. There are no stupid theories."

"Really?" It gave me hope. "What about an art heist?"

"I stand corrected." Her hand went back to the wheel. "Besides, Derrick might have answers."

That one hurt. "Who's Derrick?"

"He's my guy. I called him and he's making passports, and yes, this one I'd trust with my life."

I stewed on that one for the rest of the drive. She had a guy, someone she trusted with her life. Were they as close as we were? I'd seen three of her four cat paws. How many had this guy seen?

Olivia waited until we arrived in Suzhou before letting me off the hook. "Derrick and I have never dated."

"What?" Now I had to play it cool. "I never gave it a second thought."

"No, I mean we never dated because it was an arranged marriage. Derrick is my husband."

I could feel my stomach churning. Suddenly, I was cold, hopeless, and uncontrollably miffed. "I thought only Chinese people did that."

"Hey, when in Rome…"

"This isn't fucking Rome."

"Why do you care?"

"I don't," I mumbled. It wasn't like I ever had a chance.

She laughed as she pulled the car into a driveway. Derrick was standing in the doorway and he wasn't at all what I'd had expected.

Chapter 24

Derrick was maybe sixty years old on a good day. He stood at the front door waving Olivia over. His cane, which he needed for balance, was even older than he was. I pegged this lumpy white mass of a man at close to three hundred and fifty pounds. He lumbered on stubs of legs like a clown on stilts.

"And this is your husband?"

Olivia frowned. "Seriously, Andy?"

I reached for the door handle of the car. "How the hell am I supposed to know what you're into?"

Olivia exited first and walked with me into the modest single-story house. Built close to a hundred years ago, it looked clutter-cosy. Inside the house, I upgraded cluttered to hoard status. At least there were passageways through the junk.

"Let's see what you've got, Derrick. These passports have to be good."

Derrick's voice was gruff, struggling to get through a throat that sounded as if it still had a chicken bone from last night's supper trapped in there somewhere. "Who ya running from?"

"Chin's men."

They're bad people, Olivia. Why are you messing with them? You couldn't find an easier cause?"

A Dream Escape

She looked over at me. "Sometimes the causes come to you."

He turned toward me as he made his way to the desk across the room. "You worth all this trouble, boy?"

I shrugged uncomfortably. I was still trying to wrap my head around the fact that I wasn't on my tour with Candy and the rest of them.

Olivia slapped me on the rump. "He's worth it, Derrick."

Derrick smiled, grabbed his camera, and pointed to the white backdrop. "Who's first?"

Olivia pulled her hair back from her ears and stood without a smile. Derrick posed her for a second photo. "We need a different one for the Chinese Visa."

I was next.

Derrick took the camera over to the desk and plugged it into the computer. He brought up the first picture of Olivia, cropped it and pushed print preview. The picture came up on the screen and on a plate. The passport was placed onto the plate and held flat while he positioned it. Then he hit 'play' and in less than two seconds the picture was on the passport. He ran his thumb over the result and there was no smudge.

He finished both passports and smacked them on his hand before handing them over. "Good as real. I'll upload this all into the government registry. Give it an hour."

"An hour sounds good. We won't check into our hotel until later in the afternoon. You can take expenses from KN5647-K9."

He started typing and, within minutes, twenty thousand British Pounds had been transferred. "Want a receipt?"

"No, but I need an account opened for me and a hundred thousand Yuan put in it." She added, "Also from KN5647-K9."

He tapped away at the keyboard, pulled a Bank of China Credit card from the stack in his drawer, and typed the number in. "Consider it done, although it might take a couple days. Now tell me what you're up to, Olivia? I've heard your name on the down-low."

Olivia laughed as she took the card. "We made the down-low, Andy."

Kevin Weisbeck

I gave her a meek thumb's up. "Is that a good thing?"

She nodded. "Derrick, have you heard anything about the Three Gorges Dam on that down-low? We've intercepted the blueprints and think it's terrorism."

I humbly added, "Or an assassination of some kind."

"You got this blueprint?"

She started to unbutton her jeans. "I have it here Derrick."

My jaw dropped as she peeled the envelope off her back. My eyes took a second to register the pain from peeling the tape from her skin. She was one tough cookie. The envelope was handed to Derrick and she hiked her pants back up.

Olivia leaned over and whispered, "What? The man's my husband, right?" She gave me a playful shoulder to my chest as she slowly pulled the zipper up. I almost fell over. "Close your mouth, Andy. You look like that monkey, the one made out of a coconut, only you don't have the cigar hanging out of your mouth."

I slammed my mouth shut. "I uh, you…"

"And I'll take that as a complement."

"It, uh, was meant as one."

Derrick was pulling the blueprints out of the envelope when something caught his eye. "Oh my God. Do you know what you have here?"

Olivia and I both shrugged.

Derrick checked through everything and threw all but the blueprint to the floor. He took it over to the window and placed it against the glass with the backside of the blueprint toward them. The sun was breaking through the clouds and lit the paper up. Some of the blueprint from the front side shone through while most of it did not. From the backside, it looked like a map. On the bottom corner there were two letters and a number that you couldn't see from the front side, 4PB.

All three of us moved closer to see it. "What's that mean, Derrick? I'm sure you have a story?"

"I do. *Pinghéng de 4 gè Zhizhù*, the Four Pillars of Balance." He folded up the map and took a spot on the couch, after sliding a stack of books out of the way. Olivia took a spot on the coffee table and I looked around and decided to stand. "I'm sure you've heard of *Feng Shui?*"

Olivia offered her expertise. "It's nature's balance, mountains and water in harmony."

"Correct. Those are two of the Pillars." He scribbled that on the front of the blueprint. Then he scribbled *Zhēnxiàng* and *Cuòjué.* "These are the man-made two, Truth and Illusion. Legend calls the combination of these two, 'Chaos'."

"So, these pairs are paired, Harmony and Chaos, Nature and Mankind?" Olivia deduced. "What's the legend and what does this have to do with the map?"

"The legend goes back seven hundred years. There was a young Emperor in Xi'an who had been given a riddle from one of his people, a small child. It was a bit of a treasure hunt based on riddles and the Emperor loved the challenge. It inspired him to take it to the next level. He made a treasure map, ripped it into four pieces and made four riddles, calling each one a pillar. Sadly, nobody back then ever solved them, and the unknown prize went unfound until eight years ago."

My head cocked. "Someone solved it?"

"There was this computer geek, Nǎo Pang. Kid was real smart. Supposedly, he modernised the maps, hid them in the open, but in unexpected places. Just remember this was all just stories through the grapevine." He held up the map. "Until now."

"And there's three more maps?" I asked.

"Pillars," Derrick corrected me. "And yes, there are three more. And before you ask me where to find them, I'll tell you I have no idea. All I know is the four Pillars are Mountains, Water, Truth and Illusion. It is also said that if you unite these four Pillars, your house will be granted what you most need. It could be harmony, clarity, or a grand illusion. Most think it could be even greater. You see there was this bank heist worth millions… a security box full of gold coins. It happened eight years ago, and nothing was ever recovered."

Olivia rolled up the map, "And the old maps?"

"No-one knows. Hell, I thought these maps were just a tall tale."

"You have no idea what the kid found?"

"Huge mystery there. Nine months ago, they found his naked body hanging from a bridge with a note stapled to his chest."

"What did it say?"

"Needs and wants seldom share the same place in the heart."

I contemplated the words of that note as we made our way back to the hotel. It was spinning through my head even after my head hit the pillow. Staring at the smooth skin of Olivia's bare shoulder, I had to wonder... why wouldn't you want what you needed?

Chapter 25

Monday morning came at me like an eclectic array of thoughts dipped in chocolate. I woke up on the floor, crowded by furniture. Had I fallen out of bed? Had I fallen somewhere in the mess of Derrick's house? And where was Olivia? But this wasn't the suite in Suzhou or the dingy little shack. This was a couch and coffee table, the very table I'd hit my head on. Blood had crusted on my forehead.

I took a minute to sit on the couch, watch the television, and collect my thoughts. The morning news was all about earthquakes, a train accident, and the birth of a panda. Then I noticed the time and it put me in panic mode. Why was that? Then I remembered I had a job. This was Kelowna and I had cabinets to build.

But this was just a dream, a hideaway from the chaos of my reality? Life was crazy that way, car chases and treasure maps. It was nice to fall into a dream as simple as going to work and having a day without being shot at. But even in dreams, bills needed to be paid and life needed to be played out. In a few hours I'd wake up and Olivia would have a plan for us. The girl always had a plan.

I walked through the bedroom and remembered the naked woman in my bed. I had puked and heard a door close. At that point, the woman had disappeared, just like things do in dreams. Julie was hitting on me… just like in a dream. Was this the dream?

Hell, it was a lot more relaxing than being in China. I even enjoyed it, and why not, I was sleeping. Maybe I could figure out where that second pillar was. Shit comes to you in dreams, I'd heard. The one we had was water. That left mountains, truth, and illusion. Could one of those maps be here in my dream? Maybe I was having these dreams because this was the Pillar of Illusion? It was all starting to make sense... or was it?

As expected, the day dragged in a beautifully mundane fashion where the coffee and lunch break conversations revolved around my world in China. Julie was a no-show, so I mentioned the cat paw tattoo, but I didn't dare vary from the truth. Getting kneed in the nuts hurt like hell. I told them about the bullets, the back window of the car exploding, and kicking out the windshield. It was great stuff. I listened to their comments, looking for clues. There was no mention of the maps.

The day was winding down and with about twenty minutes left, the boss came over to me. It wasn't uncommon for him to stop by and thank a worker for making a station change, especially when they didn't get too far behind. That wasn't why he was stopping by.

"Just got a call from Julie's father."

That was odd. Julie didn't live with her parents. She probably hadn't lived with them for close to a decade. I didn't say anything.

"Seems Julie was in a car accident on her way back from the wedding."

That made sense. That was why she didn't call in. At least she wouldn't be written up. Then it hit me like a speeding cement truck, what if this wasn't a dream? "Hey. Is she okay?"

"Shook up. She's going to be spending the night at the hospital. I think they call it precautionary."

"Thank God." Then I started to wonder why I was being told all this. It wasn't like I was family and management had strict rules when it came to talking about personal affairs. Last year one of them got written up when they let it slip that Danny had Mono. Who knew we had a right to privacy and all that crap? Oddly, we all knew he had Mono. His brother Jeff also worked here and was running his mouth to everyone.

"She'll miss the week, so I need you to cover her station until further notice."

"Ya, sure. I can do that. Hey, not to be a shit disturber, but why are you telling me this. I mean I get the whole covering her station bit, but the accident."

My boss jerked his head as if he'd almost forgot the most important part. "Oh, ya. Her dad asked if you could stop by. She was asking about you."

"Really?" It came out as if I'd won the lottery. Julie had actually asked about me? Then I remembered the phone messages. In the cloudiness of waking, I thought we'd had a conversation, but those angry rants were simply phone messages.

She was damn drunk. What did she remember about the wedding, about calling me? She'd wanted to dance, and I wasn't there. Her date was likely not a dancer. Well, that was her problem because she'd picked him. Damn it, why was she messing with my stress-free time. Why, because I couldn't get her out of my mind. That's the thing about dreams, they tell you how it's gonna be, what you'll dream of, and whether or not you get the girl. Maybe there was a reason, a clue.

Did I really want to pop by the hospital? A sudden reality set in. She was hurt, but not that bad. The last time we had talked, she was angry. I imagined she still wanted to chastise me, in person, and maybe even blame me for the accident. And more importantly, I'd have to take it. I started to clean up her station. If I didn't, I'd get shit for that too. The woman was unstable, but the good-looking ones usually were.

With the decision made, I'd swing by the hospital and accept my fate. I walked to my car. We were friends, right? Besides, in the back of my mind there was an off chance she just wanted to see me.

Now I knew I was dreaming.

Chapter 26

The hospital was eerily quiet and I left the gift shop with a blue teddy bear. It was a cute one with a cowboy hat and boots. I'd heard Julie say that real men wore cowboy boots. This little guy would be introduced as Billy the Cub and hopefully it would make her think twice about losing her temper.

I stepped into the doorway and tried to gauge what I was walking into. Would she be all maimed and disfigured? Would she be fighting back the pain? Would she be changing her clothes, or loading a gun? I'd take changing. Hospitals never allowed a whole lot of privacy. I'd been in this ward once when my appendix ruptured. It was anything but fun. I was getting a bandage changed or checked every time somebody stopped by. With any luck, Julie was just sitting up in bed.

She was.

Julie took the Bear with a tired smile. "Thanks, Andy. Why are you here?"

"Your Dad said you asked for me."

"Sorry. I don't remember. Shit, between yesterday and the accident, I don't remember much."

"Are you okay? I mean it was weird not having you at work. I had to do drawer faces."

A Dream Escape

"I hope you didn't mess up my station. I've got that job dialled in pretty good."

"I broke your drill, and that template has a few extra holes in it now, but other than that..."

"It better not." She tried to sit up.

The grimace told me she was hurting. "Don't move. I didn't wreck your station. It's all good still."

"Better be."

"What the hell happened to you?"

Julie shifted to get comfortable and let her body slump into the bed. "I totalled my car and fractured my femur. It's not bad enough to cast, but it frigg'n hurts like you can't imagine. I mean, when I was a kid, I tobogganed into a tree and broke my lower leg. That was a walk in the park compared to this."

I casually pointed to her face. "Smack your head, too?"

"Shit." She brought her hand up to her hairline. "Is it that obvious?"

I had to assume she hadn't seen it. She'd banged her head and although the knock was at the hairline, the effects went a lot further. Here she was all worried about the small bandage and the cut beneath it. She should have been more concerned with the shiner. Her eye had blackened like she been made up for Halloween. "It's barely noticeable."

"Are you shitting me?"

"Ya. You've got a bit of a black eye happening."

"You're enjoying this, aren't you?"

"After what you did, I should."

"What did I do?" She was honestly puzzled.

"Well, for starters there were the phone messages. You left a few on my machine. You were a little upset."

"I was?" She rubbed her head. "You said for starters. What else did I do?"

"I was talking to Barry." I paused to let her catch up. She didn't. "He said you'd already asked him to do that favour. You know the one you were asking me."

"You lost me. I never talked to Barry."

"You were gonna ask me a favour, remember?"

110

Kevin Weisbeck

"And you said yes, without knowing what it was. I remember. It was very sweet of you. Then you couldn't because your parents needed you."

"My parents didn't need me. Barry told me you asked him first and he said no and that was why you asked me. I'm not even mad at being a second choice. I'm upset that you wanted to dupe me like that, making me say yes before knowing what the favour was."

"You didn't have to help your parents?" Julie frowned. "And you honestly believed I'd ask Barry before you? Are you insane?"

"Yes. I mean you wanted him to take a friend of yours to this wedding. He said no, so you asked me. Barry said he saw a picture and your friend wasn't that attractive, but that's not why I blew you off. I didn't want to be the fool."

"First of all, I never talked to Barry, oh wait. First of all, you are the fool. Do you think I'd ever ask that Neanderthal anything? And there is no ugly friend needing a date. He was yanking your chain."

"Oh, shit." In hindsight, I should have seen that. Barry was always pulling something. "What was the favour?"

Julie started to blush and looked away. "It sounded like a better idea before the accident. Now I'd just rather forget it. It was stupid."

"Did it have something to do with the wedding?"

"Kinda."

"Did you need me to move something or drive you somewhere? I'd have done that."

"You're such an ass."

"What? I said I'd do whatever, so spit it out."

"Nah. I don't need the favour anymore."

Wasn't it just like a woman, I thought to myself? They ask a favour, you say yes, and that's not good enough. Next thing, they have you begging them to do this favour. "I bought you a bear, so fucking tell me."

"It really was dumb and if you didn't want to do it, I'd have understood. It's just that I hate going to weddings alone... so?"

111

A Dream Escape

"What? You wanted me to go to this wedding with you?" I tried not to act thrilled beyond belief, but it was hard. I was so going to nut-kick Barry the next time I saw him. That prick cost me a date with Julie.

"I did."

I saw the control shift from me to her. I needed a quick counter. "You seen yourself in a mirror lately?"

"That's it. I take it back. Next time I'll go alone."

"No. I'd be happy to go with you." I should have known I'd never really get power. "I'm just teasing you, and hey, I think you look great."

She smiled. "Really?"

I bit down on my lip as I nodded. She looked like she'd pissed off James Brown. Still, the eyes were sweet, and they were looking at me. "What? You want me to tell you you're pretty or something? You want me to call you a hottie?"

By saying that, I'm pretty sure I just had.

"They're releasing me in a couple hours. You think you could hang around, give me a ride home? My car's kinda junked."

"I can do that."

"I haven't seen it yet. Maybe we can stop by the impound and have a look."

"They said you totalled it off. What happened anyway? Were you still a little drunk?"

"Maybe a little, but I was good to drive. I'd just picked up a coffee at McDonalds and hit the freeway. I got up to speed and this car came out of nowhere. It switched lanes right in front of me, so I swerved. I must have hit some gravel on the shoulder. The bastard didn't even stop. It was like he'd done it on purpose."

"Did you get a license plate or see the driver?"

"No, because the car didn't have plates and the windows were all blacked in. Hell, the whole thing was black."

I felt the blood drain from my face. Did she just say a black car with no plates? There was no way it could have come from my dream, could it? It could, if this was the dream. Mr Chin had gone after Julie in retaliation. I had to ask. "It wasn't a BMW, was it?"

"Why yes, it was. How did you know that?"

112

Chapter 27

It had been getting harder and harder to wake up from the dreams. I had just found out that Julie had wanted to take me to a wedding. How cool was that? Not that Olivia wasn't a catch. Where Julie was miles out of my league, Olivia wasn't even on the same planet. But wasn't it her arm, currently draped across me? I cleared away the cobwebs to get a better look.

The hotel room in Suzhou was amazing. The dresser and armoire were made from cherrywood, and the tub was the size of a Jacuzzi. Olivia had used it first and had flirted with me afterward as she walked around in her robe. Well, I called it flirting, but it was really me sneaking peeks as the front of the robe occasionally opened. She hadn't noticed the brief exposures, or my reactions. Maybe she had, and liked the attention. That would have made it flirting. After the baths we had washed our clothes in the tub and hung them up over the heat duct.

She slept in a t-shirt and panties that she'd bought from the boutique in the lobby. She had also purchased a pair of boxer briefs for me.

There was something magical about washing the stench of the Huangpu River out of one's body and then crawling into the silk sheets of a king-sized bed. She had curled up on her own side and fell asleep fast. I'd stayed on my side of the bed and done the same.

Thing was, I was still on my side and she'd been the one to break the proximity rules. She was nuzzled up against me, her body pressed against mine, her face resting against my shoulder. I'd curled my arm around her and held her like we were an old married couple on vacation.

She moaned, meaning she was waking up. Her leg found mine and her knee started to rub its way up my leg. My eyes widened as her smooth skin rubbed dangerously close to my manhood. She was so warm, so silky, so damn sexy. Her leg stopped when it came into contact with my shorts.

"Hmm, somebody's wide awake," she snickered.

It was too late to pretend I was sleeping. I looked down at her to see her staring up at me. "I uh…"

"God, you're so shy. You like me, right?"

I couldn't speak. It was like I had a bag of buns in my mouth, maybe a loaf of bread. Instead, I nodded.

"Then why so shy? I'd think you'd like my knee there."

I did, but I also remembered the elevator. It was a passionate kiss followed by that same knee, the one that had taken my breath away. It dropped me to my knees, and I didn't want that again. "Uh, the elevator?"

"You'd done something stupid. Have you done anything stupid lately?"

"I don't know. Maybe the spitball?"

She slid her hand down my chest and started across my abdomen. I was extremely glad I'd spent the last two months working out. Her fingertips stopped as they started to slither their way under the waistband of the boxers. "Just say the word."

Was she seriously thinking of grabbing me down there? Maybe I had everything wrong, and this was the dream. I'd initially thought that. Lately, I'd been waffling. China made more sense. I had to stop thinking about it. Olivia, who was now the obvious dream, wanted to put a hand on me. Should I let her? I definitely should let her. This could tell me a lot.

As a teenager I'd had a few dreams like this. They always ended the same way, me waking up with a mess in my shorts.

"Uh, word."

"Fair enough." She slid her hand further down my shorts and grabbed a handful. "Nice, Andy. You shouldn't be so hung up on keeping him to yourself."

I held my breath while she checked under the hood, so to speak. She liked what she had found and that made me smile as she started. My heart started to beat hard in my chest and my breathing started to labour. Damn her hand felt good. Her touch was surprisingly gentle, soft. If only I could make this last forever, but I already knew that soon, I'd be making a mess and this dream would be over. Until then, I'd enjoy this. I bravely slid my hand down her back. I rounded it over her butt and gave a squeeze. The woman was firm.

My eyes turned to the fabric of the tight t-shirt. The outline showed me that she was equally aroused. Sadly, I only lasted forty seconds after seeing that.

Olivia gave an innocent giggle, like we were two school kids experimenting behind the bleachers. "Was that so bad." She pulled her hand out and tried not to get any on the bed.

"That was amazing," I gasped as I tried to catch my breath. What was more amazing was the fact that I was still dreaming. I had always woken up when the orgasm started. There was no other way for this to happen.

"You look lost. What's up?" Again, she giggled. "Or not up anymore."

"Uh, why am I still here?"

She was about to run to the bathroom but stopped herself. Instead, she placed her wet hand on my chest and leaned in for a kiss. She briefly placed her lips against mine. "Did you really think this was a wet dream?"

I kissed her back. "Would have bet money on it."

"You are too cute." She looked back at the tired lump in my shorts and the wetness starting to soak through the fabric. "That's not a dream." She got up and left the room to wash her hands.

I stared at the wet lump confused. If this weren't a dream, then why would she do this... unless she really liked me.

Olivia came back, pulled the blankets up, and crawled back into bed. "For the record, I find you adorable."

"Same."

"You're handsome, nicely built, and there's a sweetness that's as refreshing as a kitten playing with a ball of yarn. Let's not over-think anything or do anything stupid to fuck it up."

"Uh, you just..."

"Do you think that was stupid?" she dared.

"Not at all."

"Good. Now that we're a something, I need to ask you a question."

"Whatever you want."

"Good. Last night you were dreaming about this Julie girl. What's up with that?"

My eyes widened. Was Olivia the jealous type? "Why bring her up?"

"You were talking about her in your sleep, something about a car accident."

"Yes. She was driving back from a wedding. She'd had a bit to drink, but she claimed she was okay to drive. Why do you care? I mean I think we've just proven it's just a dream." I looked down at the covers.

"News flash, big boy, I already knew it was a dream, but here's a thought." She was suddenly serious. "We're looking for four Pillars. We've already got water. We need mountains, truth and..."

I already knew where she was going with this. "Illusion!"

"That's right, now let's go get dressed. I think I know where our Truth Pillar is."

Kevin Weisbeck

Chapter 28

Our flight finally landed in Beijing an hour late. With new passports and a renewed hope, Olivia and I hurried through the crowds to get out of here. We, well she, knew that Mr Chin's people would be looking for us at airports and train stations.

"I didn't hurt you, did I?" She looked down at my crotch.

I smiled and awkwardly answered, "Of course not."

"Then walk faster." She gave me a push. "Or do you want to get caught?"

"Where are we going?"

"Follow without falling back too far and you'll find out." She didn't make it easy for me as she wove her way through crowds and to a waiting cab. She hopped in the back and left the door open as she slid to the far side. "*Ni hǎo*. Tiananmen Square."

I fell into my seat and closed the door as the cab rolled from the curb. "Do we have any money?"

Olivia drove an elbow into my ribs. "Not yet, and we need this ride, so shut up."

I whispered, "You've got nothing?"

"Not here yet." The elbow returned. This time I kept quiet until we arrived. "Now what?"

She was staring through the windshield. "The light should changing soon. When he stops, get out and run to the square. I'm

117

gonna run the other direction. He'll follow me, not realising you're the slow one. After I lose him, I'll double back and shit... it's green. Go!"

"But the cab hasn't stopped yet."

"Go!"

She exited the cab and ran back the way we'd came. I ran the other way, into traffic.

Olivia looked back. "Wrong direction!"

I saw her point and I made the adjustment. She was right, about the direction and the fact that the cab driver would go after her. Dodging a couple scooters and a few hundred pedestrians, I made it to the square. That was the easy part. Waiting for Olivia drove me crazy.

Ten minutes turned into twenty, and that turned into forty. Had I missed her? I did seven laps around the square, a marathon of walking. Where the hell was she?

When the hand landed on my shoulder, I turned with a clenched fist.

"Whoa, big boy. It's me."

"Where have you been?"

"How was I supposed to know he ran track in high school? And I'm still a little sore from being shot."

"Fair."

She started for the gates of the Forbidden City. Inside the grounds, we covered the area quickly. I took the one side of the courtyards while she took the other. We were looking for a painting. I almost asked a guard but stopped myself. What if the man knew Mr Chin?

When I reached the third gate there was no Olivia. That meant she had found it. I backtracked her side until I found her. "That's it? That's the painting. Doesn't look like much."

"And yet it's the most important painting in here."

Olivia and I both looked over to the man guarding it. He was four feet tall and as close to a hundred as anyone could get without having to blow out a forest full of candles.

He was also the one that explained these paintings to tourists. His story began and we listened.

Kevin Weisbeck

"At the Forbidden City there are close to fifty thousand paintings. The most important of them is this one, called 'Truth'. See that man?" He pointed to the one in the painting. "He is said to be the man who killed the truth."

I leaned in to get a better look. "How'd he kill truth?"

"Back in 1402 the land was ruled by Emperor Jianwen. He was a good ruler. He ruled with honesty and compassion. His Uncle saw this as a weakness and decided to take the throne. First, he won over the people by starting lies and spreading ugly rumours. Lies are always more believable than the truth.

Once he'd won the people over, he used them to access, and attack, the Palace in Nanjing. A general on the inside betrayed Jianwen and opened the gates. Emperor Jianwen Di was overthrown. The uncle, Zhu Di became the Emperor Yongle. Thousand of servants, family and loyal military were killed in the attack and Emperor Jianwen was caught and burned alive. His charred body was displayed to everyone as proof of the successful coup.

Yongle had killed many to get at his nephew's throne, but that was just a start. After the take over, Yongle killed all Jianwen's allies. Tens of thousands were slaughtered.

What most people do not know is that Jianwen had heard of the attack. He was about to commit suicide when an old eunuch gave him a box. It was from Jianwen's father. It held a razor to allow him to shave his head and a map to the secret underground tunnels. Jianwen escaped and hid out with the monks He was never to be found. The truth is, he was the real emperor, and the burnt body was that of an imposter, likely a loyal servant.

During Yondle's rein, in 1406, the capital was moved to Beijing. The Forbidden City was built as the new Imperial Palace and the moat was dug. Do you know where all that dirt went?"

I looked to Olivia. Neither of us knew.

"That dirt was moved to make that hill." He pointed to the hill just beyond the exit of the Forbidden City." They call it Jingshan Park. Rumour has it, Emperor Jianwen watches over the Forbidden City up on the hill. He rules us in the afterlife because he was the last True Emperor.

119

A smile spread across Olivia's face. "What's the name of the hill?"

"The hill is called Feng Shui Hill, and it was made from a lie."

"Thank you," Olivia replied as she grabbed my hand and pulled me along.

"I'm guessing you've figured it out?"

"Maybe."

We climbed the hill and stood at the top looking over the Forbidden City. Up there, the ground was concrete with raised pebbles to massage the feet. We both went barefoot hoping to feel something. Instead, we noticed the pebbles were in a pattern. That being said, there was no 4PB marking.

After snapping a few pictures of the pebble pattern, we decided to move on. It was getting late and we still needed to pick up some money. Hopefully, Derrick had come through.

At the bank I had to call Olivia, Vivian. Her passport was Vivian Dubois, and I was Jackson Steele. What was I, a porn star? "Was this name your idea?"

"It was," she answered as she stuffed the money in her purse. She handed me a hundred Yuan. "Now run off and buy yourself something pretty.

I took the bill and was about to run off when she grabbed my hand. "Kidding. Let's go get a bite and head back to the hotel."

I smiled. "What are we going to do there?"

"You're gonna go to bed while I go over these pictures."

"What?"

"I need to figure out these clues, and you need to fall asleep, go to Kelowna, and find our Illusion Pillar."

Kevin Weisbeck

Chapter 29

Julie unfolded her hands and dropped them to her side as she watched me push my way through the turnstiles and head for the parking lot. Her left arm ached as she slipped her hand onto the top of her purse and used the strap as a sling. Dangling the arm heightened the pain in her shoulder. The long sleeve shirt hid the bruising that had started in her neck and bled all the way down to her elbow. She gave me a coy wave with her good arm when I looked her way.

"Hey, Andy."

I hurried my pace. "Hey. What are you doing out? I thought you were on bed rest."

"I can only do so many sudoku puzzles. I needed to get out and get some fresh air. Do you mind driving me around? I have a couple errands to run." She put her hand up. "If you can't that's okay. I don't mean to…"

I stopped her. "I'd love to. I mean I feel like a shit for not going to that wedding."

"Don't worry about it. We can both agree that Barry is a useless turd."

I nodded as I used the fob on my key chain to open the doors of my 93 Malibu. I opened her door and awkwardly watched her get in. Should I take an arm, help her in? She wasn't the damsel in distress type. She might take it the wrong way. If I didn't, she

A Dream Escape

might think I wasn't interested. Olivia wouldn't have any part of a door being held for her or a hand being extended to help. She'd put a knee in my groin just for thinking it.

I stood there holding the door until she got seated. Better safe than sorry. When she was settled, I closed the door and went around to the other side. My lunch box got tossed on the back seat as I took my place beside her.

Julie was wearing a skirt. I had never seen her so girlie-girl. It was usually jeans and a t-shirt. Heck, it was always jeans and a t-shirt. This was a nice change. She had nice legs.

She let me gawk for a split second before calling me on it. "Never seen a pair of legs before?"

"They're not that nice." I looked up.

"Right. Then why are you staring?"

"Okay. Maybe they aren't so bad."

She batted her eyes. "Why thank you, Andy."

I laughed. "So where are we going first?"

"You're gonna hate me." This time she forced a smile. "Can we go to Shoppers Drugmart? I have to pick up a prescription and they have a sale on perfume."

"Can I wait in the car?"

"I was kinda hoping you'd help me pick one."

"I'm not sure how much help I can be. I don't wear the stuff."

She put a hand on my leg. "But you know what you like."

I looked down at the hand as if it were wrapped around my penis. Was I seeing too much into this, or was this exactly what I thought it was? I placed my hand on top of hers. It wasn't a grab, wasn't a squeeze. It was meant as a generic and very safe move, much like holding a hug a tad longer than one should. It could be read as interest or passed off as just a friendly gesture... no ring, and no, I do.

Julie read it as shy to the point of cute and wove her fingers between mine. That was a definite hand holding move because apparently, a boy like me needed the bolder approach.

I gave it a squeeze. "Perfume shopping it is."

"I'll buy you a Creamsicle."

122

Kevin Weisbeck

"A what?" I had been thinking of a buying a Creamsicle all day. I'd even shoved my hand in my pocket, hoping for enough spare change to get one out of the vending machine. I was fifty cents short, and nobody could make change. Why, of all the things she might have picked, did she bring up Creamsicle?

"Did you hear me, Andy?"

"I, uh…" This was definitely a dream? I was controlling it, to a very small degree, which made sense. I liked Julie so she had to like me. I wanted to spend time with her in order to find out more about these Pillars and there she was, standing by my car. I'd wanted ice cream, a Creamsicle to be precise, and she had just offered one up. What would happen if I changed it up? Maybe, for shits and giggles, I'd change what I wanted. Maybe I'd rather have a Dilly Bar.

"Earth to Andy. Would you rather go to the DQ? There's one on the same block. We could get Blizzards, or maybe a couple of Dilly Bars."

A smile started to form as I gave her hand another squeeze. I was in the driver's seat, literally and figuratively. "I would love a Dilly Bar." The five-minute drive to Shoppers was done in four.

Julie spritzed a Brittany Spears on her neck and allowed me a sniff. "What do you think?"

"Wow."

She glanced at the price on the box. "If a twenty-four-dollar perfume can get a wow out of you, I wonder what a thirty-six-dollar perfume might do?"

She gave herself a shot on the other side of her neck and moved her head off to the other side. I took the cue and filled my lungs with the wonderful aroma of this lovely girl in a skirt. I wanted to place a peck on her skin, maybe put a hand on her hip and draw her in for a kiss. So why didn't I. Hell, I should be able to will her back to my place and have sex with her. It was my dream, after all. Oh, but how would I explain the mess in my underwear to Olivia. My groin ached as my lips recoiled. It wasn't worth Olivia's wrath, or was it?

"Now that's a reaction." She grabbed an unopened perfume, after planting a kiss on my cheek. "Thanks."

123

"No, thank you. What are we doing next, underwear shopping, bathing suits?"

"Ha, you wish." She reached for my hand and dragged me toward the checkout. "Now let's go get that ice cream."

This had to be a dream. Julie hadn't paid any attention to me until I'd started to will it. I had to refocus. A geeky kid, Năo Pang, had put a Pillar in my dream and Julie had to know something about it. "Hey, does the word illusion mean anything to you?"

"Are you shitting me?" She followed the comment with an eye roll and a head shake, like I was being silly.

I wasn't sure what she meant by that, so I shrugged it off as an inside joke that I was on the outside of.

We pulled out of the stall and Julie was good for her word and sprung for the Dilly Bars. I'd have to buy next time. My eyes followed her lips and teeth as she nibbled the chocolate off the ice cream, her eyes occasionally looking up to see if she'd caught my attention. She had.

I knew I had to go, but it was hard. We were talking, laughing, making a connection. This had never happened. The handholding had never happened either. I stopped the car in front of her house. "I had a great time."

"Me too." She took my jaw in her hand and let her lips find mine.

The kiss had only lasted a minute, but it was all I could think about, that is, until I handed her the box of perfume she'd just bought.

The lone word embossed on the box was 'Illusion'.

Chapter 30

Olivia's eyes were locked on mine the moment I opened them. She wanted to press me for the truth, but there wasn't time. Breakfast was almost over and we had to get downstairs or miss out. Apparently, I had been talking in my sleep and she had been listening. She'd been listening to broken conversations between a girl with the nice legs and myself. There had been a perfume that had dazzled me. I'd also mumbled something about a Dilly Bar.

Olivia wasn't impressed, or maybe it was an insecurity. She merely smelled like the soap that she had used to wash away the Huangpu River, and all she had to offer me was a pillow mint.

We dressed and made our way down to the dining room before the complimentary breakfast was over. I noticed she was angry eating. "You seem a little miffed."

"Hurry up and eat," She snapped as she wrapped a few Danishes in a napkin for later. "I've got a cab coming. It might even be sitting out front."

"Are you pissed at me?" That question was wrapped in regret. I knew she was mad. Like being late for work, it was always best to face it head on verses hide from it. "I mean you seem like you..."

"Like I want to take my foot and park it up your ass? You're imagining things."

I imagined her foot buried in my ass. It wasn't hard. "Are you angry because of Julie?"

"Who?" She got up and started for the lobby.

I scooped a slice of wheat cake and tried to keep up. "Julie's the girl you're mad at. I didn't do anything."

"Hold it. Why would I be mad at her? You're the one throwing yourself at her like some..."

"Ha. Then you are mad at me." It was like I'd won a stuffed bear at a carnival. In fact, I'd only poked the bear.

She turned abruptly, putting me back on my heels. "I never had to help you."

"She's a dream, Olivia. I don't have feelings for her."

Olivia turned to the front doors of the hotel. "We have to hurry. We've already spent too much time in one place."

Again, I was running to keep up.

The cab dropped us off in a parking lot with one of the gnarliest trees I had ever seen. Olivia ran off to get the admission tickets. She waved me over.

"Why are we here again?" I asked.

"Because old people are a wealth of wisdom. These gardens have more old people than a cemetery. At any time of the day, they flock in the hundreds. They fly kites, dance, and exercise."

"Exercise?"

"They've got an area, about the size of a soccer field. It's full of that outdoor exercise equipment and full of..." She waited for me to finish the sentence.

"Old people that might be able to help us?" I shrugged. "How?"

"While the young Chinese pride themselves on who they know, the elderly Chinese people pride themselves on what they know."

I studied them as we walked to the centre of the equipment. She was right. There were hundreds and they were all working out. Ninety-year-old women stretched liked they were twenty and the old guys worked out with the vigour of young men. I was more than a little jealous. One old guy was twirling around on a bar like he was entered in the damn Olympics.

Olivia let me stew in my own world of guilt from not being able to touch my own toes. She needed answers. One group of women were taking a break and she joined them. It was simple conversation, pork or beef with rice noodles, and how well their grandchildren were doing. It took a while for her to steer the conversation toward Chinese culture and truths.

"What are you truly looking for?" The woman was close to a hundred, if not a few years over. "Come walk with me."

Olivia watched as the old woman, barely four feet tall, waddled off. She quickly took her place beside her. "I'm looking for something, but I'm not sure what it is. It should connect your culture with truth."

"The only one doing that is our Confucius. He gave us not only truth, but also the simplest form of truth. He was a very wise man."

I had caught up with Olivia and the woman after several failed attempts of showing up these old guys and I was still a little out of breath. "Does Confucius have some kind of shrine or temple?"

She looked up at me with the sorrow of a mother seeing her son failing at life. "There is the Temple of Confucius. It's on Guozijian Street. You should check it out. You might learn something."

She turned her back to us and waddled off. I almost followed until Olivia hooked me by the arm. "She's done with us. I'll check it out on my phone."

"Uh, I think we better do it later. We've got company."

She looked over to see three black SUVs rolling through the parking lot and heading our way.

"How do they know?" I asked.

"Cameras." She took my hand, and we were off and running. "Damn things are everywhere. That means he has an informant in the police department."

"You mean the police are after us too?"

127

"No, just the one that's put our pictures in the system. They're watching for facial recognition. One of these cameras gave us away."

"That's BS."

Olivia finally agreed with me on something, yet she wanted to kill me. "Run that way. I'll go this way."

"I don't think we should split up."

I looked back to see her sprinting for the trees. I was caught in the open with three black SUVs bearing down on me. Why me? Why couldn't a couple of them go after her? My legs had me running before I could pick a direction.

The bad part about being in the open was that they didn't have to get out of their vehicles. I headed straight for the Temple. There was no way they'd be able to chase me up the steps.

As I crested the stairs and looked back, I could see they were on foot. I figure three SUVs would mean six guys. There were ten. Three of them were damn tall and faster than me. I wasted no time trying to lose them. I cut through the temple, an absolute no-no, and raced down the stairs on the other side. To the left I saw a fence. In front of me I saw a fence. I looked right and saw four of them rounding the corner to cut me off from an easy escape. The fence it was.

Climbing chain link was a lot harder than I thought. I finally made it over and dropped onto the ground on the other side. I ran about fifty steps before looking back. I had cut the guys chasing me in half. Only five of them could make it over. The others were too short to scale it.

Did it matter, five guys with guns or ten? I'd die either way. Again, I was in the open and running for my life. In the far distance I saw people scattering as a black SUV chased them out of the way.

"Oh shit."

A shot was fired, and I cringed. I was still running and hadn't been hit. A few more shots were fired, and I was wondering how these guys got hired. It wasn't like I was a tiny target. Not wanting to be shot, I had to stop and look back.

That's when I saw that these guys weren't shooting in my direction.

Kevin Weisbeck

The SUV had caught up to me in an attempt to get between me and the shooters. Right when I saw the other two SUVs in the distance, the passenger door flew open.

"Get in!"

Who was I to say no to Olivia? I got in and she blew a donut and started back the way she came.

"Uh, SUVs twelve o'clock. That means they're right in front of us!"

"I can see."

She headed for them with no fear. Me, I was afraid. Two SUVs were coming at us as fast as we were coming at them. Bullets were bouncing off the windows, door panels and fenders. Then I thought of that final scene with Warren Beatty and Faye Dunaway. They were Bonnie Parker and Clyde Barrows, and they were being shot up by the police. Three or four shots in each would have killed them, but these police didn't stop until the two were fully perforated. I didn't want that.

"And you've got a plan?" I asked.

"Yep, but I can't guarantee it's a good one."

I covered my eyes as we met up with the other two vehicles. "Shit."

I waited for the impact, but it didn't come. I opened my eyes and looked back. The two other SUVs were turning around. "They didn't hit us."

"That was the plan." She breathed her own sigh of relief. "I mean we were going pretty fast. It would have been bad for everybody, including them, right?"

My mouth opened, but nothing came out. *That* was her plan?

129

Chapter 31

We hit the highway, tires howling and the other two SUVs in chase. I couldn't imagine they'd stopped to pick up the others. They were far too close. Olivia wasn't worried. She was pedal to the floor focused.

"How you holding up?" she asked.

I wasn't sure how to answer that. On one hand I wasn't dead yet, although I was kinda wishing I was. There's something about a looming death that kinda knocks the wind out of the sails.

"Relax. I'll get you home safely."

"I'm really back to hoping this is the dream."

"Holy shit! Are you kidding me? This is so not a dream. I can't even believe you just said that."

"I know. And for the record, I'm not trying to piss you off. I know you find that hard to believe, but I really like you. I like living, so I promise you, if we get away from these guys, I'll find a way to make it up to you. I was flirting with Julie, but only because she's not real. That means any attraction I may have to her isn't real."

"Really?"

"Of course."

She swerved hard, slamming my head against the side window. "I disagree."

"Ouch." I rubbed my head and scrambled for the seatbelt.

"Don't you dare put that on, just in case I need you to kick out a windshield or we have to make a quick break for it."

"I like seatbelts."

"I said no."

I did as I was told and sat quietly while she wove through the traffic. It gave me a minute to rethink the Illusion Pillar. I had to believe Julie had something to do with it because she was predominantly in my dreams. And since she couldn't help me, maybe the answer was somewhere in her workstation. I'd have to check that out tonight when I...

"Hold on!"

"I have a bad feeling about this."

She cut into an opening in the guardrail. That had us bouncing through the grass meridian and looking for an opening to the highway heading in the other direction. There was an opening, but it was small and there was traffic coming.

I stomped the floor, even though I didn't have a brake pedal on my side. "You're not..."

"This is how we separate the men from the boys."

She cut in front of a large truck hauling steel and used a small sedan to help straighten herself out. I watched the first SUV take the full brunt of the impact. It hit the guard railing hard and was almost torn in half. The second one hammered the brakes, found the opening, and entered the freeway a couple hundred yards behind us.

Olivia smiled. "And then there was one."

I was glad she could count. Hopefully, she could count us down to zero. I looked back and saw they were gaining. That had to do with our vehicle starting to sputter.

"What's wrong? Put your foot into it."

"It is," Olivia barked. She looked down at the gauges to see that the fuel tank was empty. "Shit."

I had to ask. "Why'd you grab the one with no gas?"

"It was full when I stole it. They must have hit the tank with one of those bullets."

"Wouldn't we have exploded?"

"Not if the tank was full." She added, "Not as many vapours with a full tank. That's what explodes."

"Good to know. Now what?"

"I can't believe I'm gonna say this but put your seatbelt on."

I didn't need to be told twice. When she heard the click, she hammered the brakes. Then she jammed the shifter in reverse and pinned it.

"What the hell are you..."

"Hold on."

The SUV behind us swerved to miss us and Olivia compensated. We had to be doing a good fifty mph when we made contact. I had no idea how fast the other vehicle was going, but the impact sucked me back in the seat with a vengeance.

Olivia took a second to catch her breath. "Get out! We've got to go."

I blinked away the blur and rolled my neck around. The head was still attached. I tried to get out but couldn't. The door was ajar, but the seat was holding me back. Then I realised I was still wearing the seat belt. I couldn't really remember putting it on, but I had flashes of her telling me to.

Unbuckling, I exited the mess of broken glass and twisted metal and followed Olivia to the back of the vehicle. Two head–sized dents were imprinted outward on the windshield of the SUV that was chasing us.

"Get over here," she ordered.

I did as I was told. She stepped into an open lane and tried to stop a car. A couple vehicles passed, not wanting any part of this, but a third stopped after she stepped in front of them. She ran around to the driver's door and opened it. "Get out or come with. Your choice."

The woman quickly got out. Olivia parked herself behind the wheel. "Are you coming?"

I nodded as I slowly reached for the handle on the passenger side. I looked around at the carnage. This was as real as it got, from the two unconscious thugs to the honking traffic. And then there was the smell of oil and antifreeze as it puddled under the vehicles.

"Now!" she shouted.

I opened the door and started to get in. That was when I saw a golden BMW on the other side of the highway. The back window was down. Sitting in the back seat, Mr Chin and a woman were staring at us. He looked angry, and she looked scared.

It was Julie.

Chapter 32

Iparked my car in the first open spot and raced through
the turnstile. My card didn't work on the first attempt
and I jammed my face into one of the bars. On the
second attempt the green light lit, and the turnstile moved. From
there I rubbed my cheek as I wove through the doors to Julie's
workstation.

I stopped and took a long look at the place. Julie was gonna
be pissed. Somebody had already trashed the bench, the drawers,
and all the paperwork for today. "What the fu—"

Barry walked up behind me. "She's gonna kill you when
she sees this."

"I didn't do this."

"Don't tell me. Tell her."

"She'll never see this. I can fix it."

"Too late." He held up his phone. He'd already snapped a
picture and sent a text to her. The reply had been an angry emoji
followed by three capitalised letters, WTF.

"I thought you didn't have her number, ya prick." I shoved
him. "And why'd you lie to me about that date thing. Julie wanted
the date for herself, not a friend."

"She wanted you to go with her? Oh, that's funny."

I started to round up the paperwork. I'd be building these
cabinets today and needed this information. I also wanted to see if

there was anything hidden in the directions, maybe a Chinese symbol or a 4PB. God how I wanted to find a 4PB.

Barry stood and watched for a minute before losing interest. I ignored him as I shuffled tools into drawers and templates onto the pegboard. Screwdrivers were slipped into holes that awaited them and the three screw guns were put back into their holsters. Everything was there, except the clue to the Pillar of Illusion. She had a calendar and a poster with two chipmunks in g-strings. The caption read 'The Real Chip and Dale's.' The boss would have had her take it down, but it was cartoon rodents.

I unpinned the poster and looked at the back of it. It was blank. There were no hidden messages in the calendar either, only pictures of flowers and numbers. The dates were correct, and the months were in order. There was nothing cryptic about any of this.

My work morning soon became a work afternoon, and I enjoyed the easy pace. There were no poker debts, pillars, or crazed Chinese trying to kill me here. This was a dream, and I felt I could make it as safe as I wanted. I really wanted safe. When the final whistle went, I packed up the tools, grabbed my uneaten lunch and headed for the car. Julie was waiting for me.

I noticed she was wearing jeans. "Where's the skirt?"

"And have you ogling me until your eyes fall out? I think not. And what happened to my workstation today?"

"It was like that when I got there. I saw Barry leaving though. I'm thinking he did it." I opened the passenger door and couldn't help but notice the smooth skin on her neck. Yesterday the skirt, and today the ever-sexy ponytail. What was she thinking? I stared for a second before closing the door. "He's a dead man. So, what do I owe the pleasure?"

She held up a coupon for McDonalds. "You're buying me supper. I bought yesterday."

"You know I work in a cabinet factory, right?"

"That's why the coupon. Two can dine."

I pulled the shifter into drive. "Then what are we waiting for?"

She leaned back against the door. "Question."

A Dream Escape

"Shoot."

"You asked if the word illusion meant anything to me. Why did you want to know that?" She asked but didn't let me answer. "Because I had a dream last night. I was in China at some desk being questioned by some fat guy. He had these chubby fingers and couldn't stop eating. Then we drove off in a gold-coloured BMW. I could have sworn I saw you there."

"Are you shitting me?"

"Duh." She playfully kicked my leg. "Tell me more about these dreams. If I'm gonna date you, I need to know what I'm getting myself into."

"Fair enough." I figured I should start with Olivia, because none of this made sense without a crazed woman to knee me in the nuts and drag me across China. It sounded ridiculous as I explained everything, the chases, the villains, and the story of the Pillars. I even stopped twice, but she made me continue.

"And this Olivia, she's pretty hot?"

"That's what you're taking away from this story?"

"Is she?"

"Uh, she's, uh…"

"Go ahead. I can handle it. She's just a dream. Have you two…"

"No!"

"Why not? You said she's hot, right?"

I wanted to tell her that she was too, and that I hadn't had her either. And why hadn't I been with either one of them? Was that what Julie wanted to know? This was flirting, suggestive and testing. She was setting the mood. "Yes, she is, but she's not as hot as you."

"Really?"

"I can't get that skirt out of my mind. You really have nice legs."

She kicked me again. "Ya think? What about her hair? Is she a blonde or brunette?"

"It's a little darker than yours. Too bad she wasn't blonde, like you. I've always preferred them."

136

Kevin Weisbeck

Julie slid over beside me and kissed my cheek. "Kinda crazy, but you've got all the right answers. You'll do."

My arm quickly slipped around her and drew her close. I was about to kiss her when I noticed the black BMW following us. I half-kissed her on the cheek and made an immediate right.

"Where are we going?"

"Scenic route."

"What's going on, Andy?" She looked back over her shoulder and saw the car. "What the hell is that, Andy?"

I wheeled left and pulled into the Chevron Station. "Probably nothing." I drove around the back and cut through the parking lot to the car wash next door. I grabbed the first stall. The BMW drove past us to the other side. Before they could see us, I had it in reverse and was heading back toward the Chevron. I was gone before they knew what happened.

"Good job, Slick." Her head dropped down on my shoulder.

I kissed the top of her head and took a deep breath. Her hair smelled terrific.

"Since you're buying dinner, I should supply dessert." She curled up even closer.

This had to be a dream. If dessert meant sex, then I was sure I'd like it. The thought put a smile on my face, although I'd have a hard time explaining everything to Olivia. Oh hell, I wouldn't have to worry about that until tomorrow.

We got the food to go and left for Julie's place. As I pulled up into the driveway, I noticed a black car pulling into a stall down the street.

Chapter 33

I half-rushed Julie into her house and looked over my shoulder at the car, half a block away. Mr Chin's people had found me in my dreams.

Julie was the first to enter the small one-story house. Built in 1942, the basement was unfinished, dirt floors and no windows. The yard, however, was a spacious half-acre. That's how it was done back then.

We sat at the table and ate our burgers. She hadn't seen the car. I kept the chatter about work, or more, Barry and his stupidity. I popped the last fry in my mouth and smiled. I wanted to see where this dream was going to end up. "You said there was dessert."

"Brownies?" She got up and headed for the kitchen. "I made them yesterday and saved us a couple."

Although this wasn't what I expected, brownies were my favourite. It was no coincidence. "Any ice-cream?" I knew there would be. It was my dream.

"Chocolate okay?"

"Wouldn't have it any other way."

She took the tub out of the fridge freezer and set it on the counter. That was when her phone rang. It was a girl friend. "I need to take this. I'll just be a second."

"Take your time," I said as she left the room.

Kevin Weisbeck

Once she was out of sight, I started searching for anything that might be linked to the pillars. There were the pictures on the walls, although they were straight from Walmart. The drawers were filled with silverware, tape measures and quite the collection of different tapes, glues, and paperclips. None of it helped.

I was rifling through the bookcase when she returned.

"What are you doing, Andy?"

"Why I, uh, what?"

"You look like you're about to steal something."

"No, just looking at your collection."

"Of Stephen King or Mad Magazine?"

I grabbed one off the shelf. It was 'The Shining'. "This was the first book I ever read, I mean, voluntarily. You've read it?"

"I didn't get past page four."

I chuckled until something clicked. I had an idea. I opened the book to P4, or page four to be precise. Okay, it wasn't 4PB, but it was close. Jack was talking to Ullman about the attic in the Overlook Hotel. It brought my eyes to the ceiling. Was there an attic in Julie's house?

"Come get your brownies and ice-cream, silly boy."

Her flirtatious offer of dessert quickly brought my eyes back to her. The attic could wait. There was also a cold beer. I dove into both. "Thanks."

"Is this weird?" she asked as she motioned for me to take a seat on the couch.

"I guess a little." I chose the middle cushion.

She took an end, facing me. "If we become something, everyone at work will tease the shit out of us."

She was right. The only other couple that worked at the cabinet plant were Darren and that dippy blonde, Meagan. Maybe it was because she couldn't open her mouth without saying something stupid, like guitars were invented by cavemen. That was why it was called rock and roll. They'd also invented the blues and named it after the sky.

"We know all those guys, Julie. I doubt they'll bug us too much. Don't get me wrong, there will be a barrage of snide remarks, but I'm willing to weather it if you are."

139

She smiled. "We, this, might become something worth heckling?"

"I'd like that." I stopped there, not wanting to upset Olivia too much. Was I talking in my sleep? Would she find out about this? Hell, it was just a damn dream and I was trying to find a pillar. How far should I push this? Enough beer might push it to the point of no return.

"I should be back to work in a week. The doc says I'm a quick healer. I'll be doing physiotherapy on the leg for a while though."

"How's the head?"

She reached up to rub the bruise. "Hurts a bit at night. They gave me these pills for the headaches. Pretty potent shit. They sure knock me out." She kept her eyes trained on mine.

"Sounds like fun." I stared back into her eyes, wanting to inch closer, kiss her. That was what she wanted. It was what she'd wanted for a while, but I'd never been able to muster the courage. Now, I had the courage. I just didn't need to complicate things in the real world. What I needed was the Pillar of Illusion. I took another swig of beer. "Can I use your bathroom?"

"You'll have to use the ensuite, in my bedroom. I was in the middle of redoing the main bathroom. Hey, you don't know how to tile, do you?"

"How hard could it be? I've seen it done on TV." I got up, set the unfinished ice-cream down, and poked my head into the bathroom. "Whoa. You've gutted the thing."

"Two bottles of wine and a crowbar. There was no looking back."

"No shit." I turned for the bedroom. "I'm not gonna see anything that I can't unsee in there, am I?"

"You mean like bras and stuff? There's always a chance. Be brave."

I smiled and entered. It was a man's curiosity to snoop. Julie was a smart dresser and wasn't like one of those crazed single girls, yet she was always single. There had to be a reason.

The medicine cabinet didn't divulge anything. There was the usual aspirin, Q-tips, and cough syrup. In the drawers there was make-up, lots of make-up. I took a seat, to do my business.

I thought about the attic while I sat. What would there be in an attic? This wasn't the kind of house to have stairs up to a room full of junk. This one was more the, crawl up through the closet trap door, type. I quickly pulled my pants up and headed for the closet. The accordion doors opened to what had to be the most organised closet I'd ever seen. How else could she have packed so much stuff in it.

I placed a few of the plastic Tupperware shoeboxes aside, stacking them high enough to climb on. Then I reached up and slid the trap door open and poked my head up inside. There was insulation. There wasn't a whole lot more than that. But Jack and Ullman had been talking about the attic on Page four. They'd also been talking about the third floor, something Julie didn't have.

I took one last long look before putting the door back into place and jumping down off the boxes. Julie was waiting for me just outside the closet and she was understandably pissed. Her fist caught my jaw sending me back over the boxes and tumbling into the closet.

"Get out of my house, you jerk!"

Chapter 34

Her fist was small and yet it packed one hell of a wallop. Had I passed out? I came to on my back. My clothes had been stripped off me to my underwear. And was that Julie, pinning me down. I half-focused my eyes to see the blur of a woman. Her arm was cocked for a second blow.

"Whoa. What the…"

The accent was British. "What are you doing. You're supposed to be looking for a pillar, not trying to shag your co-worker."

Blinking twice, I worked Olivia into focus. Then I looked around. We were in a modest hotel, plain but nice, like a Super 8 or a Sandman Inn. "Morning."

"Don't morning me."

"Why are you so upset. I was just in my dream. I was looking for that damn pillar in the attic. I saw a book, The Shining. P4, or page four, had the two men talking about an attic. I thought it was a sign, so I was doing the detective thing."

"Nice try. You're supposed to be looking for a 4PB"

"Close enough. Hey, are you jealous?" It turned the corner of my mouth upward.

"Do you really want to go there? You were almost in tears when you met Derrick."

Kevin Weisbeck

"Was not." I cleared my head and gently pushed her off. "I was only bummed because I realised, I don't know much about you, like what makes you laugh, what makes you want to kick my ass, and what do you miss most in life. Is that crazy?"

Olivia sat up. She was more annoyed than usual. "I laugh at other people's pain and I kick ass when I feel betrayed. I miss people with sanity. Anything else?"

"What's your favourite colour?"

"Say what?"

"Colour. What's your favourite? I peg you for a burgundy or maybe an indigo."

"Why not. Put me down for black?"

"Uh, that's not a colour. Pick something, like pink."

"Pink?" Her life had been a lot blacker than pink. From the tattoos to the scars, to the ability to take out hired guns at will, she'd been branded a tough bitch. She had never allowed herself the luxury to cry, to be vulnerable, or to be the kind of girl who liked pink.

"I'm sorry. Is this really that hard?" I could see the struggle. "Have you ever tried wearing a dress. I'd bet you'd look damn good."

"And why not put a kitten in my arms." She got up and started for the door. She stopped halfway and turned back. "I don't know why I can't like black. And how the hell do I keep you alive while wearing a dress. Maybe I throw the fluffy little kitten at the gunman. It might leave a deep scratch. Oh, and afterwards, we could go out and get a healthy kale salad or some of that tofu shit."

I sank back in the bed, wishing I'd never brought it up. "Sorry. Let me make it up to you. I'll buy breakfast."

"You got money?"

"Uh, no."

"See you downstairs." She left as I scrambled to get dressed.

I caught up with her at the elevator and wisely kept quiet as we made our way down to the lobby. Other married couples in the elevator were doing the same. It made me wonder what they'd talked about to start their day.

143

A Dream Escape

I apologised during my breakfast, beef noodles and coffee.

Olivia was typing on her phone. She was only doing it to ignore me. I tried again to apologise.

She put her fork down. "Look, I'm not like this because I'm a cold person. I'm like this because I have to be stronger than my enemy. People that have a favourite anything, piss me off. You need to be able to adapt and you can't if you have preferences. Take this food. I'm not a fan of half this shit, but my body needs energy. It might be a long day and who knows if I'll be swimming in the river, sprinting through back alleys or climbing twenty flights of stairs. You have to be ready for anything and there's no wiggle room for pink."

"Must be nice to be so on top of things."

"It is." She went back to her phone.

"I like my favourites. I love these noodles. I like blue. Both favourites."

"I'm sure you do."

"Oh, sarcasm. That's good. Very constructive."

"You mean destructive."

I was about to answer when I saw them enter the restaurant. "Shit."

Olivia looked up. "What?"

I pointed to the two men. "Do they look like…"

She looked over her shoulder. "Mr Chin's men…ya. Let's get up and head for the fire door behind the dessert counter."

"Won't that set the alarm off?"

"You want to go that way?" Her eyes pointed toward the two men, who had now seen us and were closing fast.

"Nah, I'll follow you."

The alarm wasn't loud, but all eyes were on us the moment our chairs tipped over. The two men drew their guns and gave chase.

Outside the woven walkway looped and twisted amongst the trees and shrubs. Olivia took as many straight lines as she could, and I tried to keep up. I should have had what she had for breakfast.

Olivia stopped at a wall. "Damn it."

Kevin Weisbeck

"This is a closed in courtyard."

"Not exactly." She looked over the wall to see the canal. It was about twenty feet across. "Follow me."

"What the heck. We can't jump that."

The one man had his gun pointed toward us and fired a shot as Olivia shoved me into a bush. The bullets hit the wall and chips of cement rained down like flakes of hail.

"Get up here. There's a boat coming. Watch and follow."

Olivia hopped up on the wall and jumped the eight feet from the cement wall to the rooftop of a passing boat. I climbed up and ran down the top of the wall a couple steps and stopped. She made it look easy. The two men reloaded as they darted down the sidewalk toward me. I backed up to get as much of a run as I could. I took one last look at Olivia before taking the ten-foot leap.

I bounced off the railing and fell back into the water. That had Olivia turning back. A boat window broke as another gunshot rang out.

She dove into the water and swam to me as the boat distanced itself. Ropes trailed off the side of the boat and we both grabbed for them. Bullets zipped as they hit the water. The boat dragged us down the canal, away from the hotel and out of sight of the two men.

"I'm sorry. I think I over thought the jump."

Olivia gave me a half smile. "It's okay. Our clothes needed to be washed anyway. You okay?"

"I should try to be a little more like you, you know, eating the shit I don't like and being more prepared."

"That's not who you are though."

"It probably wasn't who you were either, once upon a time."

She thought about it for a second. "That's too long ago for me to remember."

"How'd they find us?"

"I'm taking the blame on that one. They must have tracked my phone." She pulled it out of her pocket and held it up. It dripped from every hole as she let it slip from her fingers. "Paperweight now."

"They can do that?"

"I had to turn on the GPS for directions and that's all it took."

"Directions to a lead?"

"Nǎo Pang had a thing about the Japanese/Chinese war. He was really upset that the Japanese never owned up to what they did. There's a Chinese People's Anti-Japanese War Memorial Hall."

"What are we waiting for."

She looked at the cement wall as the boat dragged us down the canal. "A ladder for one thing."

I laughed. "I suppose."

"And it's periwinkle."

That caught me off guard. "What?"

"My favourite colour, periwinkle, like Alice's dress in the story, Alice in Wonderland. I also like meatloaf. It's my favourite meat, dried out and with Ketchup and baby potatoes."

"Meatloaf eh, I get that."

Chapter 35

Kevin Weisbeck

Olivia parked the stolen car in the first empty spot she saw. We'd just passed over the Marco Polo Bridge and pulled into the parking lot of the Museum of the War of Chinese People's Resistance Against Japanese Aggression. This historic spot was home to the second Sino Japanese war. China had lost many but had pushed the Japanese back.

I got out of the car. My clothes were almost dry. "So, this is the place?"

Olivia started to jaywalk across the street.

I continued, "and you think it represents truth?" I got ahead of her and beat her to the other side. The light had turned green, and the cars were coming.

"Truth is, the Japanese have never acknowledged the fact that this war ever existed. Nao Pang was obsessed with this place because the Japanese did indeed attack China and it was an atrocity on humanity."

"How could they not acknowledge the fact?"

Olivia shrugged. "They don't teach it in their schools, and they never talk about it. Such bullshit. I mean even Germany apologised for Hitler."

I held the door for her. "Fingers crossed."

"Screw luck," she replied. "We'll find it if it's here. Power of positive thinking."

"Don't mind me if that whole positive thinking thing is wearing a little thin with me. I mean, I've recently swam in sewage."

"Give it a rest, Princess. That was days ago, and you survived." She pulled out the Visa and tried it. It wasn't working yet. "Damn it Derrick."

"Are you saying no ice-cream when we get inside?"

She used the last of her money and bought two tickets. "No popcorn either."

There were four halls to the museum, that's if it could be called a museum. The main hall held the truths of what happened, that in 1931, Japan had attacked China without cause. It showed the chronological battles from start to finish up to 1945.

The second hall showed the atrocities. It was graphic and had me on edge. The third hall focused on the China Communist Party and how their guerrilla warfare tactics had warded off the invasion. The last section was the Hall of Martyrs which had a statue called the unknown martyr. There were also thousands of names. Olivia and I started through them but soon gave up. A name would be a needle in a haystack.

As with any museum, there was a giftshop and I was heading straight for it.

"Forget it," Olivia chuffed.

I ignored her. I'd always collected old maps and there were plenty to choose from here.

"Andy, I said we're broke."

"Relax. I'm just looking." I walked over to the wall of maps. There were twelve in all, showing different invasions and strategies. Back home, I had several maps that outlined the battles of the civil war. I had eighteen maps of Germany explaining how the Second World War had played out, but my favourite one of all was the map of the Great Wall, outlining the many different stages of construction. It included original routes that were never used.

"You're a child. We have to go."

"Go? Where are we going to go? This place was a blank. We have no leads."

Olivia's face twisted in a contorted surrender. She was so sure this was the place. That geek had loved the halls, loved the truth behind the stories, stories that the Japanese so strongly denied. "You can have five minutes."

"Thanks, Mom." I took my time going over the maps. "I see why the Chinese are so upset. I'll bet these battles aren't even mentioned in American history books."

"That's politics." Olivia waited as I studied one of the maps. "What's that one?"

"It's the safe zone around Nanking. It was breached and many Chinese soldiers and civilians died."

"Never heard of it."

"Not many have. I saw the story in the atrocity hall. Japanese say it never happened, and the Chinese say hundreds of thousands were killed in a six-week slaughter. It was one of the biggest lies."

"Or truths." Olivia shoved me aside to get a better look.

"What the heck are you doing?" I asked.

"You see that?"

I looked closer. "See what?"

She pointed to the bottom corner. The tack that had been holding it to the wall had fallen out causing the corner to curl. The light had got behind it and helped her see the four vertical lines and the small letter q. I shrugged until she pulled the corner out and looked at the back to see the q become a p... a pIIII to be exact.

"Whoa. That's the…"

Olivia looked up at the price. It was one hundred yuan, about twenty dollars.

I gave her a puzzled gape. "What. Just grab it and we'll run. It's not like we haven't done that before."

"They'll wonder why, of all the things to steal, we'd pick this map."

"So how do we get that kind of money?"

"Give me a second." Olivia eyed the crowd. "We can't lie, cheat, or steal it. That would be bad karma."

"Since when do you care?"

"On this, damn straight I care."

A Dream Escape

She saw two men playing mah-jong in the small concession area. They both worked here and were on a break. She walked over, me blindly on her heels. "Mind if I join you?" she asked.

The one old man frowned while his friend offered her a chair. Olivia took it and faced the generous one. "You're a gambling man I see. I'd like to play a game with you."

The old man studied her as he reached for his wallet. "I play you mah-jong."

"No," Olivia corrected. "I'd like to play a different game."

"What game," he asked as his eyebrows dipped downward.

"One where you could make twice as much as me. Here's how it works. You write down ten numbers, pick numbers between one and a hundred. Don't show me because I'm going to guess them. For every number I get wrong, I owe you twenty Yuan. If I get them all right, you only owe me a hundred, total."

"Help me understand. What do I owe you if you get nine of them?"

"I still owe you twenty for the one I didn't get. You owe me nothing."

I nudged her. "Wasn't it gambling that started this misadventure?"

She looked back and nodded before turning back to the man. His friend had a fifty out. He wanted in on this. "The only way you lose money is if I get them all. Then you owe me a hundred Yuan. Deal?"

"Okay. I'll turn around, while you pick the numbers." She slid their score pad over to them. "Write them on the back of this."

The two men argued for a few minutes as they decided on the numbers that might stump her. Then they put the paper face down. Olivia reached for it and the one man slammed his hand down on it.

"Don't worry. I'm not looking," she assured them. "I just need the energy from it."

"You no touch."

"Fair enough. Then you touch it with one hand, and I'll hold your other hand. I'll read the numbers through you."

150

Kevin Weisbeck

He held out his free hand while he kept the numbers trapped. "Okay."

"I'm going to get rid of the obvious ones first. There's an eight, an eighty-eight for luck, and a sixty-nine. I swear you guys all love that number." She pressed them both. "Am I right?"

"That's only three. Continue."

I watched as Olivia closed her eyes. "I've got an eleven, twenty-two and a twenty-three. That should be six."

"Lucky guesses," the one old man grumbled. "You need to get four more."

"Funny you say that, because four is one of them, right?"

The man pulled his friend's hand away from hers. Then he took Olivia's hand. "You go through me. You never get the last ones."

She looked around to see me smiling from ear to ear.

I was a believer. "You got this Olivia. Just three more to go."

"Three more," she paused, "to go. Thirty-two, for my friend. Not sure why you picked that one."

The one man nodded as he edged closer. "Two more."

"I know, and I'm seeing one in the seventies, I think." She let them stew. The man holding her hand was trying to throw her off by squeezing her hand harder than comfortable. She ignored him.

"Which one in seventies are you going to pick?"

"I'll get back to that one. For now, I want to say ninety-nine. How am I doing so far?"

"You got nine. Now pick one from seventies."

She pulled her hands free and put them palms together in front of her face as if praying. Then she blew through them. It was a nervous move that scared the shit out of me. She seemed stumped. The last number wasn't coming to her.

"What's wrong?" I whispered.

"I've got someone in my ear. You do know I'm try to concentrate on that last number, don't you?"

"Sorry."

"You pick last number now. We have to go back to work and want your money."

"I think you're trying to trick me. I'm getting a number, but I'm confused because I thought I'd already said that number."

The two men stared silently. Both had started to pale.

"I'm right." She waved a finger at them. "You two are sneaky. The last number is another sixty-nine."

The money was slid across to her. She took the bills and gave a polite bow. "*Xie, xie.*"

I was on her heels again as she took off to buy the map. "How the hell did you do that?"

"You tell me. You were a bigger part of it than I was."

"What?"

"You'll know soon enough." She bought the map, unrolled it, and held it up to the light. We had the Truth Pillar, as did thousands of others without even knowing it.

"Now we should find somewhere for you to get some sleep. It's getting late and we need that Illusion Pillar."

Kevin Weisbeck

Chapter 36

Back in Kelowna I did the usual get up and off to work routine. I wanted to get to the better parts of the dreams, the parts with Julie and the search for the Illusion Pillar, but my dreams didn't work that way. I had to play them out. I wasn't fully awake until the first screw slipped, and I jammed my thumb.

The rest of the day rolled along with Barry and the others tormenting me for stories. It was nice to see these guys, even if they were back home. And what were these guys really doing right now. Who was covering my station? Being in Kelowna was slowly becoming a memory. I hadn't truly returned yet. My vacation was still in full swing. And what was Julie doing? Then I remembered that Julie's attraction to me was all just a part of my dream. In real life, she was still that beauty of a gal that wanted to be nothing more than a friend. I was never a part of her world.

After work, I found myself driving over to the impound lot. If I couldn't find anything at Julie's, or at her damn workstation, then maybe it was in her car. And where was she today? The last few days she had met me by my car. Today she was absent. I had to believe she was mad at me for snooping through her closet.

I pulled up to the front of the impound yard and as expected, they were closed. I got out of my car and walked up to the gate. I could see her Jeep. No wonder she'd been hurt, the thing

153

was a mess. It had hit the ditch with such an impact that it was slightly folded at the firewall. The front fenders had buckled, and all four tires were flat.

"Shit, Julie. What a ride that must have been."

I looked up to the three strands of barbed wire above the fence and looked around for another way. I started right and walked the fence line. At the back corner, the fence curled up from the ground. The dirt was a little dug up, making it easier to crawl under. It was as good as an engraved invitation, so I dropped to my belly and started to shimmy.

It was easier than expected. I stood up and dusted myself off. Hopefully, the illusion map would be as accommodating. Julie's Jeep was fifty feet away and I ran to it. The doors were locked so I grabbed a rock. Then I dropped the rock and reached through the already broken side window. It creaked and jammed at the half-open mark. I squeezed my way in.

The glove compartment was an obvious first choice. In it I found insurance, tire warranties, and a Dealership checklist book that had never been filled out. She'd probably had the work done, but never at the dealership. I could see her Dad doing the oil changes.

There was nothing under the seats, nothing in the visors. The back seat was bare, except for the broken crystals of glass and some door trim pieces. The girl was a tidy one. I didn't see anything abnormal hanging from the mirror or in the ashtray.

The hood was popped, and I gave the engine a once over before going to the back. I shuffled through the few tools and the emergency kit. Again, it was all about the clean and tidy. This was the kind of girl who likely changed her underwear everyday. Who did that? I wasn't as diligent. I'd likely shit myself in an accident, making clean underwear a moot point.

I backed away from the trunk when I first heard the growling. A German Shepherd was standing twenty feet to my left. It didn't move until we locked eyes. Then I darted right, and the chase was on.

There was a truck beside me, so I jumped up in the box. The dog also jumped. The damn thing knocked me over the side,

Kevin Weisbeck

and I found myself hitting the ground and scrambling to get under an old van. The dog got down on its belly and started to crawl its way under the vehicle after me.

"Damn it, dog. Go away." I rolled out the other side and started for the fence. Then I imagined the dog beating me to the other side. That stupid beast had probably dug the spot that I'd used to get in. I changed direction and headed for the gate. Jumping at it full stride, I landed three feet off the ground. The dog also jumped, catching my ass.

I tried to shake myself free. He held on like a one-year-old chunk of bubble gum, stuck to the underside of a table. Even with the dog attached, I started to climb. It eventually dropped to the ground with a mouth full of denim.

No time was wasted as I made my way up and over. The barbed wire bit into the inside of my thigh as I carefully tried to manoeuvre my way to freedom. I landed on the other side facing the fence and facing the dog with my pocket in his mouth.

"Oh ya? You're not so tough now." I did a lunge for the fence and the dog did the same. After an embarrassing back-pedal, I fell on my ass. "Whatever." Then I saw the brown wallet at the dog's feet. "Ah shit."

I had to think, and then it came to me. Back at my car, I had a sandwich. I really hoped the dog liked bologna.

At the far side of the compound, I tossed the dog's next meal over the fence. As expected, Cujo followed. When I bolted back for the gate, the dog hesitated for a second, and let me go. He would eat fast.

I, on the other hand, ran fast and found that half-hole under the fence. My arms pulled and pawed me to the other side. Now to get my wallet.

"Woof, woof!" The dog had finished the appetiser and now he was ready for the main course. "Woof!"

Again, I was on the run and looking for a car to climb onto. I figured the fence would be just another chunk out of my trousers. A single leap put me on the trunk of a Ford LTD. Another jump and I was on the roof. The dog followed me up.

"Shit."

155

A Dream Escape

I jumped from rooftop to rooftop until I saw my sanctuary. Two cars were stacked, and I knew dogs couldn't climb. The gap was six feet from the pickup, and I slammed against the top car's passenger door. Thank God for roof racks. I started pulling myself up when I felt everything shift. "Huh…"

The dog was on the ground behind me barking as the top car, a Buick Estate station wagon, began sliding off the bottom one. I stepped onto the window opening and jumped back to the pick-up truck.

After a loud crash, there was silence. I looked down for the dog but didn't see him. He was likely crushed. This was my chance. The fence was quickly in sight and I thought about that poor dog as I scrambled to the other side.

"Woof, woof!"

"What the f…" I looked back as I got to my feet. Cujo was in full sprint. That had me reaching for my door handle as the dog shot out from under the fence. Damn he could run.

"Woof!"

There'd be no breathing until the door had slammed shut. I sat there with my eyes closed, praying to God. He had allowed me to live. When I opened my eyes, Cujo was standing on the hood, staring at me through the windshield. His saliva was dripping off his lower jaw.

"Woof!"

I started the car, hoping he'd jump down. He didn't.

"Fine by me. We'll do it your way." I put the car in reverse and gunned it.

The dog stayed on the hood like he had sticky fly feet. How was it possible? But how was it possible the dog wasn't crushed when that car fell? He was standing right where the car had landed. Was this dog some kind of supernatural ghost dog? Then I remembered I had more food.

I stopped the car and opened my lunchbox. There was chocolate, which wasn't good for dogs, carrots, and a bag of Doritos. Pulling the carrots out of the bag, I tossed them out the window. Cujo flinched but didn't move. Next, the bag of Doritos was opened and dumped out. He couldn't see them, so I cut the wheel and backed up a bit. The chips caught his eye. A minute later his nose was twitching.

"Smell good, don't they boy."

Cujo looked at me, looked at them, and then licked his lips.

"They're all yours."

The dog wanted to wait me out but sadly, he was given a keen sense of smell. He couldn't help himself and when he jumped down, I sped off. On the way to my place, I drove past Julie's house. I wanted to stop in, apologise, and maybe pick up where we had left off.

Then, I rubbed my jaw and thought of Olivia.

Chapter 37

I ended up at home and drifted off watching a rerun of a Grey Cup game. I opened my eyes hoping for a score. BC hadn't won a cup in a couple years. Trying to bring my world into focus, I couldn't get a score, nor could I find the TV. I rolled out of bed and walked over to the window. It took me a second to realise I was back in China, Beijing to be exact. The town was the same as when I'd drifted off to sleep, but the surroundings weren't familiar. Neither was the dog that had started tugging on my pants.

"Get away from me." I tried to push the dog off my leg.

"Leave him alone. He's just a stray." Olivia walked over and picked the dog up. He was a cross between a terrier and a poodle of some sort. His shaggy brown fur was matted, and he was a chewer and a licker. That tongue flicked at Olivia's face like a snake's tongue at its prey.

"I just had a dream about a dog and I'm still a little spooked."

"What happened?"

"Junkyard dog attacked me after I went through Julie's Jeep. I almost lost a butt cheek."

"What did you find out?"

"Dogs are strong, and they're heavy too."

"I mean about the car."

"She was a bit of a neat freak and she walloped that ditch. There were no maps, no P's or fours, unless you count the four flat tires. They were Pirelli's."

"You went through the glove compartment?"

"Of course."

"You checked out the trunk?"

"For sure, and the visors and the console."

"Great. And what kind of vehicle was it."

"A Jeep. Why?"

"Did it have a rod by the back seat?"

I thought for a second. "I think it did."

"They're like blinds. You can pull them out in order to hide what you've got in the back compartment."

"So what. It wasn't hiding anything."

Olivia shook her head. "Rolled up, it would probably be a great place to hide a map."

Suddenly I could imagine a map rolled up in the fabric. I could also imagine the dog chasing me around the compound again. "Damn it."

"Go back the next time you fall asleep." She put the dog down and let it scamper off. "For now, we have to catch a flight. We're going to Guilin."

"I hope that's a restaurant."

"City in South China. I found a lead and bought the tickets."

"How?" I thought we were broke.

"Visa is working. I also bought us coffees and pulled pork steamed buns. Here." She pulled one out of the bag and tossed it to me."

I watched as she opened another bag and pulled out a pair of pants and a shirt. "For me?"

"They should fit. You were starting to smell. I got us deodorant and toothbrushes too."

"People are gonna stop staring if we look and smell like everybody else."

"That's the plan. Now clean up and get changed. A taxi will be here in five and the flight's in an hour and a half."

"What account did the money come from?"

"No can tell. I'd have to kill you."

I finished the sandwich, bun thing, and started to change. As I was emptying my pockets, I remembered the dream. I'd bought groceries in hopes that Julie might have forgiven me and dropped by. She didn't. I'd also hit the bank and took out a hundred dollars. I should have had seventy left after buying chips, chocolate, and a case of beer. I flipped through the wallet and looked at the bills. There were three twenties and a ten.

I thought about telling Olivia, but how would I explain it? Had it been there all this time? She'd think I was holding out on her. I wasn't. Besides, she was finding her own money and keeping those truths from me. Fair was fair.

I slipped on the jeans, pulled the shirt over my head, and started for the door.

Between the flight, airport waits, and the bus ride to the hotel, it took us well into the afternoon to get settled. It was a prettier part of the country, with the mountains towering like gigantic and well-placed pylons. The tea farms and countryside were a vast change from the concrete and smog that we'd left.

"I get the mountain theme. I mean we're here to find the mountain map, but there are quite a few mountains here," I noted. "Have you picked a favourite?"

"There's a little village, that's if you can call it that. It's less than a hundred residents. We're on our way to it right now. It's called Ping'an. I've recently found out, while you were sleeping, that Nǎo Pang lived there as a child. He played in the mountains around his village. You're gonna love the place."

"Are we talking nature hikes?" A frown formed across my face as my legs began to cramp at the thought. "Don't get me wrong. I love the whole fresh air thing. I'm just…"

"Don't be such a baby. You are going to love this place. I'll even sit us at the front of the bus so you can experience every moment."

"Uh, we're at the back of the bus."

Kevin Weisbeck

"This is the bus that takes us to the bus. You see the road up the mountain is a twisted one. This bus would never make the corners."

"Really? Should I be scared?"

Olivia smiled as she turned her head away from me and watched the countryside pass us by. She didn't speak again until we got to the bus transfer. At that location there were a few stores, a restaurant, and some primitive bathrooms. I declined the tour and sat at the front of an empty bus with the cola that she bought for me.

"It's a cute place, isn't it?" she asked.

"It's beautiful. Sorry if I'm a lousy travel partner. I just have a lot on my mind."

"Like Julie?"

I gave her a faux look of bewilderment as the bus driver and other passengers started to board. It was safer not to talk about her, for now. Why was she upset about a damn dream? Sure, there was a real Julie who existed back home, but that was not the Julie I'd gotten to know over these past few days. And to her, I was a different Andy. In my dreams I had a magnetism that I didn't have here. I thought about that as I looked over at Olivia. She was stunning. Maybe I did have it here.

The bus driver closed the door as the last passenger boarded and we were off. The first mile was nice, wide road, nice views, and silence. Suddenly, the road narrowed, the drop off the embankment was a lot deeper, and the oncoming traffic thickened. The driver wheeled the bus around each corner as if he was the only one on the road. He wasn't.

I counted eight near misses with oncoming cars in the next mile, and twenty-two close calls the mile after that one. Soon the road was barely wide enough for the bus, and yet he kept speed and didn't slow down for the blind corners. At the four-mile mark, we saw the first car in the ditch. The driver's side of the car was gashed open from whatever had hit it. Three other cars and a small truck found the same fate, allowing me to realise the larger vehicles had the obvious right of way.

161

A Dream Escape

At the seven-mile mark my theory developed a hiccup. There was an abandoned bus, likely from years ago. The front end had been pushed back to the driver's seat. That was enough for me as the one we were in continued to sway around the corners, race blindly into shadows, and honk at anything that came at it. The driver had nerves of steel. I started to get up. Nobody wanted to be put through the windshield when this bus hit another one coming down the hill. Olivia stopped me and shoved me back in my seat.

"Not a chance, cowboy. You're staying up here."

Sweat was forming on my brow as the corners jostled me around in my seat. "I don't have feelings for her. You know that. She's not real."

"But she is. She's back home."

"She's a stranger in real life."

"Dreams don't lie. They just shed the illusion of who you think you really are."

"Are you saying I have a shot with her?" It was meant as a joke, something to lighten the mood. In hindsight I should have known better and kept my mouth shut.

Her fist found my ribs. It came so quick that I didn't have a chance to brace for it. I gasped as the bus hammered the brakes causing me to slip out of my seat and onto the floor. I was the only one who fell.

The horn on the bus kept a steady tone until the car in front of it started to back up. It wouldn't have a pullout for about a hundred yards. Then they could pass. I picked myself up off the floor and sat back down. I wanted to return a shot to her ribs, but the hurt look in her eyes stopped me. Well, that and guys don't hit girls.

"Are you okay?" I asked her.

"I'm good."

"I'm with you, not her. And look at yourself. You are a damn beautiful woman. I can't imagine why you'd doubt those looks."

"I'm not good at opening up and you know I don't do the whole feelings thing so let's change the subject. You got periwinkle out of me. Let's not push it."

162

"But I have to because I really care about you. What's your favourite movie? I'm a Rambo kind of guy."

She smiled as she shook her head. "I see that. You're very macho."

"Very funny. Now what's yours?"

"It's a Wonderful life."

"Wow. I have that one back home. We'll have to watch it someday."

Her smile wilted. "Ya, I'll look forward to that."

"No seriously. I'll make us popcorn."

"Back home?" Her look sobered.

"Hey, I don't care if it's Canada, or here. We'll figure that out."

The bus stopped again and this time it was in a parking lot. We had arrived.

She shot me one of the saddest winks, knowing that day would likely never happen. "Come on. Let's go see what our room looks like."

"It's getting late. Maybe we'll watch it on the movie channel, after supper." I could smell something cooking. The aroma lingered in the cool mountain air.

That brought the smile back to her face. "You're cute."

I didn't understand what she meant by that until I saw the room.

Chapter 38

The last few days had been hard for me, although the growing fog hadn't helped. That morning haze seemed to be taking longer to shake. Even flights and cab rides had me drifting into a no-man's land of thoughts. My interest in Olivia, and Julie, had helped clear the head a bit, but that wasn't my only problem. What bothered me most were my legs. They were cramping up and felt like stone. I'd noticed it since the swim in the Huangpu River. Maybe I was coming down with some kind of sewer water fever. That river was like swimming in a toilet bowl. Regardless, both Canada and China were leaving gaps. A part of me was fading into the ether.

Kelowna, however, had a lot more holes and events that either didn't add up, or were lost entirely. It had to be a bug of some sort, something that brought a mild fever and a tingling in my back. I put my wrist up to my forehead. It was warm.

Today had started with an alarm clock and a lunch being made, but for the life of me, I couldn't remember what I'd made, or sitting down at any point and having it.

At least the work part of it was over. I swiped my way through the turnstile and started for my car. The corner of my lip curled upward when I saw Julie standing beside it. The smile wouldn't last long.

"Got a call from the impound. Said somebody broke in and was going through one of their vehicles. He said the dog gave the guy a good scare. I told them that was nice, but why call me?" Her eyes narrowed. "Do you have any idea why they'd call me, Andy?"

"I can explain."

"You broke into my Jeep. Why would you do that?"

"How'd they know?"

"They've got cameras everywhere. I had to go down there and watch the videos. The one guy was a real slimeball. They wanted to press charges."

"Shit."

"I talked them out of it."

"Thanks."

"You broke into my Jeep. What's next, my house? Oh wait, you've already done that."

"It's not like that." But I remembered her hitting me because it was exactly like that. "Okay, maybe a little, but I can explain."

"This outta be good."

"Not really, because you're not going to believe me and if you think you're mad at me now…"

"I've learned to expect the unexpected from you, so shoot."

My mouth opened and nothing came out. Should I say anything? What would happen when she finds out this is all a dream. She's not real and neither was her accident or what we had. She might play along, although I seriously doubted it. She'd be hurt, betrayed. It would crush her. And what did it matter? She wouldn't believe it. Neither would I… if I were the dream. Was I the dream?

"I really shouldn't say anything."

She grabbed me, spun me toward the car and shoved me into it. Then she grabbed a handful of my crotch and squeezed.

"Damn it, Julie. That hurts."

"Good. Now start talking."

"Like I said. You're not going to like this, but you, this, the accident, and even now, it's all just a dream. You're not real."

She squeezed harder. "Does this feel like a dream?"

"Ouch. Stop." I put my hands on her shoulders and gently pushed her back. Her grip loosened and she dropped her hands to her side.

"Do you think this Olivia chic is the real one now?"

"She's more real than this." I lifted my t-shirt up to reveal some bruising left by Olivia's punch to the ribs. "She did this to me before I fell asleep. And for the record, I piss her off too. It's not just you."

"You probably fell out of bed and landed hard on your side."

"Oh, I wish it was that easy." I sat her on the hood of the car and started to tell her about Nǎo Pang, and the Pillars we'd found. "That was why I was rummaging through the Jeep."

"You're scaring me, Andy. I don't care what you think is going on in those China dreams, but it's not real. This is real."

"No Julie, this is not real."

"Is that why you were going through my Jeep?"

"We need to find the Illusion Pillar. It's why you were run off the road."

"No. I was run off the road by an asshole. You need to go to bed and sleep this off. Damn it, Andy, you look fucking worn out."

"It's okay." I put a consoling hand on her shoulder. "I'm sleeping right now."

"What are you saying, you and I... the kissing?"

"In the real world, you and I both know you're out of my league. We've never dated or even talked about it. You listen to my stories about China like the rest, or maybe you don't cause I'm not there telling them. Either way, there's no us. You're too good for me." I gave her a second. "If it's any consolation, I'm loving the us part of these dreams."

"Andy, you need help."

"No, I need the Pillar." I didn't want to go back empty-handed. "I need you to do me a favour."

"A favour?" Julie asked.

"This will prove my story, if you're willing to have an open mind."

"This should be good. What do you need?"

166

Kevin Weisbeck

"We need to go to your Jeep. You need to unroll that rear compartment cover thingy. I think there's a map hidden in it."

"A map."

"Actually, one of the Pillars. It's the Illusion Pillar. We already have Truth and Water. You see what I'm saying, Feng Shui is the Harmony, and Chaos is Truth and Illusion, or Zhēnxiang Cuòjué."

"And if we go to the Jeep and it's not there, will you go home and get some sleep?"

"You do this for me, and I'll do whatever you want."

"I know I'm enabling you, but let's go."

She hopped in the front and I quickly wheeled the car out of the spot. I knew the map was there, it was my dream. I also knew that after I proved it to her, I was going to make a move on her. Be damned if Olivia gets jealous. I'd always liked Julie, and this was only a dream relationship. Olivia would have to understand.

At the auto wrecking yard, I wore a hat that I had in the trunk, and sunglasses to get past the girl in the office. The Jeep was still unlocked. Julie popped the back open and we both looked at the blind. She reached for it and I stopped her. "Please, can I?"

I pulled it open to see two words, written in thick felt pen.

Time's Up.

167

Chapter 39

Once again I woke up scrambling for answers. The bed was small, and the room was bare. There was one window, more a small pane of glass roughly placed against the hole in the wall. The door was a set of six-foot planks held together by shorter ones, on hinges that were browned with age. Was this a barn? The sheets however were as white as a fresh blanket of snow and they smelled like rainwater. The room itself was no more than eight feet wide by twelve feet long. Hopefully, this place wasn't costing us too much.

Olivia burst through the door letting the morning sun run an attack on my senses. "You getting up soon? They're starting to cook breakfast."

I could smell the bacon. It was likely the reason I was awake. That aroma travelled. "Give me a second."

She sat on the bed beside me and put a hand on my forehead. "Are you not feeling good?"

"I'm okay. The brain wants me to stay in bed. This is quite the place."

I was remembering now. Just like I was remembering the shack they called a kitchen, and the old lady that cooked supper last night. Everything was cooked in hollowed bamboo tubes placed in a fire. They had minimal electricity. Last nights meal was lost in the fog, but I knew I liked it, well, I think I did. I turned to get out of bed and stumbled.

Olivia caught me. "They've got coffee. Looks like you'll need a strong one."

"Legs are a little stiff. That's all."

"Too bad. I see a day of hiking. How'd you do on that Illusion Pillar?"

"Not so good. I'll tell you at breakfast." I massaged my legs as I slipped on my pants. "What is this place? It sure is quiet."

"This is where the Mountain Pillar is. I can feel it. I was nosing around, and they all remember Nǎo Pang. They told me he was here just last year. He stayed for a week and then he was gone. I doubt it was a coincidence."

I nodded as I slipped my shirt over my head. "You said they have coffee?"

She took my hand. "I'm buying."

"What? They take Visa? Do they even know what plastic is?"

"Visa is everywhere." She led me out the door and down a path that hugged these eclectic shacks. It was obvious that there were no building codes here. The homes, built like barns, sat nestled together like the mountains. There was no symmetry, no paint and nothing from the twenty first or even twentieth century. The weathered boards, all brownish black, twisted and clung to each other with nails recycled from old countryside sheds. There was power to some of the buildings, the wires either nailed or hand-tied to whatever worked. And amongst it all, there were the people. They worked, smiled, and kept out of the way of the tourists that visited. Sure, it was their home, but a paying guest meant a few more panes of glass, or a handful of nails.

Outside the restaurant, the old lady was stuffing tubes of bamboo into the fire. Olivia let me go inside and order the coffee. I put in the order and quickly returned to the doorway.

Olivia crouched down. "*Ni Hǎo*."

The old woman briefly looked over to her. "*Ni Hǎo*."

"Do you speak English?"

The lady continued stuffing tubes. "I do some."

A Dream Escape

"Do you know a boy, Năo Pang? I went to school with him." Olivia made the gesture of opening a book. "School." "School. Năo Pang smart boy."

Olivia nodded. "Smart boy. Did you see him last year? He told me he was coming out this way, said he missed the mountains."

"Năo Pang loved the mountains. He..." She gestured walking with her fingers.

"He liked going on hikes?"

"Yes. Hikes."

"Did he have a favourite one?"

The old woman nodded. "He like one most of all." She pulled a stick out of the fire and used the burnt end to draw on the flat rocks of the ground. She drew a series of squares, the village, and then the lines of the rice fields. She pointed up the hill and then drew a square at the edge of the field. It must have been a barn or a shed.

"Is it a nice hike?" Olivia wanted her to think they were just wanting to enjoy the sights.

"Rock steps, beautiful mountain tops."

"It goes to top?" she told us.

A man came with the two cups of coffee and I handed one to Olivia. "What are you thinking?"

Olivia smiled. "You best have a big breakfast."

Our meal was quickly eaten, and we were on our way. I started counting steps but stopped at five hundred. I'd lost interest in the hike before it started. The only thing that kept me going was the sight of Olivia, ten steps in front of me. She was a beautiful woman, so confident and strong, and yet she had a vulnerability that was enchanting. It could even be considered cute, unless she heard you.

"Hurry up, Andy. You're falling behind."

"Don't you want to stop and just take it all in?" It was my way of asking for a break.

"When we get to the top, and find the map, I'll let you have a treat."

That had me moving again. Did she have chocolate, chips or… Oh, I wonder if she was talking about a kiss.

Her smile hinted that it would be worth my while. "Coming, Dear."

She laughed and continued. After eighty more steps we stopped. An old building, stripped of half the boards and nails, was just ahead. There were only ten pools of rice to wade through.

"I didn't bring my rubber boots, Olivia."

She took off her shoes, rolled her pants to the knees and gave me a kiss on the lips. It was passionate and a hint to what was to come, that's if I followed. Then she turned and took that first step. The mud and water only made it halfway up her calf.

I took a second to catch my breath and started rolling up my pant legs. "It's a damn good thing you're cute."

We waded through the pools of rice, being careful not to trample the crops, and slowly made it to the other side. I climbed out first and held out a hand. Olivia took it. As she made her way out my foot slipped on the muddy bank and I slid ass first into the water. Olivia fell flat on her back as her hand slipped from mine. She landed in the pool as if getting ready to make a snow angel.

Sitting in the rice pool, I watched as she slowly pulled herself to her knees. My chuckle soon became a laugh.

"Good move slick." She climbed on top of me and placed her muddy hands on either side of my face and pressed her dripping wet body against me to make sure I was as wet as she was. It was followed with a kiss.

I kissed her back and mumbled, "are we having mud sex."

She stopped the kiss and pushed herself up. "Nothing until we find that map. You need incentives, not rewards."

"I'm good with both."

"Business first, Andy." She got to her feet and pulled her wet shirt over her head. Over at the cleaner side of the pond she washed it and used it to get the mud off her face and arms. Then she wrung it out and put it back on.

I just stared at her tanned skin as the beads of water rolled over the curves. I didn't start washing my face until her shirt was back on. "How far from here?"

"We're almost at the top of the mountain. It can't be far."

There was a trail that led past the barn. It ascended another couple hundred feet before we were there. We stopped and looked out over the valley. It was easy to see why this kid liked hanging out here. Rice fields sprawled in all directions, hundreds of years of work. Generation after generation broke their backs for these stepped pools.

I put my arms around her and pulled her in for a hug. "Wow, eh?"

"Wow is right." She dropped her head on my shoulder.

The moment lasted until I saw the pile of rocks. We did the same thing in Canada, using rocks in the tundra to mark direction or boundaries. A long triangular rock was pointing to a tree off in the distance.

The tree was a large Banyan tree. Over-sized branches towered to the sky in a crooked mess of sticks and leaves. The trunk, about three feet in diameter, had several cracks and gaps as the roots spread over the rich dark soil like gnarled fingers on a monster's hand. It didn't take long to find a tube. It was bamboo and had a top carved from a larger piece of wood. I pulled it off, pulled out the map, and spread it out on the green grass. It had the pillar markings in the bottom corner.

"We found it," Olivia howled.

"We..." I turned to see Olivia's shirt and bra hanging on one of the branches.

She unbuttoned her jeans and slid the zipper down. "Are you ready to see that last cat paw?"

Chapter 40

It was an infomercial that woke me. Why did those stupid things always come on at twice the volume? I watched it through glazed eyes. A large Chinese man was selling vacations to China. He looked strangely familiar until I could clear my head. It was Mr Chin, and he wasn't selling vacations, he was selling real estate in Shanghai. And it wasn't real estate as much as it was burial plots. I grabbed for the remote and turned it off.

After a few minutes, I looked over to the clock on the wall. It said it was three-thirty in the morning. I got off the couch and headed toward the bathroom. As I sat, I thought of Olivia and my reward for finding that third map. Again, I hadn't woken up with a mess in my shorts. That meant Olivia was real, and I clearly had a girlfriend. We also had all but one map. We were close. My thoughts quickly shifted to Julie. She had to be the connection to the fourth map. Maybe it wasn't in Julie's Jeep, or her attic, but it was around her somewhere. Why else was she so prominent in my dream?

After I finished my business, I zipped up and washed my hands. Then I grabbed my keys. Julie wasn't that far from my place and be damned if I was going to let her hold me back. With the fourth map I could have what my heart desired. Hadn't I already found it with Olivia? Maybe it wasn't the maps, more the pursuit. She was a world out of my league, but she liked me.

The lights weren't on at Julie's place, which was a surprise. Waking her wouldn't make me popular, but it might put an end to these pillars, and perhaps these damn dreams, if I could find it. Worse case scenario, we might get to share a moment. I felt a twinge of guilt, but it passed.

I rang the doorbell, but Julie never answered. There was no response to a heavy knock. I stepped over to the window, cupped my hands on the glass and peered in. The place was a mess. It was like she was looking for something, maybe found it, and abruptly left. Around the back of the house, I found a window that wasn't locked. I popped the screen, climbed through, and stepped in the cat's water dish. She didn't have a cat, but I'd heard she often watched her neighbour's Ragdoll Persian.

Inside, I checked the bedroom first. I expected to open the door and find Julie fast asleep. She wasn't there. Nor was she anywhere else in the house. Had she gone to her parents? Did she do that kind of thing?

It didn't matter. What mattered was that I had her place all to myself. I turned a light on and started to go through her dresser, her closet, and through the stuff under her bed. I rifled through the living room and kitchen. After that, I started in on the rest of the house. It took just over an hour to realise she had already found the map, because it wasn't here. Why the hell had I brought it up, and was that why she was interested in me?

I looked back to the window. It was time to go, but I decided on the back door. Why climb through a window when you can use a door. The damn thing wasn't even locked.

"What the f..." I opened it and thought about locking it on the way out. I didn't. Maybe, Julie didn't lock it for the neighbour, for dropping off felines on a whim. It would have been nice to know that an hour ago.

Looking at my watch, it was time. I had to get back to Olivia. I'd obviously drifted to sleep after sex. Hopefully, she'd be waiting for me.

174

Chapter 41

Olivia was still there, dressed, and sitting with her arms wrapped around the legs that were tucked up into her chest. I took a minute to drink her up while the fog in my head dissipated. She looked content, happy. I slipped on my pants, moved beside her, and gave her a peck on the cheek.

She continued to stare out over the valley. "I get why that kid loved this place."

"It's pretty breathtaking."

"How would you know," She laughed. "How'd you sleep."

"Sorry about that. I must have drifted off after we… you know."

"No, I don't. What happened, Andy?" She turned her head and her eyes landed squarely on mine.

What was I supposed to call what we'd just done? It would answer a few of the questions in her head.

"Can I call it making love?" I asked. "I mean, I feel like I should be calling it something macho, like shagging or doin' it, but it felt way too wonderful for that."

She leaned in and kissed me on the lips. "I think love making works."

"I especially liked it when you…"

Olivia quickly snapped out of the moment. "Shhh."

"What did I…"

A Dream Escape

"Someone's coming. Quick, this way."

She gathered up the maps, her clothes, and the shoes while I grabbed my shirt. There was a stand of Osmanthus trees, and it made good cover. We watched as two men appeared. They were dressed in black suits. Oddly, you didn't get a lot of suits up here, unless they were looking for something, or someone.

They had found a path that skirted the rice pools and were studying the grass that had been bent down. They did a quick pan of the area. The one man took off his suit jacket, folded it nicely, and laid it down. Then he took a seat in the grass, facing the forest.

I put my mouth up to her ear. "What are they doing?"

"They know we're here and they're waiting us out."

"How long before they give up?"

"Dunno." She looked behind us. "Longer than I want to wait. Let's see if we can find another way back."

"What? In there?"

"It's called a forest."

"I know what it's called. I'm guessing you don't watch horror movies. They all start like this you know."

"Such a man one minute and all boy the next. What am I going to do with you?" She took my hand and dragged me deeper into the woods. "I'll protect you."

The trail disappeared after fifty feet and thickened until we were bushwhacking. Branches snagged our shirts, tore at our skin, and left me wondering if we shouldn't just give ourselves up. Fallen branches cracked under foot and others snapped off trees as we pushed our way through. Those sounds carried.

"I can hear you two trying to leave." The man's voice bellowed. "That's okay. Mr Chin knows you will come to your senses soon. He wants those maps."

I opened my mouth to respond, but Olivia slapped her hand over it.

"It'll take half a day to get through that forest. By then we'll be down there waiting for you. We'll talk then."

I moved her hand. "I vote we go down those pond things?"

"We wouldn't make it far before they shot us. Besides, there's no busses leaving for a couple hours." She started moving again. "Let's work our way back and I'll have a new plan by the time we get there."

"Okay." I took two steps and screamed.

"Andy, what are you doing?"

My eyes were frozen over her shoulder. She looked back to see what I'd seen. Fifty yards away a dark shadow was sleeking its way through the trees. It was much larger than a rabbit, not quite as big as a unicorn, and it had hungry yellow eyes.

"What is it, Olivia?"

"I'd rather not say." She shoved me. "Just head down the hill. I've changed my mind. I like the rice field escape plan."

"Why? What's back there?"

"A rather large cat."

We stumbled over downed trees and slid down the steeper embankments. When we reached the edge of the rice fields, we could see the valley again. The murk of branches, leaves and shrubs were behind us. So were the yellow eyes. Halfway down the steps the two black suits stood staring. One had his gun drawn. He waved it in the air and made an open gesture of putting it back in its holster under his jacket.

"We don't want to kill you two. There's no need. We have something you want and I'm sure it will bring you to your senses. Mr Chin wants to meet with you and set up the trade. He's a patient man, but even he has his limits. He'll be in touch." They turned to walk away, and then stopped. "And be careful. The forest is full of Panthers, but I'm sure you know that already."

I had to think Mr Chin was bluffing. Everything that was important to me was here. She was standing knee deep in mud. Back home I had a dead-end job. They could have it, and my car. There was a comic book collection and a few frozen pizzas in the freezer part of the fridge. It wasn't like I was worth anything.

Olivia kept an eye on them as she started working her way through the pond. "This time, let's not get so wet."

Behind us we could hear branches being snapped as the shadow with yellow eyes continued to lurk.

She gave me a playful shove. "And hurry it up, would ya?"

"Yes, Dear."

Chapter 42

The bus ride down the mountain wasn't any safer than the ride up. It was truly remarkable that more people didn't die in this twisted game of chicken. I wasn't the only one thinking this either as everyone on the bus had their eyes either trained on the road or closed. For some, it was important to know when the impact would come.

When we arrived at the bus depot, twenty-four wobbly legs left the bus and not one person tipped the driver. Olivia had picked a seat near the back of the bus this time. Love, or something like that, was growing between us and she was enjoying the stupid things, the hand holding, the childish conversations.

"What's next?" I asked.

"We get on the next bus and hope there's Wi-Fi. We still need one pillar."

"Julie doesn't have it, not that I'd be able to bring it back with me even if she did."

"I hear what you're saying. I wasn't sure how you'd pull it off either."

"I could have it tattooed onto my body," I offered.

"For the last time, Andy, those are dreams. There's no grabbing a map or bringing it back. There's no getting a tattoo, crazed junkyard dogs and there's no…"

"No what?" I asked. "Blonde with a crush on me?"

Kevin Weisbeck

"I didn't want to say it, but yes. You do however have a fairly hot brunette sitting beside you. You could do worse."

"I've done worse, a lot worse."

"Okay, I think it's time you learn when to shut up and take a compliment without sounding like an idiot."

"Good luck with that," I added. "Are you hungry?"

"Nah. I'm heading for the bus. Maybe you can find me something." She gave me a kiss, knowing I was going off on a quest for food. "Actually, here's fifty Yuan. I'll take a pop if you can find one."

"I can do that."

Her ass gave me a little extra wiggle as she went up the steps. I watched for a few seconds and then shook the spell. I was hungry and looking for anything I could recognise. A burger would have been great, yet non-existent here. And it couldn't be fish. I'd grown to hate fish.

A small row of shops constituted a mall, of sorts. There were teas, local spices like star anise, and there was fish. I kept looking. I found t-shirts, hats, and books about the Great Wall. I laughed at those. The Great Wall was hundreds of miles away. Talk about desperation souvenir shopping.

I was about to give up when I saw two kids carrying a bag of candy. They went left so I went right. I didn't have to go far. The first thing I saw was the shrimp flavoured potato chips. They were beside the squid flavoured ones. That had to be a joke. One shelf down I found the soft candy. It wasn't a burger, but it wasn't fish flavoured either. The pineapple twists looked good and so did the mango balls. I grabbed both. There was Pepsi, and I gathered up a couple for the road.

The cash register was in sight when I saw the rack full of silk scarfs. It didn't take long to see one that would look good on Olivia. It was black with a flowered pattern of what looked like a periwinkle blue, her two favourite colours.

When the lady rang everything up, the total was sixty-five yuan. Thing was, I wanted the candy, the pop, and the scarf.

"Will you take fifty?"

The young woman shook her head. "Sixty-five."

179

A Dream Escape

I pulled out a Canadian twenty. "You take Canadian money? This bill is worth a hundred yuan. You'd be getting a deal."

"No funny money."

"But I..."

"Excuse me." It was the woman next in line.

"Uh, yes."

"I'm Canadian. I have a few extra yuan. I'll take the twenty for fifty yuan."

"But that's not..." I stopped myself. There were no banks for miles. "How about seventy-five?"

"Fifty."

We exchanged bills, I bought the stuff, and stormed off.

When I stepped on the bus, Olivia was fixed on her phone. She didn't look up when I handed her the Pepsi. She was reading and had to finish the paragraph. I put a candy up to her mouth and she trustingly opened wide.

"Got my change?" She started chewing.

I handed her the thirty-five yuan without thinking. Olivia looked down at it briefly and stuffed it in a pocket. Then she finished reading the article and turned her phone off. "What else did you buy?"

"Huh?"

"Fifty yuan for candy. Did you get a few magic beans too?"

"I, uh, you don't..."

"Come on. Hand it over."

"Okay. I bought something else."

"No big. What did you get? Did you find squid chips? Because they're amazing."

"I was hoping to give this to you later." I pulled the scarf out of my pocket. "Here you go."

"Oh, wow. I'm sorry. I didn't think you'd do something like this." She held it up to her face before draping it around her neck. "I love it. Thanks."

I noticed the price tag was still on it. In Canada, the clerks always removed those things. The scarf alone was fifty Yuan and Olivia didn't need to know that.

She also saw the sticker. "Not to be ungrateful, but do you have any other money on you?"

"I didn't use your money for this. I used..." It sounded bad any way I said it. "I used my money. I had a few Canadian dollars."

"When we were starving in Shanghai..."

"Oh, I didn't have it at that point. I'd have shared if I did."

"How'd you get it?"

"Forget it. You wouldn't believe me."

"Try me."

"Remember when I got bit by that dog, in my dream at the junkyard?"

"That was a dream. What does it have to do with this?"

"In that dream I went to the bank."

"It was a dream, Andy. You can't bring shit back from dreams."

"How do you explain it then? I fell asleep broke and woke up with close to eighty dollars."

"You must have had it before. You just didn't remember."

"We were hungry. Believe me, I checked my wallet. I was broke. In my dream I took out a hundred and bought close to twenty dollars worth of food. It's the only thing that makes sense."

"Andy. This is impossible." She shook her head and started to play with the end of her scarf. "But I'll let you prove it."

"How?"

"Next time you fall asleep, get more. Drain your account. I mean it's not real money on that side, but it spends pretty good on this side."

"Okay. I will."

Again, she shook her head. "That's sarcasm, Andy. Oh, and thanks for the scarf. It is beautiful."

I handed her the rest of my Canadian money. "Not much use until we can exchange it, but its yours."

"But..."

"Not to worry. I'll be sure to get more."

"Thanks." She raised her brow. "Oh, and I found something, so we're flying to Xi'an."

Chapter 43

Seats twenty-seven E and F meant that Olivia had a window and I was stuck in the middle seat. Luckily, the aisle seat, d, was empty. I'd managed to stay awake for the beef noodles and watched intently as a stewardess napped through the take off. The woman's head nodded and bounced as she sat belted into the fold up seat. She'd obviously had a long day, or a run of late nights. I could relate.

My day had been equally long, with the hikes, the first-time Olivia sex, and the suicidal ride down the mountain. I'd survived it all as yesterday rolled into tomorrow. It was getting dark, so I closed my eyes and let my mind drift back to Kelowna.

For no particular reason, I staggered to the freezer part of the fridge. I had to see if I still had five frozen pizzas. I did. A pepperoni one was pulled out of the box as the oven got dialled to four twenty-five. Then I tossed the pizza on the middle rack without a pan.

I went through the living room on my way to the bedroom. Everything was just as I'd left it. The bedroom was still a mess. I took a second to stare at the bed. It had been a week since I'd dreamt of that dead hooker. In the closet there'd be a box. It had a few trinkets from my childhood and a handful of rare comic books.

The value was about two hundred dollars. Was that enough for Mr Chin? Did he think they were worth anything to me?

The box was there. What else did I have that was worth anything? Through the window I could see my car. That wasn't it. Under the bed I had a few girlie magazines and a safe. I opened it to see a few old photos and a hard drive. There was nothing on it other than more photos, some favourite audio books, and a lot of music. Seeing all this meant that Mr Chin had taken nothing of mine. He was bluffing.

I made my way into the bathroom and grabbed my toothbrush. I started scrubbing and didn't stop until I could smell the pizza. The little sweaters that had coated my teeth were spit down the drain. Although Olivia didn't seem to mind, they drove me crazy. I ran my tongue over my teeth and smiled as I made my way back into the kitchen.

The pizza was starting to brown the cheese up nicely, so I slid it out and started cutting. The first bite was hot, but I managed to open-mouth chew it without blistering any skin.

I picked up the phone and dialled Julie. There was no answer.

"Damn it, pick up already."

Two more slices were slapped together like a pepperoni sandwich. I'd been half-asleep when I dropped by her place earlier. It was time for another visit.

The back door was still unlocked. I walked in and gave the house one last walk-through before starting to clean up. Sure, it wasn't my place to do that, but what better way to go over everything. There was still no map. This was either a waste of time, or I was missing something.

I took a second to pan the room from the door. I did good work. Maybe Julie wouldn't be so mad at me now, or she'd be doubly pissed, because I was in her place without asking. It was one of those no-win deals.

On the way back to my place I decided to humour myself. I stopped by the bank and walked up to the machine by the door. My card was slipped into the slot and I asked it for two hundred dollars. I had that and then some.

Insufficient funds.

"What?" I'd just been paid and other than the car payment and the phone bill, I should have had money. I asked for a balance and got two dollars and thirty-seven cents. "Are you kidding me?"

I hit print, yanked the receipt from the machine and stuffed it in my wallet. Then I went home, had a slice of cold pizza, sat on the couch, and turned the TV on. Jeopardy was starting.

A two-card hand, a flop, the turn, and a river.

"What is Texas Hold'em poker, Alex?" I said aloud.

On TV Derrick had also answered poker but forgot the Texas part. He lost two hundred.

"Idiot."

Which poker game has all losers match the pot for the next round.

"What is Guts?"

I nodded off before the next answer and left this world thinking about Julie. She was avoiding me, likely at the parents. To her I was certifiable, with all this crazy talk about dreams and pillars. It was a lot to take in, but she was part of it. I guess the truth hurts.

My eyes opened as the plane touched down. That jostled me in my seat. Was it a rough landing, or had I been that out of it?

"Welcome back sleepy head," Olivia said as she flicked my bangs out of my eyes with her finger.

I tried to focus. "What time is it?"

"About four. Stay awake and I'll buy you breakfast, that is unless you're sitting on a wallet full of hundreds." She smirked as she laboured at holding back an, I told you so.

"Well, little miss smarty pants, I did go to the bank. Thing is, I'm broke." I pulled out the slip that claimed two dollars and thirty-seven cents.

Olivia looked at it. "How long has this been in your wallet?"

"It's today's."

Kevin Weisbeck

"Uh, date's smudged."

"No way. I just…" I grabbed it back and studied it. Part of the year was all you could read clearly from the date. The rest of the receipt was perfect. I'd smudged it when I pulled it from the bank machine. "Damn it."

"That's okay. I'll still buy ya breakfast."

Chapter 44

The plane emptied quicker than usual. It was a redeye and that meant no children and very few tourists. It also meant little talking and few rules. The ones that had managed to stay awake had had the run of the plane, including helping themselves to snacks, juices, coffee, and sodas. Olivia was one of them. She managed a few conversations, acting the part of a semi-seasoned tourist. She'd heard rumours of the emperor's army of clay and with any luck a few of the locals had too.

She took my arm. "I learned a few facts about our Terra Cotta Army."

I shuffled through the airport, still dazed from switching worlds. "Do tell."

"Nǎo Pang had a thing about this place. Much like he loved Ping'an, he hated Xi'an. He claimed the whole Terracotta Army was a hoax."

"You said you were buying breakfast?" I was feeling better, the fog lifting. "Do we need a cab?"

"Cab or shuttle. Doesn't matter."

I stepped out in the street as a cab tried to race off. The brakes chirped to a stop. I opened the back door to let her in.

She took a seat and shifted over to give me room before giving the cab driver the name of the hotel. "That was kinda brave, for you."

I put my arm around her and ran my tongue over some of the smoothest teeth my mouth had ever seen. They were clean enough to give me the courage to kiss her like a teenager. She didn't fight me.

"Not in cab. No. No. You stop now."

I stopped and Olivia apologised to the driver. She explained we were newlyweds. China was our honeymoon.

The cab driver smiled. "That nice, but no kiss in cab."

"No kiss," she replied. "What are we doing, Andy?"

"Here we go." I pulled my arm back.

"What?" she asked.

"Well, you've come to your senses. I knew this was too good to be true."

"It's not like that. I live in China. You live in Canada. You have a girlfriend. Remember Julie?"

"Julie isn't my girlfriend. And didn't you say she was a dream? Now you're jealous of her?"

Silence.

"Come on Olivia, talk to me."

She remained silent until we got to the hotel. "What do I say, Andy. She's blonde, probably cute, and she lives in Canada. I don't. It's simple logistics."

"I kinda like it here, except for the random shootings, the swims in the polluted rivers and Mr Chin."

Olivia chuckled as she got the key from the front desk. "No bags. Lost at the airport. If they call, please come get us. I need my curling iron."

The man behind the counter nodded.

"You sold that quite well," I whispered.

"We don't need the attention. What is it about me that you like?"

"For real?" I looked at her. "To start, you're beautiful. I'd be lying if I didn't tell you that those long legs and that lean hourglass of yours hadn't pulled my eyes right out of their sockets the first time I saw you."

"So that's it? I have a hot body?"

"It was at first, but since getting to know you, it's so much more. You're playful, you have a strong personality, you're funny and you think like I do."

"How do you figure?"

"You trust a very limited group of people. Where some would say you're a skeptic, I call it being a realist. People like us don't own rose-coloured glasses. We know all they do is tint things. That doesn't make it any better."

"Does Julie have those glasses?"

"She does, and she needs them to see the world that she likes. She doesn't do exciting."

"I think we do too much of it."

"I agree. So, what do you see in me?"

She opened the door to our room and flipped on a light. "You're a pain in the ass, but you're real. I don't see the games. Either you're too stupid to lie or you're just one of those old-fashioned honest types. You're also kinda cute."

"Kinda?" I flopped on the bed. "I'm kinda adorable. And what brought this all on?"

"You need to know a few things about me. I'm more than a little broken, but I think you get that. You need to see the scars, see if you could live with them."

"Scars like you don't like clowns, or you hate Birthdays?"

"No." She started to unbutton her shirt. She let it fall off her shoulders and land on the floor behind her. Then she unclasped her bra and let it fall open. It also slid off her shoulders and landed behind her. "So?"

Oddly, I hadn't noticed them until now. Why was that? I'd made love to her on the hill and seen her near naked body in Shanghai when she walked to the bathroom. Olivia stood there vulnerable, expecting to be judged. I was doing just that with my eyes as I took it all in. One scar crossed over the left side of her collarbone and ran a diagonal across her chest. There were three shorter ones an inch apart that ran across her right breast. They looked deep at one point and had sliced through the nipple. Below her left breast her ribs had been branded like she was cattle. The triple S's were burnt into her skin leaving them red and raised. She turned around.

At some point her back had been whipped. There were scars from thirty to forty lashes. They'd healed nicely, but that didn't stop me from imagining the flesh being torn off her back in strips like bacon, and the scarring that would have been under the skin. How did I not see this?

Olivia gave me a couple minutes to stare, judge, and to change my mind. Julie, she was sure, had never been beaten or lived the life that she had. Julie wasn't broken. In fact, if she was to wager a guess, Julie was a pretty little thing with a life of sock hops and lollipops. There was a good chance she'd never slept in the streets or befriended drunks, drug addicts, or runaways.

It was a shame too, because Olivia's people were painfully honest and had lost the need to hide from their past, much like a woman loses her modesty after having a baby. Nothing like doctors, nurses, and interns staring at your bare crotch every five minutes. They poke and prod while you wail in pain hoping to pass a watermelon-sized child. Still, people like Olivia seldom went a day without a finger being pointed.

She turned back to me expecting to see the look. She wouldn't hold it against me. I came from Julie's world, not hers. My arms were wide open as I stepped toward her and wrapped myself around her.

Nothing but loving and positive energy poured out of me.

"I'm broken. You know that, now."

"You're not broken. You've just had all the bullshit knocked out of you."

"You don't think I need a few minutes on a shrink's couch?"

"We all do, but I wouldn't change a thing. That being said..." I wiped a tear from her face. "I think you sprung a leak."

She angrily wiped at her cheek. "Tell anybody and I'll..."

"You'll what, cry, beat me up, knee me in the nuts. I'm okay with that, as long as it's you doing it."

"Oh great. Now it's my turn to wonder if you're all there." She twirled her finger around her ear. "Any toys in the attic, Andy?"

"The box is full, but we're already dating. I think that means you're stuck with me." I smiled and dropped my hands to her ass and grabbed. "Besides, some of those toys might be fun."

"Again? Really? It's like flicking a switch with you, isn't it?" She jumped up and wrapped her legs around my hips. It caught me off guard and we fell backward onto the floor.

There'd be no sleeping.

Chapter 45

I held Olivia's hand as she stepped off the bus. The beauty of her vulnerability had washed away all the scarring, inner and outer. She became unguarded around me, relaxed, and I needed that.

"Stop it," she half scolded.

"Stop what?" I asked.

"That goofy shit you're doing. It's annoying and we still have work to do."

"Can do." I waved a hand in front of my face, turning a shit-eating smile into a serious looking smirk. It only lasted a second before the smile returned. "Sorry."

"You're a child." She continued, "Nǎo Pang thought this was a hoax? That would be a pretty elaborate hoax. I mean eight thousand clay soldiers, each one with its own facial expressions. That's a lot of work."

"It is."

Olivia kept my hand tightly clasped in hers. We were off the bus now and shuffling through the front gates. "Did you know that no country has ever inspected these figures?"

I shrugged. "It's China. They don't share well."

"True enough. Nǎo Pang figured, actually strongly believed, that these soldiers were not even made by the Chinese."

"Now who's talking ridiculous?"

"He believed they were made in Italy and Greece and then secretly brought over."

"That's absurd. You couldn't keep that a secret."

"Did you know that one hundred and eighty-two people died in the excavation of these soldiers."

"Died? How do you die brushing away at the dirt with paintbrushes?"

"Doesn't sounds so crazy now, does it. The sight is heavily guarded and on the odd occasion someone escapes with a terra cotta finger or small piece of an arm. The Chinese now seed the sight with pieces, pieces made in China."

"That's stupid."

"Not really. They do it in Paris and Versailles. They scatter chunks of marble at the base of the statues. That way people grab the chunks instead of breaking off pieces."

"So, if Emperor Qin Shi Huang didn't make these armies of clay, why the elaborate story?"

"That's the million-dollar question, except we're not after a million dollars. We're after the map. Nǎo Pang thought it was a hoax and because of that, I think he hid the map here. I say we scout it out like a couple of cute tourists and hope we get lucky."

"What's happened to you. You went from kneeing me in the nuts, to hand holding, rainbows and fluffy kittens."

"I know. I don't like it either."

"I never said I didn't like it. I'm just used to the bad-ass Brit."

"Maybe I should body slam you on the pavement."

"I'm sure you could." I took a defensive stance. "Or we could just find the map."

We started in the main building. It held hundreds of soldiers lined up in rows four wide. Trenches, cut deep into the earth, looked too clean, like they'd been cut by a loader's blade. Who would notice that though? Everyone was taking pictures of the soldiers, and the horses.

"See any maps?" She asked.

"Nothing." I took her hand and led her out of the building. "If you were Nǎo Pang, where would you hang out? I mean if these things are fake, he sure wouldn't waste his time on them, right?"

"Good point." She put her hands on her hips and looked around. "If he's right, it's all fake."

"There's a movie house. Wanna go watch some propaganda?"

"Can't hurt. Let's hope they've got popcorn."

The movie, much like the grounds, told a story of the First Emperor's unification of the seven kingdoms. He had created currency and ruled with an iron fist.

Finding nothing here, we left the theatre, checked out the other two buildings and came up blank. Olivia was thinking out loud. "What do we know?"

"The Emperor wasn't liked. He had a busy reign, build the first version of the Great Wall and Grand Canal. How'd he die?"

"Mercury pills," she answered.

"Why the hell was he taking those?"

"Someone told him it would give him immortality."

"Seriously, or were his Alchemists trying to kill him? Surely they weren't that stupid."

"Sticks and stones, Andy." She waved a finger at me as we entered the main courtyard. "Maybe this isn't fake. If everyone hated the Emperor, then it makes sense that the people would want to assassinate him. At the very least they'd want to overthrow his Kingdom, and that eventually happened."

"The people were poisoning him?" I seemed to be getting left behind.

"Maybe not directly, but what if they were behind it somehow? If he died, they could rise up, except they'd need weapons."

"Lots of weapons," I admitted.

"There were eight thousand iron swords here. Each Terracotta soldier had one. The farmers supposedly raided this area and took them."

"Wouldn't they need a map to execute their attack on this place?"

"It would have helped." Olivia suddenly had an idea. "Come with me."

"Where else am I gonna go?" I followed her to an opening in the courtyard.

She looked around and stopped. With her right foot she tapped away at a bronze plaque amongst the tiles. Then she stepped on the corner of it and put a little weight down. It moved.

"What is that?" I asked.

"The symbols are north, south, east, and west."

There was also a star, like the ones you see on a map.

"It is loose," she added.

Which didn't mean much. A few of the tiles had become loose. How many thousands of people walked over them each week? That being said, it was likely the only truth here, and our only lead.

"You want me to dig it out?"

"No. I mean not yet. There are too many people. We'll wait until it gets a little quieter and then I'll give you a diversion."

"That's why you're the boss, Boss. What are we going to dig it out with?"

"I say we go to the gift shop and see if they sell souvenir bottle openers."

"You're too good at this. It's scary."

"I heard they have donuts here."

"A woman after my heart. If they have donuts, I'm loading up."

I devoured four donuts and bought a terracotta soldier bottle opener. It was sturdy and the handle was a good size.

Olivia tossed the last bite of her donut in her mouth and headed for the door. I put the bottle opener in my pocket and trailed a couple steps behind her. I kept my distance so that I could watch her walk, which I loved, and because she'd told me the plan, fall back and be ready.

She made her way over to the steps that led down to the Exhibition of Ancient Weapons building. There were three steps in total, and she went down two of them without incident. On the third one she rolled her ankle and dropped hard. I heard the shortened scream as she fell.

Two people came to her aid, followed by several others. Within a minute a crowd had gathered. All eyes were on her. I squatted down and started to twist the corkscrew between the bronze tile and the one beside it. It was halfway in when a hand tapped my shoulder.

I looked up to see a couple staring at the gathering. I quickly stood up, stepping in front of the plaque.

"Excuse us. Any idea what's going on over there?"

"I heard some celebrity was signing autographs. I eyed the woman and pegged her for a stay-at-home housewife. Do either of you know an Ellen DeGeneres?"

"Seriously," the woman snorted.

"That's what I heard."

With that, she dragged her husband toward the crowd. "Thanks."

"No problem," I muttered to myself as I knelt back down and pulled up on the corkscrew.

Olivia was sitting now. A trickle of blood ran from her hairline. She had put the cut there with her ring after she fell. She acted dazed and the crowd watched on. The poor thing was hurt. A doctor took a look at her ankle and massaged the tendons while another man ran off the get a wet cloth for her head.

After a few minutes, she tried to stand. The doctor wanted her to remain sitting, but Olivia was persistent, claiming to be fine. They helped her to her feet, and she sat at the edge of a planter. The cloth came, as did a first aider with a kit. She looked over to me while the cut was attended to.

The first aider cleaned the wound, bandaged her up and ran a flashlight over her eyes. After that, she was given a clean bill of health and three quarters of the crowd had moved on. One couple was asking about Ellen DeGeneres.

"Thanks, I mean *xie xie*," Olivia said as she got to her feet.

The woman nodded, packed up her things and left. Her radio had just informed her there was a young girl in the Main Exhibit that had skinned a knee.

Olivia headed my way, dodging the crowds. She didn't see me. She stopped and looked toward the main gates, no doubt wondering if I was waiting for her. She likely wondered if she'd been played. Could I have left without her?

My hand playfully slipped around her waist and I pulled her in for a hug. I tapped her on the head with a rolled-up map. "How ya doin... hey, why'd you hurt yourself?"

"Blood makes for a better crowd." She looked down at the map. "You got it. Does it have the mark?"

"It does."

"We should get going."

"No argument here."

The gate was in sight when her phone rang. She answered it without slowing down. "Hello?"

Now she stopped.

"What do you want?"

There was another pause while she listened.

"I'll tell him. Call us back in an hour, and we'll need proof."

She hung up and slipped the phone into her pocket. "Change of plans."

"What?" I blurted. "No way. Why? I thought we were going to ignore him. He has nothing."

"They've got your friend, Julie."

Chapter 46

B ack at the hotel, Olivia put the last map with the others. We waited in silence for Mr Chin's phone call. I couldn't help but wonder if she was okay. How did she get trapped in this mess? More importantly, how were my dreams getting sucked into this craziness. None of it made sense. Olivia watched my reaction as she tried to gauge where my head was at.

The phone rang once, and Olivia answered. "Is she there?"

She listened for a few seconds and then handed the phone to me. "He wants to talk to you."

I put the phone on speaker and set it on the table. "I need to speak to Julie."

"I'm sure you do," replied Mr Chin. "I want something myself. I'm sure we can help each other out."

"Let me talk to her." I found my voice cracking.

"Andy?" The voice was Julie's. "Who are these people?"

"It'll be okay. I'll come get you. They don't want you. They want me."

"Why? What did you…"

"That's enough." It was Mr Chin. "I'm mad at you, Andy. I'm also pretty happy. I hear you have my maps, so I'll make this simple. These maps, when put together give the owner what they want, what they need most. "We can both win. For you, that's

Julie's and your freedom. Hand them over and you can have the girl and two airline tickets home. You'll have your life back. I give you my word."

"When do you want to meet?"

"Fly to Shanghai. I'll leave money for the tickets at the Xi'an airport. Bring the maps. The next plane leaves in three hours."

"And if I don't?"

"Each day I'll send you a picture of Julie. She'll change before your very eyes and it won't be pretty." He paused hoping for a response. There was none. "Look, Andy. You get what you want, and I get what I want. It really is a win, win."

"It is." I hung up and handed the phone to Olivia. "I guess we're going to Shanghai."

"Shanghai it is."

She walked over to the bed, lifted the corner of the mattress, and gathered the maps.

I walked over. "Wanna put them together?"

"Not really?"

"You mean after all this, we still don't get to see what these maps are about?"

"It doesn't matter anymore. They belong to Mr Chin now."

I took her hand. "Are you angry?"

She shook her head and gave me a kiss. "We should go down to the lobby and get a cab. The plane leaves in three hours. That's not a lot of time."

"You're right."

I got out of the cab and took Olivia's hand. I was finally understanding how these airports worked. Still, Olivia was the one who went up to the counter to buy the tickets. It took a few minutes and she continued to use the fake passports. Mr Chin didn't need to know everything. She paid with the Visa, leaving Mr Chin's money at the counter.

"Okay. That's done. Want to get a bite to eat?"

I shrugged.

"Come on. I know you're hungry. You're always hungry."

"You think they sell nachos anywhere?"

Olivia forced a smile. "They've got a pizza place. It's not very good, but it looks the part."

"I could do pizza."

"Don't get excited. I said it looks the part."

We made our way to the place and ordered a deluxe, holding anything that came from the ocean. It was better than expected.

"You know you can't trust him," Olivia warned.

"I agree. I learned that at the poker table. Then there was the dead hooker and the small favour. The guy's been lying from the start."

"So how do you want to handle this?"

"We trade, the map for Julie. Are you okay with that?"

"It's your call," Olivia answered.

"You're upset. Come on, don't start closing doors on me now."

She put her slice down. It wasn't really that good, and she wasn't that hungry. "Julie needs you to save her. You can't do that and keep the maps too. Only in dreams do you get to have it all and this..."

"I know, I know… is not a dream."

The overhead speakers announced the flight number. It was boarding.

"Let's go." She took my hand and pulled me up from my chair. She held it all the way to the gate. Then she let it go, gave me a hug, and handed me my ticket.

"What's this?"

"Your tickets. There's one to Shanghai and two from Shanghai to Vancouver, for you and Julie." Olivia kissed me and a tear started down her cheek. She had never meant to fall in love. She'd let her guard down. This was her own damn fault, and she knew it.

"Where's yours?"

"You need to save Julie and stop acting like she's just a friend. You owe her that." She started to back away from me. "Now go, and don't let her down. Stay on your toes. Everything

199

happens for a reason, even the maps. You don't need to force anything."

"Olivia no. I thought we…"

"You thought wrong, but we did have fun. We both know Julie's a better fit. This…" She motioned to China and the craziness, "isn't who you are. Just don't forget me."

She turned and started to walk away. I stood dazed. "Olivia, please…"

"Don't beg, Andy. You're better than that." She kept walking without looking back. "You don't need broken."

Chapter 47

I reluctantly found my seat. It was by a window. Olivia had always taken that seat. It wasn't a selfish thing, just that she'd never flown and found the clouds fascinating. It was surreal, like she was in a safer place, like heaven. It was one of the few things that calmed her.

For me, the seat added to the trepidation. I was alone. Olivia had decided that our worlds didn't belong together and, as much as it hurt, a part of me understood. I couldn't live in China, not after all that had happened. I'd made enemies and seen the fat rolls of the country, so to speak.

But how could I have let her leave that easily? It wasn't the scars. I hadn't even seen them when we'd made love. All I saw was the softer side of her. It was like climbing over a prison wall and landing in a world of waterfalls, pools of clear water, and unicorns. Maybe that was it. I didn't belong in that world any more than I belonged in China. That was her world and she'd spent a lifetime arranging everything, the fears, the red flags, and the hideouts. I had a place like that myself, things I didn't share because then I'd have no where to hide in case the world went south on me.

I had to suppose that everybody had a spot, that one place where they could hide from the harsh realities. Sure, there were the odd ones who gave up their hiding places. They'd enter into a blissful relationship with their mate, no walls, and no secrets. Could that really work?

The plane sucked me into my seat as it launched down the runway and up into the clouds. I looked out at the white fluff and it pressed hard against my chest. I slid the cover of the window down. It loosened the pressure.

Soon, the stewardesses were getting the drink carts ready. People were milling around and the line-ups to the bathrooms began. I'd flown enough to know there was always an initial need for them, like most people held it for the flight. I always went at the airport.

And what was Julie doing at this moment. Was she tied up in a chair, locked in a room? Had they hurt her? She came from the same world as I did. We made kitchen cabinets, earned a modest living, and hung out with family on the weekends. Unlike Olivia, we had friends that owned homes or rented apartments and they all seemed to have jobs and things in common. I didn't know any drug addicts and the only drunk in my life was my Uncle Stanley. He was a happy drunk.

I wasn't sure what Julie had, but she'd never mentioned any addicts or drunks. If truth be told, we never talked all that much. Our only conversations consisted of the weather, or the weekends. Only in my dreams had we bonded a friendship. In my dreams I had kissed her. These were the dreams that Olivia had tried to warn me about.

Resting between my legs, I had the four Pillars... four maps that when figured out, would grant the owner what they truly wanted, and what they truly needed. I'd have to hand them over to Mr Chin if I wanted to get Julie back, and I would. I didn't want her getting hurt over this. It was my mess.

But there was nothing stopping me from having a look.

I opened the tube and slid one of the maps out. I saw the marking in the bottom right corner. This was the water map (Feng), and the front was a blueprint to the Three Gorges Dam. The back was blank. I rolled it up and took it, and the others, to the bathroom. Although the light was poor, when I held it up to the light, the back of the blueprint allowed certain lines from the front

Kevin Weisbeck

to show through. It was indeed a map. It looked like a map of sewer tunnels like the one I'd been in with Olivia. There was an X in the heart of it. At the top I saw one word, Huating. It was a suburb of Shanghai.

I grabbed the next map. On the one side, I saw a detailed map of the Emperors Palace in Xi'an. This was the illusion map (*Cuòjué*). I held that one up to the light. The other side also had a map to the sewers in Shanghai (Huating) and the X was in the exact same place. It made no sense. I grabbed the last two maps and held them up. Again, I saw identical sewer maps, the word Huating and the X. Then I noticed a few slight variations. Looking closer I saw quite a few variations.

Each map had the same tunnels. Each map had an X, but on each map, different gates were open and locked. I thought about if for a second as someone knocked on the door. "Just a second."

I rolled the maps up and shoved them back in the tube as I made my way back to my seat and sat down. Four maps, four different routes to the same spot. Why?

"What's in the tube?" the woman beside me asked. She was an attractive Asian and young enough to not care about the social disciplines of minding one's own business.

"Pardon me?"

"You're guarding it. Whatever's in it must be important."

"I'm just a little OCD, paranoia thing."

"OCD isn't paranoia. It's a control issue."

"You learned that in university?"

"I'm a professor."

"How old are you?" My initial guess had been twenty-two or three.

"Twenty-nine."

"You've aged well."

"That's perspective." She added, "did you know that the average is four?"

"You lost me."

"Everything that is, and that has happened, has four perspectives. There's the future, the present, the past and the illusion. Each perspective is different. Like I'm twenty-nine. I feel

203

good at twenty-nine, but when I was a child, I thought that was old. As I age, I'll wish to be that young again. The illusion is the transition of these changes."

"If you say so."

"Think about it." The woman went back to her book.

I indeed gave it some thought. Perspective times four, past present and future, not to forget the transitions.

That was when it hit me, and I understood the four Pillars.

Chapter 48

When the plane landed, I couldn't get off the damn thing quick enough. I saw Mr Chin's men waiting and promptly ducked behind the fattest man leaving our plane. I'd also given the woman, who had sat beside me, money for her to distract them. She did a good job pretending to think that one of them was her cousin. She hugged him and talked a mile a minute. By the time she admitted the mistake, I was in a cab.

I got out at the Bund and checked my funds. Olivia had slipped me a hundred Yuan and the airline tickets. The girl at the airport got half for her performance and the cab driver took forty. That left me ten to buy a pad of paper and one of those pens that wrote in four different colours. It was all I'd need.

In the little shop where I bought the pen and paper, I left a tip, the balance of the money. For that, the shopkeeper allowed me to use a shop window to copy one of the sewer maps. I taped it to the glass and roughly traced the routes. Then I took the pen, clicked the blue ink refill, and started to circle the open gates.

The sewer had metal gates between tunnels, and they were all supposed to be locked. I had seen one of the gates. It had an electronic keypad. Was it fair to believe that this Năo Pang had somehow hacked the computer system? Could he have these gates locking and unlocking on a pattern, or more like four patterns?

A Dream Escape

But what kind of time had to pass before each change was still a mystery. If I had a map, I could figure it out. I also knew which locks had been broken. They were the ones that Olivia had first showed me after we'd dove off that damn tour boat.

"You take too long." The man said. He had agreed to help me, but the change was a little over five yuan. It wasn't much.

"Here's a fiver." I had a Canadian five-dollar bill. It was worth twenty yuan.

The man took it and frowned. "Two more minutes."

"That's worth twenty yuan. Give me five."

"Two." He moved in closer. "What you draw?"

I had finished the first colour, grabbed a different map, and started circling the open gates in black. "Ever watch TV?"

"You on reality show?" His eyes widened as he looked around for the camera. There had to be a camera.

"I am. If I win the money, I'll remember you."

"You any good?"

"I'm ahead of everybody so far."

"Ho damn. This my lucky day. You take your time. I get you a pop."

"Thank you. I'll mention your generosity to the producer." I finished that map and started in on the third routes with red. I didn't write which colour was which, just in case I lost it, but I used the colours wisely. Black was truth, red was illusion, blue was water, and green would have to be mountain… cause of the green trees on a mountain. Made sense to me.

I was just finishing up when the man returned with a soda and a business card. "You give this to your producer. I helped."

"Thank you. I need to go, don't want anybody passing me."

The man practically shoved me out the door and threw a bag of candy in my pocket. "For energy. Go. Go!"

I folded up the copied map and tucked it in my jeans behind my back as I ran down the street. I had to get the real maps to Mr Chin.

The man wasn't in his office, but it was Mr Chin's building. He had to be close. The girl in the lobby office got on the intercom. "Mr Chin says you can go up now."

"Uh, no. I'd prefer he come down here."

"He's a very busy man."

"You did tell him Andy, right. He's expecting me. I haven't eaten much in the last couple days, so I'll be in his restaurant. That's if he's still interested in what I've got."

The woman repeated what I said and then hung up. "Mr Chin will be down in a couple of minutes. He is bringing a guest. He says you can help yourself to whatever you want."

"He's such a kind man." I turned and entered the restaurant, loaded a plate with syrup-drenched waffles, and grabbed a beer. I had them half finished when Mr Chin entered with Julie and two bodyguards.

"Mr Andy, so good to see you."

I put the fork down, pushed the plate away and stood up. "Always a pleasure, Mr Chin."

We shook hands. I looked over to Julie. "You okay?"

She nodded.

"Please have a seat, Mr Andy. She is fine, as you can see. Do you have the maps?"

"Not on me. That would be stupid. We need to let Julie go first."

"No maps, no freedom."

"You'll still have me. I'll give you the maps after I know she's gone. Then it'll be just you and me. We know who wins and it's not me. House rules and this is your house, right?"

Mr Chin rubbed his temples. "If you cross me, I will kill you."

"I know. I wouldn't be that stupid."

"Okay. She can go."

I got up and started to walk her to the door. I remembered the business card and pulled it out. "Go east two blocks and then head for the river. You'll see this shop along the way. Tell the man that the guy with the maps gave it to you. He'll ask if you're on a reality show. Say yes. Tell him we're still in the lead. Got it?"

"What's going on Andy?"

"We don't have time for this. Head for the shop down by the river and I'll try and get to you as soon as I can. If I don't show up by the time he closes, thank him, and get to the Canadian Consulate. They'll take you to the airport." I handed her an airline ticket. "Take this flight out of here."

"I can't leave you like this. You're not making any sense. And who's this Chin fella? Why is he doing this?"

"Don't worry about it. I'll either meet you at the shop or the airport. Then we can get the hell out of here. Promise me you'll get on that plane regardless. I have a better chance of pulling this off if I don't have to worry about you."

The fear in my eyes had her nodding. "Okay, okay. I'll go."

Watching her run down the street, it eased my nerves a bit that she wasn't looking back. She knew this wasn't a game.

Now it was time to walk back to the table and deal with Mr Chin. My beer was half empty, so I finished it… liquid courage.

"The maps, Mr Andy."

I set the bottle down. "There's a tube in the bushes by the front door."

Mr Chin and his men followed closely behind me. I reached inside the bushes and produced the tube. Mr Chin pulled the maps out and I let him study them for a few seconds. His focus was like that of a child watching their mother icing a cake, knowing that as soon as it was done, they'd be getting a slice. That had the two bodyguards leaning over to steal a glimpse.

That was what I was hoping for. I used that opportunity to bolt.

Chapter 49

The two men immediately gave chase, but the old saying is true, that a person can always run faster scared than another can angry. The two men were angry, and I was scared shitless. I sprinted through the crowds and didn't look back. I side-stepped as many people as I could but knocked the odd one down. And while Julie had gone east to the river, I chose west.

After four blocks of football manoeuvres, I stopped and looked back. I didn't see anybody, so I ducked into a building. It was a woman's department store. Standing amongst the bras and lace panties, it didn't bother me as much as it should. I needed to catch my breath.

"Can I help you, Sir?"

I spun around and saw her. The woman was a tall and beautiful Asian. Her knee length black pin-striped skirt hugged her hips and the white blouse showed just enough cleavage to make her cute, but in a refined way. "Sorry. I just…" I gulped a couple more breaths. "I just out-ran a clown."

She giggled. "My English isn't so good. Did you say clown like at the circus?"

"I did. He was making balloon animals and he sucked, so I used a couple of his balloons to make one of those wiener dogs. It looked better than the crap he was twisting up. Then he hit me and started chasing me." It surprised me how quick and easy these stories came out.

"That's terrible."

"I think I lost him. Hey, if you have any balloons, I'll make you a puppy."

Again, she covered her mouth and giggled. "I have no balloons. I wish I did."

"That's okay. I really should be going. I think I lost him." My breath was back, no thanks to her beauty. "You saved me from the evil clown. I thank you for that."

She stood there and gave me a polite wave as I retreated out the door and back into the crowds. Mr Chin's men were nowhere in sight, so I started back toward the Bund.

Walking along the railing, I checked the wall for the gate. It took a few minutes and several awkward leaning sessions, but soon the gate came into view. It was hanging partially open.

The smart thing would have been to wait until no one was looking, but as the day played out, I was finding myself neither patient, nor smart. I did, however, wait until there were just a couple people in the area. When it was safe, no one looking, I climbed over the railing and jumped. There was no time to start climbing down. Somebody would see me for sure.

I reached for the gate as I fell. I caught it with one hand and managed to thread a leg through the bars. This prevented me from falling into the river. The pain shot through my leg as the bottom railing squeezed my thigh.

"Shit, damn, argggg!" I hugged the bars as my face twisted in pain. "This shit better be worth it."

Pulling myself free, I looked down at my leg. There would definitely be a bruise. Soon, I was at the concrete walkway. As if I was there only yesterday, I sat back and leaned against the rounded wall. The grey water passed by in its trough and I dared a sniff. It wasn't as bad today as it had been.

Behind me the map was digging into my skin. I reached back and pulled it out. As primitive as it was traced, I didn't need a lot of time to orient myself. "Okay then. I am here and I want to go here." I pointed to the X.

It looked like ten city blocks, which wasn't too bad. It also looked like the route might go through about eight tunnels and each one had several junctions, which meant numerous locked or unlocked gates.

This might take a while.

Chapter 50

D own the tunnel I lumbered. I didn't want to stay at the opening. It reminded me too much of Olivia. As much as I wanted her here, I didn't want her to get hurt. This had started with my screw up. I thought I'd lost a few dollars in a poker game when in fact it was tens of thousands. She had taken me under her wing and in doing so, had been dragged into the quagmire.

"How hard could it be?" I muttered as I trace the map with my finger.

The first gate was up ahead, and the sparsely spaced lights put a dim glow on everything. It was a dusky light that allowed me to see the way, yet it hid much in the shadows.

The first gate was locked, but that was okay. I was headed in the right direction. The next one should be unlocked. I stopped at a light to check the map. As I'd hoped, the second one was open. That combination put the maps on either the Feng or Cuòjué routes. That also meant that I should hurry to make the next one while it was still unlocked.

I didn't make it. Since it was locked, the maps must have changed to Shui. It was the only ones that would have this gate locked. Was this a fifteen-minute cycle then, an hour or…

Up ahead there was another junction. It was taking me away from the X, but that was okay. I needed to find the pattern. I got to the gate and it was also locked. It shouldn't have been. That meant this had to be a ten-minute cycle. That was how long it took to get there. Then I noticed the three green lights on the lock's control panel. There was only two when I left the last gate. Three could be Zhenxiang or Shui. Since Shui was two, Zhenxiang had to be three... maybe?

I waited the ten minutes, that seemed like thirty. The stumps I called legs were starting to stiffen up so I stretched as best as I could. The lights changed. Now there were four. The gate was still locked. I ambled back to the first one. It was unlocked. I went through it and it closed behind me. After a couple minutes the lights changed again, this time to one. The gate I'd just passed through was locked.

Ah ha. There was a pattern, but it was still a little sketchy. I knew three was Zhenxiang, or was it? I ran to the next one and by the time I got there it was open. The lights were back to two. That made this one a Cuòjué, because the first one had been either a Feng or Cuòjué with one light on. If this was Cuòjué then the first one was Feng. My head began to swim in the options.

I ran to a corridor light and quickly scribbled the info down. I'd colour coded the gates. Red was Zhenxiang or three green lights. Four lights were Feng or the green circles, Shui was two green lights or the blue circles, and the black circles were one light.

That meant the next gate would be locked, but only for one cycle. It would open for four lights. I caught my breath and took my time walking to it. Four lights were lit when I got there, and I quickly made my way through it.

With two lights, I could make the next three gates if I sprinted. If I missed the last one, I'd be trapped for a full set of cycles. Since I was likely racing Mr Chin's men, I'd have to hurry.

The light changed to one and I got myself ready. There were a couple deep knee bends and a stretching of my quads. The light turned again, and I was running. I sprinted to the first gate and slammed it against the wall, barely slowing me down. The next one also got shoved out of the way as I raced for the third. I had to make it.

A Dream Escape

The tunnel darkened as I ran. One of the tunnel's lights had burnt out and it slowed me down. I stuck out a hand and tried to run it along the wall. That had me running too close to the side. Twice I caught the edge and almost rolled an ankle.

I'd been crippled to a fast walk and the ten-minute mark was coming up fast. Then I spotted the green lights. I was almost there. Thank God. I didn't want to be stuck in the dark for thirty minutes. I didn't want to be stuck anywhere for thirty minutes. Then the green dots started to flash. It brought me back to a sprint.

I dove for the door as the lights changed. My body bounced off the concrete floor as I rolled through the gate.
I dusted myself off and did a quick inventory on the pain. There were skinned knees, a sore shoulder and I'd wrenched my wrist. It was all minor stuff.

"If only I could see in the dark. There was an orange glow off in the one direction so that was the one I chose. At that light I re-oriented. The next gate would open in ten minutes and there'd be a two-gate sprint, if there were lights. Then I'd take a breather as I back-tracked two gates. Then it was another three-gate sprint to the finish.

I folded the map and put it away as I sucked in a deep musk-filled breath. The air was cooler, damp, and as the gate opened, I started to run. Both gates were open as expected and I took my breather on the way back. This was almost too easy.

These breaks were bad as they gave me a chance to think. Was Julie safe? I imagined she was, as long as she'd done what I'd told her. And how was Olivia doing? Was she missing me as much as I was missing her? Damn it, this sucked. I'd finally found someone who got me, and then she leaves. She was my unicorn, and yes, they did exist.

I got to the gate and tried it. It was locked. That was okay. That gave me a couple minutes until my three-gate sprint. With any luck the lights would be working. And what was it that I wanted? What was it that the Gods thought I needed most? Was it cash? Who couldn't use a bit of extra cash? Maybe I could give some to Julie, for her troubles. I could try and get some to Olivia. If anyone deserved some, it was her... or did she? I still wanted to know who this Ms Prescott was, and what kind of bank accounts she had Derrick dipping into.

The green lights started to flash.

The gate swung open as if on a spring. I charged left and gave it all I could. It was hard to believe I was an athlete once, but that was before the frozen pizzas and reruns of Jeopardy. The couch had turned my six-pack into a keg and the frozen pizzas turned lean legs into stumps. I was by no means a right off, but my better days were definitely fading in the rear-view mirror.

The second gate swung open just enough for me to slip through. The next one was three hundred yards away. I could do it.

My legs burned as I plodded along. The sprint had waned. I still had time as long as I didn't slow down. I'd done some jogging in the past, five and ten kilometres. My side was reminding me how long ago that was. And why did I stop jogging? Was it because I'd slowly given up on finding that special someone? If I made it through this, especially if I ended up with a bag of cash, I'd start jogging again. I'd start dressing nice. Hell, I'd even try hitting on pretty girls again. Tom Petty was right, even the losers get lucky sometime.

The gate was in sight and my drunken-like jog escalated back to a run. I landed against the gate and it swung open. It held me up as I gasped for the dank breaths. I needed a couple minutes to get my legs back.

Two hundred yards further and around a corner there would be an X. It would mark the spot. As I started walking toward it, I couldn't help but wonder what the Gods thought I needed? Right about now I'd settle for a glass of clear water, or a cold beer. Yes, make it a cold beer and a bottle of oxygen.

Chapter 51

The light got brighter as I closed in on the corner. These weren't the spaced tunnel lights that cast the amber glow that helped me to see. No, this was some industrial job that could have lit Candlestick Park. I rounded the corner and saw that the light was coming from the ceiling. The area had opened up and the ceiling, if that's what you'd call it, was quite a bit higher.

I had to stop walking and let my eyes adjust. Damn, it was bright. If my eyes weren't deceiving me, there was a block sitting under the light. Shielding my eyes, I crept toward it as if it were alive. That was when I noticed it wasn't a solid block. Fine lines defined what might have been a lid.

Crouching down, I placed both hands on it. At first glance the block didn't seem out of place, but one would have to wonder why it was here. This was a main junction of tunnels. What purpose would a block have, except to mark the area as a junction? And how many workers had walked past it or sat on it having a coffee break or a cigarette. Without the maps, it wouldn't have had any significance.

The edge was smooth as I ran my fingertips over it. Then I gave it a shove. I half expected the lid to slide off and half expected it to hinge open. It didn't do either. I got up and walked around it, slowly, deliberately. I had bought a box one time. It was a wooden

216

one, oak, or teak. It had been on a table at a yard sale. I'd walked by it twice, even picked it up. It spoke to me, but I had no reason as to why. Then the lady who owned the house took it from me. She pried the long side to the left, shoved it back half a centimetre and then slid the face off. It exposed a secret compartment. I thought it was the coolest thing and was ready to give her forty dollars for it. She only wanted two. Sold.

Setting my hands firmly on the block, I pried away at the top again. I tried front to back, side to side, and then at different angles. It didn't move. Then I tried using the palm of my hand in a hammering motion. Maybe the damn thing was stuck. How long had it sat here? I gave it a good smack in the corner and this time it did budge. It didn't slide side to side. It twisted. I dropped to my knees and pulled on the corner, while shoving on the adjacent one.

The top of the block twisted a full ninety degrees before stopping. Then I shoved side to side, front to back. It moved an inch away from me and stopped again. I proceeded to tap, slap, and push on it.

Nothing.

Then I pulled up on the overhung edge. It hinged open.

"Shit ya. That's what I'm talking about."

Inside, there was a cloth bag. It was the size of a frozen turkey and the same colour. I lifted it out. Damn thing weighed a hell of a lot more than any frozen turkey I'd ever lifted. Was it gold, platinum? I kicked the lid down and dropped the bag on top.

"What are you?"

The bag was tied and tagged. That was when my jaw dropped. The tag had a name on it, and it wasn't mine. The name was Chin. "What the fuck." Then it hit me. He had the real maps.

I pulled the tag off and threw it to the ground. Sure, my map was traced, but I was the one who found it. I worked on the knot. It had tightened a bit from lifting it, but I managed to get it loose. Soon it was coming apart and the top of the bag was opening. I helped it along by tugging on it.

The bag was filled with gold coins. There had to be hundreds of them. I pulled one out and studied it. It was aged, and it was Chinese. Better than that, they were stamped out of gold. Melted down, they'd be worth hundreds of thousands of dollars.

That would do me just fine. I tossed the coin in the bag and turned to the tunnel I'd come from.

"Wait, Mr Andy. Where you go with *my* treasure."

I looked over my shoulder to see Mr Chin holding up the tag. He had two men with him.

"It doesn't say Mr Andy. It say Mr Chin." He walked over and took the bag from me. Then he pulled out a coin. "You know what these are, don't you?"

"I have no idea."

Mr Chin used both hands to carry the bag over to the block. "You not know then, what these coins are worth?"

"Uh, their gold. Maybe a couple hundred dollars each."

"These coins are worth twenty-four hundred dollars each." His eyebrows lifted as he watched me do the math in my head.

"That's damn near three million dollars?"

"You not so stupid after all." He looked around. "Actually, you are here, and being here make you pretty darn stupid. You got away earlier. I thought you'd be on a plane by now."

"Are you taking all the coins?"

"Yes."

"All of them?"

"I'm sorry, Mr Andy. The name on the tag, it say Mr Chin." He turned and snapped his fingers.

The one man walked over and picked up the treasure. He was a burly bodyguard, so it wasn't that hard for him. I watched as the man started for the gate and stopped. Mr Chin looked at his watch and also headed for the gate. The three lights changed to four and he opened it.

"So that's it?" I asked. It all seemed so anticlimactic after all I'd been through.

He had his back to me as he held the gate open for the man carrying his coins. "Of course not, Mr Andy." He snapped his fingers again.

On hat cue, the other man pulled his gun out and levelled it on me.

Kevin Weisbeck

"No wait. I'll go. You'll never see me again. I promise."

"I have heard that story too many times." He tossed the nametag on the ground at my feet. "Tag say Mr Chin. My house always win."

The first shot hit me in the chest. The second shot almost found the same hole as the first one. The flow of blood coming out of me was immediate as I dropped to the ground.

"Fuck you." The words came out wheezy as I tried to look up at him. It was the best I could do.

"No, Mr Andy. Fuck you."

Mr Chin didn't look back as the three of them made their way through the gate and down the tunnel.

The lights dimmed as I faded. Would I be in Kelowna when I pass out? I'd gladly take the world of kitchen cabinets and frozen pizzas right about now. Too bad those were dreams. Then I saw the tag on the ground in front of me. I strained to read it. It didn't say Mr Chin anymore. I picked it up for a better look.

It had my name on it.

Chapter 52

The lights returned briefly and I was floating. Arms and legs were weighted. I tried to move but couldn't. The stench of grey water had been replaced with... what was that smell? It was sweet, like blood, cleaners, and sunshine. This was the transition, I thought to myself. This was my path to heaven. There was a light. Actually, there were several of them. They passed by me like highway lines as my body moved closer to them.

Then the darkness returned.

When I awoke the second time, the usual fog and silence almost startled me. For weeks I'd been trapped in a country of over a billion people. The traffic, the crowds, and the nights that never seemed to settle down were gone. In China, there were far too many people for quiet.

I drank the silence up, much like a survivor in the desert drinking up a mirage. I tried to remember the tunnels but couldn't. I wasn't in them anymore. I remembered I'd found gold, and I'd been shot. This happened in the sewers beneath Shanghai and the security system had gates that had been hacked by a kid. He'd turned the underground into a labyrinth of locked and unlocked passageways. How could anybody have found me there?

"He's awake!"

The voice was a woman's. She repeated herself as her voice faded from the room. All I caught as she left the room was the blonde hair and the blue jacket. It was a blur as I slowly reeled it all in. I was in bed. Was this my home? I looked around, definitely not my room. I looked beside me, glad to see no nude poker dealer.

Everything was coming into focus. This was a hospital. The fact was confirmed when the woman came back with two nurses and a doctor.

"Morning, Andy. I'm Doctor Evans. How are you feeling?"

I opened my mouth. The first word was a whisper. I swallowed and tried again. "I'm alive?"

"You can thank this girl." He motioned to the blonde. I looked over to see that it was Julie. "She was the one who had called the police."

"Hi Andy." She gave a shy wave.

"Julie?" I focused on her. "How'd you figure out the locks?"

"The what?"

"I had a map. Mr Chin had a map. You didn't. How'd you ever get to me?"

Julie slowly turned to the doctor. "What's wrong with him?"

"Andy is still processing. The shooting took quite a toll."

I had been through a lot, but I was resilient. I'd also learned from Olivia to pay careful attention to the details. Part of those details were that the doctor and both nurses were Caucasian.

"Where am I?"

"KGH," The doctor replied.

"That's impossible." KGH was the Kelowna General Hospital. They would have had to fly me thousands of miles. They wouldn't have done that, not after being shot, and I had been shot. "What happened to Shanghai?"

"See Doctor," Julie gasped. "He still thinks he's in China. He probably thinks Mr Chin shot him."

"Oh no. Mr Chin didn't shoot me." It was coming back to me in crushing waves. "His bodyguard did. Mr Chin took the coins."

221

A Dream Escape

"You have to help him Doctor." Julie moved in closer. "He's lost a lot of blood. It might take a few weeks for him to sort it all out. You were a part of it so maybe you can help. Just understand that, for him, this world in Shanghai was as real as Kelowna."

I stared with my mouth open. "Delusion? Shanghai is real." I looked around. "This is the frigg'n dream. Has anyone seen Olivia?"

"There is no Olivia," Julie replied. "Do you remember getting me kidnapped."

"Good, we agree on that." I wanted Olivia but remembered that we'd gone our separate ways. She'd slipped back into the cracks that she called home. She'd have no idea what happened after I got on the plane in Xi'an.

"You kept calling the guy Mr Chin, but that wasn't his name," Julie continued. "And this guy's not a billionaire. His name is Nao Chang, and he owns the Rice Bowl Restaurant, down by the Lakeshore."

"In Kelowna? That's not possible. I was shot in the tunnels under Shanghai."

The Doctor interrupted. "Your friend is right. You were shot in the old KVR tunnel up in Myra Canyon."

"I definitely remember locked gates and a box full of gold coins…and there was a tag on the bag. It said Mr Chin at first, but then changed to my name."

"No Andy, you remember forest trails and a briefcase full of paper money," Julie corrected.

My eyes darted between them, waiting, hoping for one of them to crack. They'd giggle or give some sign that they were kidding. It wasn't funny. Yes, I'd been shot in Shanghai and yes, I had been found in the sewers. Nobody giggled. I turned to Julie. "Okay, if this is real, tell me why you were kidnapped."

"I was in the wrong place at the wrong time. I was dropping by to see you when I found two men ransacking your place."

"You were dropping by, eh. I'm calling bullshit. You and I aren't that close. I mean we say hi at work, but you've never dropped by my place. Why would you do that now?"

222

Kevin Weisbeck

She gave everyone an impish smile. "You'd missed a couple days and didn't call in. We were all curious. I drew short straw."

In my dreams we'd kissed. She'd been in an accident. If Shanghai wasn't real, then those dreams must have been. "Have we ever kissed?"

"Pardon me!"

I rubbed my face and put my palms together in front of my lips. "You're saying we've never kissed, and that Shanghai isn't real. This is fucked up. I was in China. I was flying in planes, going to museums, and gathering maps. In my dreams I went to work, and you had an accident in your Jeep. It was in the compound over by the old Western Star Truck Plant. I broke into that place and got bit by a dog."

"That compound was closed years ago," Julie said. "And I drive a Honda, Andy. It's all I've ever owned."

"Really? Barry said you owned a Jeep."

"He lied. It's a nineteen-eighty Prelude."

My heart sank as I listened to her story. The man who shot me was a drug dealer and all that had happened was a whole lot of local crap. None of it made sense. The smell of the Huangpu River was still permeated into my skin. It was real, and so was the anxiety I felt while I was digging that map out of the Terracotta Warrior Museum. I'd seen a black shadow with bright yellow eyes as I trekked through the mountains above Ping'an, and I'd done it with a woman that had changed me like no one else could. Why would they want to take that away from me?

I needed this to be real.

"Hello. Is this Andy's room?"

The woman stood in the doorway. She had one hand on the doorframe as she politely leaned in. She was wearing dirty jeans and a tank top. Her long dark hair hung loosely in front of her. Still, I saw it immediately. It was the scar that ran over her collarbone and dove under the fabric.

223

Chapter 53

I gasped. "It's you! Oh my God, you're here."
She walked in slowly, cautiously. The police officer that guarded the door accompanied her. "She said she knows you."

Olivia's eyes flipped between the doctor, the nurses, and the blonde girl. "Are you... Julie?"

"I am. Who are you again?"

"She's pretty," the woman said as she ignored the question and let her eyes rest on me. "Are you okay? I heard you were shot."

"Twice." Not that I was proud of the fact. "You have to tell them what happened. They think it all took place here."

She moved in beside me. Her hand moved toward mine and then stopped.

I noticed. "Is everything okay?"

"It's been two weeks since we went our separate ways. I didn't expect to see you again."

"What do you mean, two weeks?"

The doctor answered for her. "He doesn't know how long he was out."

I didn't take my eyes off Olivia. "What are you talking about, Doc."

"You've been in a coma for two weeks. Your friends have been taking turns dropping by."

Kevin Weisbeck

"And you, Olivia?"

"I didn't know you were shot until this morning. I was trying to forget you. It's not that easy." She reluctantly took my hand. "We broke up. Do you remember that?"

"Sort of. We were at the airport in Xi'an. You didn't think we could pull off this whole dating thing when we came from different worlds. I kinda got it at the time, but you were all I could think of when I was in those sewer tunnels."

Julie shrugged. "You were shot in a tunnel on the KVR. There was no sewer, Andy."

Olivia corrected her as she took a tighter grip on my hand. "Nah, it was the sewers of Shanghai, and I should have been there. I mean, we were a good team in Ping'an and Beijing. I was stupid to let you out of my sight."

Julie crossed her arms. "No. There was no Ping'an or Beijing. Why would you tell him that?"

"Because in his mind he was there, and he fell in love with a girl named Olivia. They went through more than you could ever imagine, and I can't, won't, take that away from him."

She still got me, and I loved it. "Wait. A girl named Olivia? What do you mean? Is that not your name?"

"No, but you started calling me it and it stuck. Besides, I kinda liked being an Olivia. She was a pretty bad-ass bitch."

"That's because you're a bad-ass bitch, right?" Suddenly I was worried. "You're not on the debate or chess team, are you? Cause nothing about you should be nerdy."

She let go of my hand. "Girls like me don't get to be on the debate team. We usually get arrested or chased out of abandoned buildings. If I'm being honest, I'm Courtney and I'm not the girl you remember from China. We were never there. It's a place you visited, and a place I've always wanted to see. I live on the streets and don't have much of a purpose. It was fun playing the Bond girl."

I reached out for her hand and hooked a finger. "But…"

"The adventure was real," she assured me.

"It was." I pulled her closer. "I'm not letting you get away again."

225

A Dream Escape

Her face twisted. "You remember what the body looks like, right?"

I remembered the scars. "And you recall my reaction?"

"You're an incredible man, Andy, if that's your real name." She leaned in and gave me a kiss. "And I haven't had a home since I was fourteen, which makes it hard to send flowers."

"Hey, it's me you're talking to. I'll find a way." I tried to imagine living in the streets. "You don't do drugs, do you?"

"That's one thing I never understood. Too much suffering, and death."

Julie interrupted. "Hold it. You were with Andy before he got shot. Do you know what happened to him?"

"I was with him for two weeks. Granted he remembers it differently than it was, but that made it fun. It was like we were in a movie or acting out a play. I don't usually get to be anything special to anybody. I was special to Andy."

"How did I meet you?" I asked.

"We met at a poker game. It was in the back room of the Rice Bowl Restaurant. You came in for a pick-up and I was working there as a waitress. My boss, Nao Chang, talked you into a poker game. I thought you were cute and tried to warn you, but you were gonna win big. Thing is, you lost big, and he lied about the stakes. He said he'd forgive you if you delivered a package."

"A map of the Three Gorges Dam."

"No, a kilo of cocaine wrapped in Brown paper. I figured you were a little rattled, so I decided to tag along. You kept telling me it was a dream and that you weren't worried about Mr Chin. You were gonna throw the drugs in a dumpster. I wouldn't let you."

"You eventually started calling the package the Shui Pillar after talking to my stoner friend Derrick. I don't know what you two talked about, but it started the whole adventure. I'd met some odd people in my day, and you were up there, but you were also very kind to me. I must say, you sparked something."

"Yes, that was the Water Pillar. There were two sets, Harmony and Chaos. Feng-Shui was the Mountain and Water

Pillars, or the Harmony ones. The Chaos Pillars were Cuòjué-Zhēnxiàng, Truth and Illusion."

"And the Cocaine didn't get delivered?" Julie asked.

"No. Once it had become the Water Pillar, Andy wanted to keep it. We went on the run. The first night we hid out under the bridge at Hot Sands beach. That became your sewers. We went there again after jumping over the side of the Fintry Queen paddle-wheeler Restaurant. You forgot your wallet and we couldn't pay the bill. Our waiter chased us to the back of the boat.

That first morning when I got up, you were gone. It shook me a bit. I thought I'd never see you again, but you showed up that night. You kept saying I was a dream. I thought that meant you liked me, but you really thought you were sleeping in your bed at home making me up. Do remember how I proved you wrong?"

I blushed and quickly changed the subject. "So, if we weren't collecting maps, what were we collecting?"

"Your maps were actually things that would put Nao Chang behind bars. You were adamant to do that. Quite the elaborate story started brewing. I was a little confused at first, but it grew on me. I heard all about a contact book, a.k.a. the Truth Pillar, and we stole it from his house. You acted like it was some museum in Beijing. He had bad art in his place, and you described it all as ancient artifacts. You were like a curator and sold it well."

"That was the Chinese People's Anti-Japanese War Memorial Hall. I remembered seeing it when I was in China."

"Yes, that's what you called it. When were you in China?"

"I went on a tour and just got back. It was great, but it wore me out."

"That is so cool." Courtney replied. "We also got a video of this guy with someone other than his wife. That was our Illusion Pillar and we found it in a floor safe at the restaurant."

"He was cheating on his wife with another woman?" Julie asked.

Courtney tried not to giggle. "I didn't say it was a woman. The last thing we found was a gun at the foot of Knox Mountain. His son had used it in a drive-by shooting. A stray bullet had killed a young girl and the cops wanted to find the killer. That gun was registered in his son's name. Kid was too stupid to use an anonymous gun. He'd buried it out at Paul's Tomb."

"And we found it."

"We did and with that we had enough to put a few people away. Do you remember the cougar, Andy, on Knox Mountain?"

That wasn't the only thing I remembered about that place. We exchanged smiles.

Courtney continued. "They found us and gave us an offer we couldn't refuse."

I thought for a second. "That must have been when he kidnapped Julie?"

"You got it. Julie for all of the above."

I looked over at Julie. "You were in the wrong place at the wrong time."

"Yes, and I was in Kelowna."

"So why did I think it was in Shanghai?"

"Morvans's Syndrome," the Doctor explained as he broke his silence. He'd been listening to the stories and going over the information from my chart. "It sounds like you were with Julie and the gang at work during the day and with Olivia, or Courtney each night. You would have been awake for a very long time. If my math is right, you'd gone two or three weeks with nothing more than cat naps."

"You lost me, Doc. How is that even possible?"

"There's a form of psychosis that blocks the adenosine triphosphate (ATP) from reaching the cells. Adenosine is what causes you to want to sleep. If these receptors get blocked, and that happens when there's a physical break in a sleep pattern, it significantly reduces the need for sleep. At best, an hour a day usually suffices. Without the ATP telling you to sleep, you don't. I read a paper on this when I was an undergraduate."

"But if I'm awake, then I should know what really happened, no?"

"After a few days of no sleep you'd start to hallucinate. It wouldn't be long before these realities and hallucinations blurred. Part of your life was likely made up and Shanghai, being as recent as it was, would have been a big part of it. Some things, like work and friends might seem accurate, but the hallucinated parts would soon take over."

"Wouldn't I die without sleep?"

"Morvans's Syndrome is very lethal if left without treatment. The longest on record for going without sleep is about three weeks. It almost always ends with death. You were probably on track to break the sleepless record, or at least die trying."

"But I felt great. How close do you think I was to dying?"

"Let's just say, getting shot saved your life. What you needed was the two weeks in an induced coma to rest your body, and to break the cycle."

Just like the legend had said, I would receive what I had needed most, and that was sleep. That was why the tag had changed.

"And this Morvans's Syndrome turned a drug dealer into a Chinese businessman and had Julie flirting with me?"

"It would explain things. You were living a double life of Harmony and Chaos."

I tried to absorb it all. "So, the sewers, maps, the gold..."

Courtney took a seat on the bed beside me. "There were definitely shreds of truth to some of it, but the majority was pretty contorted. Your nights in Kelowna were filled with days in China. I mean, we did have a bad guy chasing us, and we totally pissed off a lot of people."

"What about the..." Andy willed her to know what he was talking about. It didn't work. "You know... that girl in my bed?"

Julie frowned. "A what?"

"Andy thought he had sex with a hooker who died," Courtney explained. "The reality of it, my friend OD'd beside you at a friend's house, and I took her to the hospital. You didn't have sex with her and she's doing fine now. She's actually signed up for some artsy dry-out retreat. But this here, this is your reality. So... I'm not sure where that leaves me. I'm a bigger part of the messed-up side of it all, the side you'd want to forget."

"We've been through a lot."

Courtney nodded. "We have."

A Dream Escape

Just then, Julie remembered the envelope. "Dang. I almost forgot this. The police stopped by today and dropped it off."

I took it from her. "What is it?"

"Crime-stoppers pays money for solving crimes. You two solved that little girls murder when you brought that gun in."

I opened the envelope to see a cheque for two thousand dollars. "Hey, do I still have a job to go back to?"

"Of course. They're all concerned."

"And I've still got three weeks, worth of vacation?"

Julie shrugged. "If you say so."

"I mean, I didn't miss any time during this whole whatever this was?"

"No. You've haven't missed a day."

"Great, cause I'm gonna take a few weeks off. I can use the time to heal up and maybe, if she's interested, take my girlfriend to China. It's kind of a cool place, even though the time zones are a little weird. You fly into the day after tomorrow and end up coming back to yesterday. What do you say?"

"Sounds messed up, in a fun kinda way. I'm in." Courtney's eyes sparkled in a mix of excitement and fear. "And the name's Olivia... ya nerd."

Other Novels by Kevin Weisbeck

Madeline's Secret

Madeline suffers from amnesia when she wakes from the car accident that killed her sister. Her parents, husband, and small child are all strangers. As she accepts these people into her new life, she uncovers a secret, one so dangerous that it could ruin her if it ever got out.

Johannes

A Madeline's Secret Companion Book

In the days that followed the death of his parents and girlfriend, Johannes is visited by a pair of friends that he hasn't seen in over a decade. Fast Eddy Cruiser is the one that used to look out for him when he was a teenager. Heidi, his high-school sweetheart, was the one he needed that protection from. Having these two people back in his life could only mean one thing. Trouble would be as certain as the emotions of a relationship that didn't end well.

The Darkness Within

A victim of his own bad choices, Johnny Pettinger is stranded following a plane crash in a remote mountain wilderness. His injuries are serious, but they're not the only factors preventing him from getting home. In order to do that, Johnny needs to shine a light on the very reason for his being there, the **Darkness Within**.

The Divine Ledger

Detective Violet Stormm is a woman on a mission. She'll do anything to catch the man responsible for a series of gruesome murders. Victor Wainsworth is the man doing the killing. He's fuelled by a ledger, a book that not only holds the names of his next victims, but clues to the **Eve of Humanity**.

Book One in the Eve of Humanity Series

About the Author

Kevin Weisbeck is a Canadian author, born in Kelowna, British Columbia and currently living in Okotoks, Alberta. He's had several short stories published in magazines and newspapers, and currently has one in McGraw-Hill's iLit Academic Program.

He can usually be found on the couch with his laptop in front of him and his Ragdoll cat, Franklin, on his shoulder. It's not an ideal writing set up, but Franklin doesn't mind. Otherwise, Kevin enjoys hiking, kayaking, camping, photography, and golf (when the weeds and water don't get in the way).

Made in the USA
Columbia, SC
11 October 2021